"**W**hy are we going so fast?" gasped Deirdre.

"How else are we to bring you safe out of the country, if not before your charming duenna raises the countryside?"

"You must not talk that way about Aunt Cassandra!"

"Aunt Cassandra?" He chuckled softly. "I took her for a very dragon of respectability, playing the stern watchdog over your harmless youthful pleasures. Is that not the usual relationship between fair young beauties and elderly dowagers?"

"Aunt Cassandra is not an elderly dowager! Perhaps she is almost thirty, but you would not think it."

"Would you not?" Again the strange, wry chuckle, as if he were amused at some secret game. "I swear, she tongue-lashed me like a true harpy."

"No, she did not." Was this the way one talked to a desperado who was abducting one? "She merely warned you not to take me, and now you have done it, she will have the constables after you directly."

The stranger smiled in a sly fashion. "I think not," he said. "I think not."

MY LADY QUIXOTE

Phyllis Ann Karr

FAWCETT COVENTRY • NEW YORK

MY LADY QUIXOTE

Published by Fawcett Coventry Books, a unit of CBS Publications, the Consumer Publishing Division of CBS Inc.

Copyright © 1980 by Phyllis Ann Karr

ISBN: 0 449-50037-3

Printed in the United States of America

First Fawcett Coventry printing: April 1980

10 9 8 7 6 5 4 3 2 1

"I have painted Bevil's character as black as I conscientiously could," said Lady Cassandra, "but to your good mama, his title outweighs all youthful follies. I really begin to be afraid, Deirdre, that you must reconcile yourself to becoming the Viscountess Fencourt."

Lady Cassandra's niece by marriage sighed and bent her blond head over her embroidery. "I know he's the catch of the season," said Deirdre in her soft voice, "and any number of other girls are green with envy . . . Oh, but that's just what makes it so unfair!" she burst out—with a sudden furious jab of her needle that caused her aunt to fear for her fingers. "Any one of them would have been so happy—and it must be me instead! Why couldn't he have been safely married to somebody else two years ago, before I was ever brought out?"

"The old earl would agree with you, but I imagine the countess would say, with your own mama, that 'he was fated to wait for just the right wife.' " Lady Cassandra tried to say this in a jesting tone, but it was not a morning in which her niece was disposed to smile and make the best of life.

"But I'm *not* the right one!" Deirdre exclaimed, breaking the embroidery cotton in her agitation. "I don't believe there can be such a thing as the right wife for Lord Fencourt! And I know he's not the right husband for me!—And I *hate* society!"

Lady Cassandra waited a few moments, until Deirdre had rethreaded her needle and seemed to have composed herself. Then she said, very gently, "Nevertheless, dear, tedious as society is at times, it does have its little compensations. As do wealth and titles. Shall I ring for tea?"

The girl ignored this question. "Oh, I know poor Mama means it all for the best, and thinks she's done something grand for me. But, Aunt Cassie, all I want is George!"

Lady Cassandra laid her own needlework aside and put one hand lightly on Deirdre's wrist. "But if you had not been introduced to Bevil, in all likelihood you would never have met the Reverend Mr. Oakton at all. Come now, dear. . . it may well be that, after all, the viscount is almost ready to settle down to a quieter life. Don't you think, if you make even a little effort, you may be able to find a few of his brother's good qualities in Bevil?"

Deirdre shook off the older woman's hand, exclaiming, "I thought at least I could talk to you—but you're like all the others! It's all very easy for you, Aunt Cassandra—everyone knows you only married my Uncle Darnham for convenience—you didn't have to give up the man you loved, and who loved you if he would only face up to his parents and cut out his beastly brother!"

She rose, threw down her embroidery, and dashed out of the morning room, leaving her aunt to sit gazing after her in stunned silence.

In her late twenties, the Lady Cassandra was barely ten years older than her husband's niece. Had she so soon forgot the pangs of youth? It was quite true that she had married the complaisant Lord Crump (the Baron Darnham), her senior by a quarter of a century, strictly for convenience—both his and hers. The death of his first wife had left the baron in need of a woman to keep his household in order, help preside over the dinners and small gatherings he enjoyed from time to time, and provide him occasional conversation and other small comforts. As long as his wife fulfilled these comparatively light duties, he allowed her to do exactly as she wished the rest of the time, asking few questions and expecting fewer answers. Thus, by her marriage, Lady Cassandra had gained the social status of a matron, with relatively few of its restraints. She had as much freedom as a respectable woman could have, and it was largely her own quiet tastes that kept her quite respectable.

But what Deirdre did not know (indeed, what very few people knew, or at least troubled to remember after all these years) was that the staid, self-possessed Lady Darnham had once loved—deeply, fervently, with all the heart-rending passion of first youth. True, she had never been forced to give up her heart's choice for a more impressive match arranged by parents and relatives; she had never been torn between love and social expectations; but only because he had been snatched from her by a fever.

She had known at once, that same sunny afternoon she was told, that there would never be another to take his place in her heart. Nevertheless, she had gone through the motions, appearing at fêtes and crushes, allowing various gentlemen to call on her, even attempting to give one or two of them a fair chance of earning her affection, all to satisfy her family—and, a little, to prove to herself that her capacity for love had truly died with her first lover. It had, and the proof was a sort of comfort to her.

Then the opportunity had come for this match with Lord Darnham. Cassandra's family became almost ecstatic: She might be the daughter of a marquess and her prospective husband a mere baron, but she was past twenty-six and her brother and two married sisters had long since begun to despair. Even her widowed father, who would not have been completely sorry to keep his oldest daughter at home managing the household, had seemed to welcome the prospect of marrying her off at last. And Cassandra herself, who in earlier years had refused three offers from much younger, handsomer, richer, and higher-ranking noblemen than Lord Darnham, now accepted the middle-aged baron with hardly a second thought, precisely because he did offer a passionless, comfortable, convenient marriage.

Nor had the last two years given her cause to regret the decision. Love was dead, but married status and the management of her own household had their consolations. She had even come to think that she would welcome a child. Why, she was even free to hope that her first child would be a daughter! Lord Darnham's line was assured in two grown sons by his first wife.

And so it was that the deep emotion of her early youth had brought her to cheerful enjoyment of her unimpassioned but amicable marriage. But had her present content, growing like fresh summer flowers over a peaceful, well-tended grave, dulled her sympathy for another young girl in love? Had the young girl she herself once was been buried so very completely along with her dead lover?

Lady Cassandra put her hand again to the brooch at her throat, the paste diamonds she wore almost constantly, her one keepsake from Charles Porter. It was little more than a trinket—Charles had not been rich—but it was priceless to her for his memory. Two years ago, only weeks before her wedding she had almost lost even this memento, to a highwayman. By great good luck, he had been one of the few robbers in the country who were in fact what outlaws were supposed to have been in olden times, and what common footpads would no doubt be foolishly considered, a generation after they had finally been eliminated—a gentleman thief. She owed her knight of the road a considerable debt, not so much for the precious trinket (which she had retained largely through her own efforts), but rather for putting to rest the last lingering suspicion that she might, perhaps, still hunger for romance.

The door reopened and Deirdre came slowly back into the morning room. Her large eyes were reddened, and she still dabbed at her uptilting nose with one of her late father's handkerchiefs, which she used when not in company. "I'm very sorry, Aunt," she said in a small, cautious voice. "Pray forgive me. It shan't occur again."

She sat and bent once more over her embroidery, sedulously intent upon her tiny blue stitches. So she has the propriety, thought Lady Cassandra, to seek formal reconciliation at once, but she is still shy of returning to me from behind the cloak of formality. Or has *she* yet forgiven *me*? She was in desperate need of sympathy, and I gave her social platitudes instead.

With a pang, Lady Cassandra reflected that she herself was in all likelihood her niece's one hope for a confidante, at least here in town. Deirdre had no sister or brother, and her mother, who should have been her first refuge, had in the matter of this marriage set herself up from the outset as leader of the opposition. The child had been introduced to many other girls in the polite circles through which she had fluttered like a timid moth since being brought out a year ago; but any intimate friends of her own age and sex she had left in Steddinghill, three counties away. Even her lover, as nearly as her aunt could determine, was intent on striving manfully against his unhallowed passion; and, although the viscount himself seemed at times eager, through carelessness or deviltry, to throw the pair together, the vicar, as a loyal brother and as a conscientious young clergyman, had thus far eschewed anything resembling a private interview with Deirdre. As for Deirdre's abigail, the woman was simply impossible—excellent for clothes and coiffures, and good for absolutely nothing else.

So the lonely girl had unburdened her heart to her uncle's second wife, and received only an echo of the worldly wisdom she encountered on all other sides. Small wonder that Deirdre had burst out with such vehemence! Lady Cassandra must do what she could to remedy the situation, and as soon as possible.

"Deirdre," she said, gently, reaching out and covering her niece's hands with her own, "there was a young man once whom I truly loved, and who loved me."

The girl glanced up, as if wishing to trust the older woman, then quickly turned her blue eyes downward again. "But you didn't marry him. Was he a younger son?"

"He was an only son. He was the clerk in my uncle's law office in Holtborough, and most of his earnings had gone to support his widowed mother and to provide a dower for his sister. He had little money, but that would not have stopped us."

Deirdre looked at her again, as if wanting to ask, "Then, why?" but no longer quite daring to frame a pert question. Cassandra realized that she must have been speaking with more emotion than she had intended. Drawing a deep breath, she went on.

"He used to write verse plays in his spare hours. I

helped him with two—indeed, we wrote most of *Queen Mathilda* together. I would give much to have his manuscripts. But his creditors had ransacked his lodgings before I could arrive there."

"He died?" whispered the girl.

Lady Cassandra nodded, an unbidden soreness in her throat. "A sudden fever."

"Oh, Aunt! Oh, I am so sorry!" Embroidery slid unheeded to the floor as Deirdre leaned impulsively forward and threw both arms around Cassandra's neck. "Oh, dear, dear Aunt Cassie, can you ever forgive me?"

The quick, vital emotion of the younger woman took Cassandra a little aback for a moment, then, conversely, bolstered her own habitual composure. "Oh, my dear, of course you couldn't know. Now then," she continued briskly, settling Deirdre back in her chair, "shall we ring for tea?"

Ringing for the maid had the desired effect of encouraging Deirdre to wipe her eyes, recover her needlework, and regain at least outward composure. Niece and aunt said little for the next half hour: Lady Cassandra feared to break the mood with idle chatter and also sensed that Deirdre was still dangerously close to tears. Not until the girl was sipping her second cup of tea did Cassandra judge it safe to say, "I speak of Charles very seldom, and to very few. Not that it is a closely guarded secret, but that some things are better left private and unspoken. I trust you, Deirdre, with my old sorrow."

The girl nodded solemnly. "I understand, Aunt Cassandra. I will be very . . . discreet. As discreet as you have been about—about the Reverend Mr. Oakton."

"Perhaps too discreet. It seems I've been of little help to you."

"Never mind. I don't suppose anyone could help. If you can be so brave about—about Charles, I will be brave about George. But even if something should happen to Bevil after we're married, I still couldn't marry— I mean—" Deirdre broke off in some confusion, ending helplessly, "I mean, Heaven forbid that anything *should* happen to him, but . . . "

"But if anything *is* to happen to the viscount, it had

much better happen before the marriage than after," Lady Cassandra supplied with a wink. "Don't worry, dear; it will take more than an unguarded remark on your part to bring down misfortune on that young nobleman's head."

Deirdre giggled in nervous gratitude and bravely emptied the last of the tea into her dish. Lady Cassandra studied her niece over the rim of her own cup.

It was, indeed, unjust that, when at least half the eligible young women in their circles were sighing for the Viscount Fencourt, his fancy should have lighted on Deirdre Chevington, who would be far happier with the Reverend Mr. Oakton and a vicarage. But what had justice had to do with Charles Porter's death? The world did not turn for the just, but for the clever.

Nevertheless, though Charles Porter was dead, George Oakton was alive; and in her own heart the Lady Cassandra determined that Deirdre should have an opportunity for romance.

2

No one whom he could not trust, and few of those whom he judged he could, knew of Sir Roderic's activities on the king's highway. To the respectable circles of London, he was an almost stodgy gentleman of irreproachable, if vaguely mysterious, personal conduct. If he was never seen in his cups, that was credited to morality of near-puritanical standards. If he was never seen at the gaming tables, that was only meritorious prudence in one whose family fortune was generally considered, while still more or less adequate, none of the highest. If he kept a single servant in his town house, that was no more than might be expected of a man who spent so much of his time in the country and who kept so aloof from social affairs when he was in town.

It was largely due to the success of this cover that he was able to continue dodging Bow Street, lesser beadles, and the hue and cry year after year, when the active life of a common footpad could often be measured in the months. Where most of them had few means of turning stolen goods into the ready, save through channels known to the thief-takers or through old-fashioned attempts to sell personal items back to the victims, Sir Roderic was careful to take only cash or such small items as he had his own means of liquidating in his home county; and where other gentlemen of the road spent most of their off hours roistering with their fellows or bedding with cheap wenches in unsavory taverns, he could fold his mask into his handkerchief once more and blend at his ease into decent inns and respectable neighborhoods.

Nevertheless, the life had taken its toll on him. Although still handsome, in a stern, undandified way, he looked older than his actual years. Thanks partly to this premature aging, but more (he flattered himself) to the rarity of his appearances at social events, to the notorious state of his fortune, to his taciturnity and known inclination toward bachelorhood, girls were no longer thrown at him as they had sometimes been in earlier seasons. He did not regret these assaults by dreamy-eyed maidens and desperate mamas—his aim was to attract as little attention as compatible with the dual role he must play, his pleasure was to distract himself in solitude with books and tobacco and an occasional sally to the theater or opera. Sometimes, however, he allowed himself to envy other men his age, respectable in fact rather than mere appearance, now sharing their homes with loving helpmates and watching their children grow up around their knees.

He was surprised, but not displeased, when Lady Cassandra paid him a visit at his house in town.

Lady Cassandra was one of the very few in London who knew him in both his capacities, as gentleman and as highway robber. He had met her two years ago, when he held up her coach and in a moment of foolish theatrics demanded the brooch of paste diamonds she wore on her dark bodice. She had given him no rest until she won the bauble back, and only because it had been a gift from her long-dead lover. And yet this female Quixote claimed to have put away all romantic impulse!

They had glimpsed each other perhaps a half-dozen times during the subsequent months, usually at the opera; they had exchanged a few civilities and a smile and quietly gone their separate ways again. And now the Lady Cassandra had come to pay him a morning call, as casually as if he were either an intimate friend or an acquaintance to be cultivated according to the common rules of *politesse.*

Studying her card, he began to direct old Jerry, his single servant, to show the lady to the drawing room, but quickly changed his mind. The drawing room was frayed and faded beneath its layer of dust; and even were it not, he had little use for the tawdry mock-elegance of the décor wreaked upon the room almost twenty years before by one of his deceased brother's favorite doxies. No, he could not picture the Lady Cassandra in one of the spindly travesties of a Chippendale chair, against a background of crumbling velvet.

But the library, which was preserved to his own taste, being virtually the only room he used besides his bedchamber and the kitchen, where he often took his meals with old Jerry—the library, with its solid dark oak furniture from the century of the Stuarts, the leather and gilt spines of its rows of shelved books, the gloss of daylight from the heavily leaded window, and the ruddy glaze of a fire in the carved stone fireplace . . . yes, that would provide a far more suitable background for the chestnut hair, deep brown eyes, and low, rich voice of Lady Cassandra Darnham.

"Show her to the library," he directed his servant. "Light the fire—three logs this time—and see that we are left undisturbed."

Jerry nodded and winked before hobbling away. Sir Róderic combed his graying hair and wound a muslin scarf around his neck with unwonted care. Lady Cassandra would not have come for mere chitchat. She would have some definite, perhaps inscrutable motive for this

13

visit. And even if she had not . . . He shrugged and turned his own steps towards the library.

"My gallant Captain!" she greeted him, turning from a study of the titles on the shelf to the immediate left of the fireplace—the works of Aquinas, Descartes, Hobbes, and Hooker. Old Jerry had already kindled the fire, added the extra logs, and departed; and the lady, unconventional as ever when it suited her, had poured out two small glasses of sherry.

"My clever lady." He accepted one of the glasses and raised it. "To your continued health and happiness."

"To your continued success and profit." They sipped, then sat in the two seventeenth-century armchairs, facing one another at a slight angle before the fire.

"The estate of matrimony appears to agree with you," he observed.

"I have been sublimely comfortable these two years past. But my niece, I fear, will be less fortunate."

"Your niece, Lady Cassandra? I believe your sisters are both younger than yourself, and your brother shirking his duty by delaying his choice of a bride."

"My husband's niece, Miss Chevington. She was brought out last season."

He shrugged. "She would not yet be twenty, then. An early age to consider oneself unfortunate in life."

"She is nineteen. An early age to be made unfortunate in life. Her mother is determined that Deirdre shall marry the elder son of the Earl of Rotherhithe."

"Bevil, Viscount Fencourt, eh?" Sir Roderic stretched out his hand for the poker and attended to a sluggish log. "While my judgment seconds yours as to the marital desirability of that young want-grace, I believe that young girls tend to look on him in a different light."

"My niece does not. Her heart is inconveniently fixed on the earl's second son."

"I do not know the man."

"I doubted you did not." Lady Cassandra sipped her sherry. "The Honorable Mr. George Oakton is in orders. He has been these fifteen months the vicar of Plover-chase."

"A living, I take it, controlled by his father the earl?"

She nodded. "A very earnest and serious young
14

churchman, nevertheless. They met last Christmas at Rotherhithe Castle."

"And why did not this earnest and serious young cleric offer for her himself?"

"He had not known her long enough before her engagement was announced to his brother. The Reverend Mr. Oakton, however, would make far the better husband for Deirdre, both by temperament and by calling."

"But not, it seems, by his eagerness to cut out his brother."

Lady Cassandra's small, symmetrical bosom rose and fell in a soft sigh. "No, alas! He might have done so had the match been merely of the viscount's inspiration, but it met with the immediate and hearty sanction of both the earl and the countess, and George is far too sensible of his filial duty, family obligations, and position as shepherd of the country flock to run counter to his parents' wishes."

"Unfortunate for the young woman. But you and I know, my lady, that one survives even the loss of a lover."

"You and I know it, but Deirdre does not." Lady Cassandra paused for a moment as if reexamining Sir Roderic's words. "I did not know, Captain, that you also had lost a love?"

"How should you have known of Hannah?" he answered, regretting the trace of bitterness that must have crept into his last statement. "You did not badger the fact from me by stealing a treasured keepsake and forcing me to endanger body and reputation in order to win it back."

"Had I found my body and reputation seriously endangered two years ago, Captain, would I have come here today alone?" She paused again, gazing into the fire, its light flickering bronze-gold on her straight nose and firm chin. "But should not we, of all people, have the greatest interest in seeing one young girl, at least, happily united with her true lover?"

"Who has not the gumption to win her for himself," said Sir Roderic with a snort.

"Who has too much propriety to make the attempt without our encouragement," Lady Cassandra corrected him, leaning forward as if suddenly giving free rein to her enthusiasm. "Yes, it will be much more difficult, seeing we cannot take him into our confidence and prepare him beforehand, but I am still confident the thing can be managed."

Sir Roderic emitted one of his rare chuckles. "My Lady Quixote! Could you not have found a likelier Sancho Panza than such a hardened criminal as myself?"

"Quixotic?" she ejaculated in surprise. She had one blind spot, then, in her defenses: Apparently it had never occurred to her that the adjective must certainly apply to any matchmaking scheme she had conceived which would require the gracious services of a highwayman. She had too ready a sense of humor not to laugh when it was called to her attention, but too firm a purpose to relinquish her plans. "Quixotic, if you will," said she, "but, unlike the good don, I am going into action with my eyes open to reality and my plans well laid in advance."

"Let's hear these plans, then," he said, resigning himself to the inevitable.

She rose and began pacing the narrow space between chair, fireplace, and bookshelves, as if she were a general instructing her staff. "During the first part of next month, we are to stop for a fortnight at Derwent Abbey so that Darnham can hunt with Lord Harkendell. Derwent being not quite fifteen miles from Rotherhithe, of course Deirdre must take advantage of our stay to visit the earl and countess, and her intended—should Bevil deign to stop for a few days with his parents. You know the country?"

"Not well. I have been through it, but not on business matters."

Cassandra drew a folded piece of paper from her pocket, opened it, and smoothed out a neat, hand-copied map on his knee. "The Reverend Mr. Oakton tends the souls both in Ploverchase and here in Little Tiptree," she continued, pointing out the sites with one long forefinger. "As you see, there is a low, wooded hill, Ploverchase Hill, between the two villages. Whenever he wishes to reach Little Tiptree quickly, our vicar always takes the footpath over this hill. The road from Derwent to Rotherhithe runs along here, about two miles south of Ploverchase Hill."

"Well?" inquired Sir Roderic.

"I will arrange to be riding with Deirdre in my phaeton back from Rotherhithe Castle. We shall arrive just south of Little Tiptree shortly before sunset. I am sure you will have little trouble finding suitable cover from which to waylay us along that stretch of road."

"But not, this time, to abduct yourself."

"Of course not! This time, as you will have divined, you are to carry off my niece. Hide with her on Ploverchase Hill, among the trees near the footpath. I will meanwhile suffer a severe fit of hysteria, necessitating my immediate removal to the house of Mr. Bellew, the apothecary in Little Tiptree. I will insist that the Reverend Mr. Oakton be summoned to my side at once. When he comes hurrying over Ploverchase Hill in response to my summons, you will naturally allow him to rescue Deirdre."

"And this is all you wish me to accomplish? Such a trifle seems hardly worth the effort."

"Trust me, Captain," she bantered in reply. "Once we have made George Oakton the hero of such an adventure as this, it will go hard if we cannot turn the situation to Deirdre's better matrimonial prospects."

"And possibly to my appearance on the new drop at Newgate—and this for the sake of playing matchmaker to a young Pyramus and Thisbe who mean nothing to me."

"You surely cannot think I would see my gallant captain swing? No, this will be as safe a venture as any you have undertaken."

"Indeed? And are you so well acquainted with the ordinary hazards of my avocation?"

Lady Cassandra smiled and returned to her chair, bringing the decanter of sherry to refill their glasses. "I do not aspire to teach you your craft, Captain. I leave the finer details of your role, perforce, to you. But Thomas, my coachman, is entirely reliable—we can depend on him to direct what hue and cry Little Tiptree may raise in the wrong direction, well away from Ploverchase Hill. You may have to dodge the apothecary's boy on his way

17

to Ploverchase, but he will be concerned only with summoning the Reverend Mr. Oakton. While the vicar will succeed in rescuing his beloved, I can hardly imagine you being held by a gentleman of the cloth, possibly accompanied by a very young doctor's lad. And the constabulary of both villages are the true descendants of Dogberry and Verges."

"Who muddled their way to success despite their lack of talent," he remarked. "But I think you have been studying Goldsmith and Sheridan more closely than Shakespeare, my lady."

"Perhaps," she replied, with another smile, refusing to be baited again. "But you must think more highly of me than to suppose I would permit you to come out of the adventure with nothing more than the warm sense of having done a good turn."

"The warm sense of having done a good turn I could endure. The damage to my reputation when I am apparently bested by a country vicar will be more difficult to surmount."

"As you yourself pointed out, the country between Derwent and Rotherhithe is not your usual place of business. As I began to say, not only has Darnham been a generous husband, but I have, besides, a sufficiency of my own. It will happen that I shall be carrying enough cash in my purse, which you will naturally steal along with my niece, to repay you financially as well as emotionally. I will not be wearing my brooch this time," she added, touching the paste jewel at her throat. "Or, if I am, you will know that something has gone amiss, content yourself with the purse alone, and ride at once from the vicinity. If worst comes to worst, we will swear you are not the robber who held us up."

"Your coachman Thomas, unlike our guileless churchman, being in it from the beginning. Will the girl also know it is mere play-acting?"

"I would prefer she did not. Deirdre is perfectly well able to play a part—she has proved it by smiling and being amiable for two seasons to dour dowagers and boring old officers. But it would give her a far more memorable evening if she thought it all in earnest."

18

"Yet if worst comes to worst, she will swear I am not her abductor?"

"At a word from me breathed in her ear."

"So I am to carry off a terrified and struggling young girl, hold her quiet without injuring her in the woods on a hilltop until the right young vicar comes along the footpath, then allow her to scream or otherwise attract his attention at precisely the right moment?"

Lady Cassandra winked. "Judging from my own experience, I believe you more than equal to the task. Indeed, if I were less sure of Deirdre's affection for George, I should apprehend her losing her heart to *you.*"

"You flatter me. No, there are too many gray hairs on my head, and wrinkles on my brow, for a young maid's fancy. But one suggestion, Cassandra. Do not fall victim to the vapors. No one acquainted with you would find it credible. Devise some other reason to send for the saintly Reverend Mr. Oakton."

Her brown eyes twinkled. "I have your word then, Captain?"

Perhaps for no one else would Sir Roderic have committed himself to such an enterprise—for no one else, that is, unless he should someday yield to the similarly madcap temptations which very occasionally intruded themselves into his own thoughts. Besides, the affair might be amusing. "Such as it is," he replied, "you have my word."

She rose and stood beside the mantelpiece, holding her glass so that the sherry glowed in the firelight. "Say, then—how much shall I carry in my purse?"

He also got to his feet and stood at the other side of the mantel. "As you have left the finer points of my business to me, so I leave that delicate question to you."

She smiled and lifted her glass toward his. "To the happiness of our young lovers."

"To the comfortable outcome of our venture," he replied. They touched glasses lightly and remained gazing for a moment into each other's eyes.

"And suppose," he asked, "that I leave the chit and abduct you a second time, my Lady Cassandra?"

"Then you will take me to some hidden haunt of yours and we will play another game of chess and wits, my gallant captain. But you should not refer to the heroine of our forthcoming adventure as a mere 'chit.' "

3

"Out, out, out!" said Marie Cluzot, putting three fingers to her *viscomte's* silk neckcloth in an effort to push him back through the open door of the inn chamber.

Laughing, he twisted away and reached out one hand, heavy with cameo rings, to tickle her. She slapped it down and retreated to the far side of the bed, where she made a great point of fluffing the pillows.

Bevil came all the way into the room and closed the door behind him, its latch shutting with a click. "Wicked," said Marie. "do you not see I must air and clean this chamber and two more this morning?"

"Daily bedmaking, as some profound thinker of modern times has observed, is a waste of time. Especially"—the viscount flung himself down accross the crumpled sheets—"when the bed has not had worthy usage between makings."

The chambermaid picked up a duster and waved it in his face to make him cough and to disarrange his light hair. Then she turned and bent part way out the window to shake the duster. "Ah, yes. You will have your wicked way with me and then go and marry your fine English lady."

It was not the first time Marie had tickled his face with a duster, and he accepted it with equanimity, merely sitting up to dab his even features with a lace handkerchief. "Permit me to give you another lesson in our barbarous Anglo-Saxon, *mon petit chou*. The word for Miss Chevington is not 'lady,' but 'chit.' "

. "But this 'chit,' you are engaged to her."

20

"Only as a matter of convenience, *ma mie*. Only as a matter of convenience."

Marie put down the duster and proceeded to tug at the bed linens as if trying to unseat her *amour*. "Yes, I have heard of these 'weddings of convenience.' In France, we were more honest. Off!"

The viscount obligingly rose from the bed. "Oh, very much more honest," he said, winking one green eye. "That's why your good pater cast you off without a sou for running away with that penniless adventurer of yours, is it not?"

"He did not cast me off. I cast him off, poor stupid *père*, who was so stupid he would not leave our poor France when he could. But I am still *la Comtesse d'Azalaine, mon ami,* and I do not play the lady-in-waiting to one of your 'weddings of convenience'!"

He laughed. "Lord, you don't really think I intend to marry the Chevington chit?"

"Ah. So you intend to have your wicked way with her also. But to have her trust, you must make the betrothals before all the world, and you think that to have my trust you need only to make your little promises in secret, like a little plotting mouse, to me only."

"I hadn't thought of having my wicked way with her, actually," remarked the viscount, tapping one long forefinger meditatively against his cheek. "Thank you for the suggestion, *ma mie*. Though, for that matter, I haven't enjoyed your favors either, to speak of."

"No, because I am not so silly as your English chits, to lose my head for a promise and a few smiles."

"Indeed. And were you so virtuously suspicious in regard to the promises of your Scottish adventurer?"

"Monsieur Kinross promised only to escort me safe out of France and across the Channel—no more. And Monsieur Kinross kept his promise very faithfully."

"As will I, sweeting."

"Ah, but which promise? That you have made to me, or that you have made to your fine young English lady?"

At last she had scored. Bevil blushed slightly before replying.

"Damme, an engagement ain't a promise. I've hardly exchanged two words alone with the girl. It's simply a social convention—a sop to public opinion for a few months."

"But the public opinion, it will not smile if you should wed only the Comtesse d'Azalaine?"

"My glorious *comtesse* of the brooms and dusters, you should be aware by now that public opinion will eventually come around to almost any little prank I might care to put on it. But meanwhile—"

"But meanwhile, you are ashamed to tell your fashionable world that you wish to marry a mere chambermaid. You are afraid to go to your father and say, 'I wish to marry the Comtesse d'Azalaine, who has lost her family and all her jewels and papers to *la Terreur* and must work as a chambermaid at the Grain and Grape.'"

"Lord, no! I'm not afraid, I merely detest family scenes. Pater stamping around calling you an adventuress—and we can't really prove otherwise, y'know—Mater fluttering about weeping and calling for her smelling-bottles and whatnot—and both of 'em at me every time I showed my face at Rotherhithe, to drop you and marry a nice little English chits like Miss Chevington—"

"But if you marry me first and tell them later, then there will be no family scenes?" Marie pouted, knowing that her pink lips made a very pretty pout, and thumped the bolster into shape.

The viscount shrugged. "Of course there will be, but we can avoid 'em. After all, what will Pater and Mater and brother George be able to do then? You and I, *ma petite*, will only need to take a house in town for half a year or so, until they come around to accepting you. For now, let them rest in blissful ignorance."

"You are wicked, wicked. You lie to your parents, you lie to your English lady, and I think you lie to me. Out!" Picking up her broom, Marie put the handle beneath his chin and this time succeeded in propelling him from the room. She closed and secured the door, then sat on the bed and smothered her giggles with a pillow.

Marie Cluzot had started her career as lady's maid to the real Comtesse d'Azalaine; but that unfortunate noblewoman, having been guillotined, had no further use for the title on this earth, and it did nobody harm if another took it for herself.

Yes, Marie was in fact the adventuress Bevil's parents, the Earl and Countess of Rotherhithe, would call her if their son were openly to announce an engagement to her. Someone, no doubt, would search over the long lists of victims, and then—besides explaining how her papers had been lost and her jewels stolen, Marie would have to theorize at great length on how some poor innocent had been mistaken for the Comtesse d'Azalaine by the vile Jacobins.

For the present, it did very nicely to pretend she kept her title a semiguarded secret, in shame at having been reduced to earn her daily bread as a menial. The revelation, artfully made to chosen guests at chosen moments, had earned her much sympathy and numerous gifts. The once or twice an acquaintance had remembered the name of the Comtesse d'Azalaine as one of the victims, a few carefully rehearsed exclamations of horror and tears of indignation at the Tribunal and its careless cruelty had been enough to disarm suspicion. But in this affair of the Viscount Fencourt, it would be much easier if her story were not examined too closely too soon. When she would be the Viscountess Fencourt, she could snap her fingers at any who whispered; then, it would be a greater scandal to the Earl of Rotherhithe's family for Bevil to divorce her than for them all to accept her identity as the Comtesse d'Azalaine and her tale that another poor, nameless unfortunate had been guillotined by mistake under that title, with the rest of the family.

Bevil might suspect, but no matter. She thought he was secured and would elope with her in any case. If he did not—ah, well, she could at least tease and bedevil him while she had the chance, pretending she did not like his scheme with the Chevington lady. In truth, she liked it very much. At present, if the Earl and Countess of Rotherhithe had heard of their son's visits to the Grain and Grape in Little Tiptree, they must believe her merely another of Bevil's passing amours, and not worth investigation. And to—what was the word?—to hoodwink them, so that they believed their son would marry this silly "chit," and then, when it was too late to prevent it, find him married to a chambermaid *comtesse*—ah, what pleasant sport!

And if she were mistaken, and Bevil was not secured? There were other noblemen in England who would feel first pity, then interest, and finally passion for a poor, pretty French *comtesse* who had only escaped just in time from the Terror, lost all her family and wealth, and been reduced to menial employment. She would go to London and choose the best of these noblemen.

Marie tossed her head, ran her fingers through her thick black ringlets, and went back to fluffing the pillows.

Meanwhile, at The Willows, Steddinghill, near Epworthy, Huntingdonshire, Mrs. Henrietta Chevington was rereading the latest letter from her child.

Darnham House
Wednesday morning

My Dearest Mama,

Uncle Darnham and Aunt Cassandra send you their warmest regards.

We went yesterday first to Harrow's and afterwards to Mme Deltouche. Madame has a beautiful ivory-white satin which Aunt Cassie says would set off to perfection the lovely old Brussels lace you gave me. Altho' Madame seemed much more eager to sell us a rather quaint brocade, with very pale powder-blue roses on cream. I suppose because the brocade is 7d. more the yard; but Aunt Cassie says that we must make some sacrifices occasionally, and as expense is to be no object, we must interpret that both ways and sometimes buy what best pleases us even if it is less expensive.

Monday last we met Bevil in the Park. He has a new roan mare, very handsome and mettlesome. He calls her Calpurnia, or Calpie. He also wore a coat trimmed in blue, that I had not seen before, but which he said was quite old. He gave us good-morning very handsomely, and sends you his regards. We shall probably see more of him when we visit Lord Harkendell at Derwent Abbey in a fortnight.

Do you remember Pearl, the cat I wrote to you about, that Aunt Cassie took in from the streets two months ago next Thursday, and washed and called in the veterinary surgeon to examine? Pearl has had a litter—three lovely soft kits, one yellow, one gray and white, and the last one a very fluffy dark gray we think may turn tortoise-shell like its mama. Pearl watches us very suspiciously all the while we hold the dear little creatures, as if she will pounce the moment we move a little finger too quickly, but she purrs loud as a drummer the whole time. Aunt Cassie has promised I may have one, or even two, so soon as they are old enough. I think I will choose the gray-and-white. The first day I held them, the yellow would only crouch in my hand uttering its tiny little mews, but the gray-and-white very quietly and boldly went exploring in my palm, peering out and putting its paws over my fingertips, full of determination to make its own way in the wide world. And perhaps also the dark gray, if it does turn out as lovely a tortoise-shell as its dam.

I hope the viscount will not object to cats.

We look forward eagerly to your coming down next month, and wish you a safe and pleasant journey. Lady Aldiston's carriage was waylaid Monday evening, but she says she has lost more money in an evening at Pharaoh, and as the robber did not touch her jewels, to hear her tell it, it was "rather a divertissement than otherwise." But I'm sure I would not wish such a "divertissement" for you, dear Mama! However, Uncle Darnham says that if one approaches London in full daylight, the danger is not nearly so great as people say; and if you prefer, we shall send Cousins Frederick and Peter to escort you safe.

With the hope that this finds you in good health,

Your loving
Deirdre

Skimming through the paragraphs dealing with kittens and highwaymen, Mrs. Chevington concentrated upon the descriptions of Deirdre's meeting with Bevil and choosing the stuff for her wedding gown, as proofs of her happiness in the match. The widow sighed in contentment and folded the letter again, filing it carefully away with her daughter's earlier missives. What a happy scheme it had proven, to send Deirdre to live with Crump and his new wife! Thereby not only giving her opportunity to acquire town polish, but—still more important—introducing her into circles where she could meet such a catch as the Viscount Fencourt. But there! Had she not always known her daughter was fit to capture the heart of the very cream of young noblemen, if only given the chance?

She did not guess, because she was too proud of her child to see it, that Deirdre cared no more for the viscount now than she had at first, that she mentioned him in her letters only for duty's sake. She did not guess the effort it cost her daughter to refrain from writing of the Reverend the Honorable George Oakton, vicar of Ploverchase. She only saw that Deirdre *did* write of the viscount and of her wedding gown; and she assumed, because she wanted to assume, that her child mentioned Bevil with affection and wedding preparations with eagerness.

The next time Fencourt paid a visit to his *amour* at the Grain and Grape, Marie twitched one light brown hair from his studiously casual coiffure. "So you are to marry this chit of yours a month and a half after she has been visiting here so close at Derwent?" said the chambermaid *comtesse*. "The sand is running out, *ma mie*—if you will leave her and prove yourself honorable to me, you must do it soon!"

4

The Reverend the Honorable George Oakton had been advised by his bishop to thunder against atheistic revolution, and by his patron and father to preach on something gentle, which would not disturb the dozers, of whom his lordship was usually the chiefest.

The bishop's directive had been general, to all preaching clergy of the diocese, while the earl's had been specific. The bishop would probably not be at St. Swithin's in Ploverchase this Sunday, while the earl conceivably might. Mr. Oakton, moreover, could think of few populations less likely to copy the excesses of the Jacobins than the combined congregation of Ploverchase and Little Tiptree. As the final argument, for once filial respect coincided with personal taste.

The young vicar chose for his text Luke 23:34, "Father, forgive them; for they know not what they do," got his thundering done with early by observing that the disorders across the Channel were effects of zeal which knew not what it did, and proceeded quietly to his main head, the duty of Christians to know, and how they might learn with the least incommodity to their daily lives.

Knowing that Miss Chevington was not unlikely to be in the congregation this Sabbath, he had labored much of the week on his sermon, and had been more than usually mindful of the possibility that it might someday be printed and used to bore young people on Sunday afternoons. As well as drawing homely examples from the lives of his parishioners ("A Christian must know the seasons for comforting words or helping hands as a farmer knows the season for haymaking and a dairymaid churning knows when the butter has come"), he tried to insert sly little conceits relative to the whimsies of fashion, the difficulties of selection at fancy shops, and the inconveniences of an ill-tuned pianoforte, such as he hoped a young lady might find at least mildly amusing.

Sometimes he could not but glance down at Miss Chevington, who had, as hoped, appeared with her party, to see whether she appreciated his efforts. Almost always he was rewarded by glimpsing a smile on her delicate, wistfully thin lips. Her aunt, who sat beside her, seemed to smile perpetually; but one could not always be sure whether Lady Darnham were smiling at intentional or unintentional humor. The young cleric found Lady Darnham slightly daunting, and her proximity to her niece helped him remember his duty not to look too often in that direction.

The earl, Lord Darnham, and several others were

comfortably asleep, while the countess watched her younger son with absentminded content. Her elder son was absent. Bevil had either not yet come up from London, or had again, in his undissembling way, chosen bed as more comfortable than church on a cloudy Sabbath morning. Lord Roger, who had accompanied a party of his guests to St. Swithin's even though St. Mary's, Meadfield, was actually closer to Derwent Abbey, was either listening with shrewd appraisal or pursuing his own thoughts behind an excellent mask. As for the rest of the congregation, they were, as usual, for the most part respectfully attentive, or at least tolerant, having learned by now that the young vicar would not strain their endurance with too long a sermon, as his predecessor had habitually done.

Lady Cassandra glanced from the vicar to her rapt niece, and smiled to herself. Very soon now—only a few more days. Darnham would hunt with Lord Roger on Wednesday. The earl would join the hunt, as would, indeed, most men of parts in the neighborhood, leaving Sir Roderic a clear field for the charade. It was fortunate that neither the Countess of Rotherhithe nor her younger son, the vicar, cared for fox-hunting, the former using delicacy of constitution to excuse herself, the latter his studies. Lady Muriel had already extended the invitation to Lady Cassandra and her neice to dine quietly with her on Wednesday; Mr. Oakton, who would doubtless return early to his vicarage so as to be out of temptation's way rather than remain with Deirdre in so small a party, would thus be conveniently at hand for the rescue.

Cassandra's one annoyance was the thought that the viscount might take it into his head to come down to Rotherhithe this week. If so, he might join the hunt, or he might, in a gesture toward keeping up appearances, elect to help entertain his betrothed at dinner. This latter course might put him on hand to join the hue and cry. Suppose he were taken into the secret, to insure against his getting in the way? Cassandra was confident he would not break his heart to lose Deirdre. But, on the other hand, he must have some reason of his own for maintaining the engagement, or he would not have offered; and, unless his motive was to throw Deirdre
28

together with his brother George—which was not only a very curious mode of matchmaking, but also argued more exertion on another's behalf than one could easily credit to the viscount—he might not appreciate having his own plans upset. Moreover, his temper was far too fantastical to be relied upon. No, best keep him in the dark. If his humor held him safe in London, all would be well; if not, surely between herself and Sir Roderic, they could keep him from doing any great mischief to their charade.

The highwayman had spoken of perhaps attending a service at St. Swithin's in order to take the measure beforehand of this callow cleric whom he must permit to rout him. The captain was certainly not present this morning. Perhaps he had come on an earlier Sunday; or perhaps he had decided such an appearance would fix his features too distinctly in the minds of the local folk. No matter. Her captain was well able to improvise.

The vicar's gaze had moved from Deirdre for a few minutes. Lady Darnham glanced at her husband nodding beside her and, in a moment of mischief, pressed one fingertip to his elbow. Without unfolding his arms or lifting his head, he opened his nearer eye and solemnly winked, as much as to say, "These young clergy expect to be fallen asleep on—keeps 'em on their toes." Cassandra gave his elbow a pat before returning her attention to Mr. Oakton.

As the party lingered outside after service to exchange compliments and genteel gossip, Lady Rotherhithe, taking two pinches of snuff to revive herself, condescendingly observed to Lady Cassandra that the latter was "prodigious kind to keep an old woman company when the rest of the neighborhood would be chasing over the countryside from morning until—I shouldn't be surprised—midnight."

Lady Cassandra politely pretended to believe that by "old woman" Lady Rotherhithe was referring to her great-aunt, the Dowager Marchioness of Wildergrise, who was visiting at Rotherhithe Castle, and who had not come out this morning. "It can be no hardship to help bear Lady Wildergrise company. Besides, foxes may be found anywhere in England, but your ladyship's society only at Rotherhithe."

"Still, I think you were considered quite the horsewoman in your day, were you not?" the countess went on. "But perhaps you begin to find the sport tiring at our time of life."

Lady Cassandra glanced over the other's shoulder at her niece and Mr. Oakton, who were speaking earnestly of nothing in particular near the church door. "Indeed," she agreed gravely with Lady Rotherhithe, who was at least a quarter of a century her senior and behaved as if the difference were even greater, "we find other sports better suited to our declining years."

"Very wise, I'm sure. The last hunt, they did not come home before half-past three in the morning, and some of them not even then. Would you credit that several of the party stopped the rest of the night at a local carriagehouse and hardly came in time to dress for dinner next day? Well, well, I look for Bevil before Wednesday —but whether he will dine with us or take the field, I don't pretend to prophesy."

"He may well wish to try his newest mare. In any event, we should not persuade him too strenuously to stop at home simply to be surrounded with female company."

"Bless us, ain't his brother George to dine with us also? And shouldn't he find his own dear little bride-to-be more exciting than a scruffy fox? But he is such a scapegrace, that boy!" Lady Rotherhithe shook her head, displacing a few grains of the powder she still affected despite Mr. Pitt's tax on the stuff. "I really do hope for marriage to steady his character. Such a dear, sweet child! We might have searched a good while before finding him a titled young lady with such sweet manners."

Lady Cassandra correctly interpreted this as a complaint aimed at Deirdre's mere gentility. The countess would not have thought herself truly satisfied with anyone under a duke's daughter as her Bevil's choice. Perhaps, thought Lady Cassandra, he has offered for Deirdre largely to pique his mama. The idea might be worth musing upon. Any point which could conceivably be of service in transferring Deirdre's engagement from the elder brother to the younger was carefully stored up in the aunt's armory. Meanwhile, she said aloud, in answer to Lady Rotherhithe: "Indeed, Deirdre's fortune in attracting your son quite overwhelms us all."

Lord Darnham, who had come up beside his wife after exchanging his own comments with the earl, coughed. "Be raining any minute now," he remarked, nodding in the direction of his niece and the vicar.

Lady Cassandra followed his hint. "Then I must not keep your ladyship out here talking. To be the cause of your being rained upon—it would be unpardonable!" She was on the point of adding that dirt would also ruin the ruffled hem of her own new muslin gown, but checked herself. It would hardly do to let the countess suspect her of flippancy so soon before the important negotiations to come.

Darnham had already taken it upon himself to separate Deirdre and Mr. Oakton, so it only remained for the two parties to make their mutual *adieux* before taking leave of each other.

The rain, when it finally came, late that morning, was a mere shower, after which the clouds parted. Lady Cassandra took the opportunity for a walk before dinner about the park, to enjoy the sunlight glistening on the fresh raindrops caught amongst the autumn foliage. Lord Crump presently joined her, nor was she sorry of her husband's company. She had been reviewing in her mind the letter she would send, by tomorrow's first post, to Sir Roderic, under the direction of "Mrs. Trendennis," and she welcomed the chance to rest her thoughts awhile from her plot.

" 'In your day,' " remarked her husband with a chuckle. "Should join the hunt, m'dear, and show her ladyship your day's just beginning."

"Ah, but don't you see how much younger it makes her feel to pretend that the rest of us are aged?"

Lord Darnham poked thoughtfully with his walking stick at the lichen on the nearest beech tree. "I think you have it, m'dear. Odd thing, that. Her ladyship's much older than I am, but I think I'm a year or two her senior in years."

"Look!" Cassandra pointed to a long-brushed red-brown blur that suddenly raced across the path some yards in front of them.

"The fox? Yes, I believe 'twas . . . Take the field with us this week, Cassandra."

"And who would escort Deirdre to Rotherhithe?"

"Let Deirdre join us, too. We'll find excuses to give her ladyship."

"Do you wish to embarrass our poor niece? You know what an inexpert horsewoman she is."

"No reason for her to be. Has a very good seat, has Deirdre."

Lady Cassandra innocently pretended not to catch the double entendre. "She would have a miserable time of it, riding all day and on into the evening."

"No more miserable than she'll have of it at Rotherhithe. Look here, m'dear, if Bevil comes down, they'd much better be surrounded by the hunt than face to face at the castle. And if he don't come down and dine with you, she'll be face to face with his brother, and you having to listen the whole evening to her ladyship."

"Lady Rotherhithe, taken in reasonably small doses, affords me very good amusement." Cassandra linked her arm through her husband's and patted his plump hand. "There will be other foxhunts. And you must not worry about my being dull on Wednesday. Believe me, Darnham, I shall have very good sport of my own."

5

"I must tolerate him," Deirdre admonished herself, concentrating more on that thought than on the song she was singing. "I must learn to tolerate him." The task seemed to grow more difficult, rather than less so, with every meeting. When she had been away from Bevil, Viscount Fencourt, for some time, she could frequently gloss over his objectionable qualities and reconcile herself to her future. After all, if a young man were so universally considered an enviable catch, there must surely be some reason for it. It could not be entirely his face, figure, title, and fortune that other young women saw in him, could it? No, he *must* have amiable qualities which she could not see at present, but which would become visible in the intimacy of marriage.

At least being married to Bevil would make her sister to Mr. Oakton, and that would make possible very long conversations with the vicar in the family circle, and that was something. Something, however, which did not comfort her as much as it might have.

Chance encounters with Bevil in the park usually did little to upset her hopes for a reasonably tolerable wedded life; he would doff his hat and pass on after a few polite pleasantries which cost comparatively little effort to overlook. But parties like the present dinner at Rotherhithe Castle would rip the whole delicate fabric of her wistful fantasy to shreds. Why had he not joined the hunt instead, if he meant to ignore her for most of the evening and treat her with his offhand possessiveness during the rest of it? Even allowing for her newness to such society (she had lived all her life until the last year and a half quietly in Steddinghill with her mother and no higher society than Sir Hugh and Lady Violet), and for her inexperience in matters of the heart and of courtship, she thought it could not be quite natural for an engaged lover to spend so little of the evening with his betrothed. Yet whenever he did condescend to favor her with a few words, she found his careless compliments more distasteful than his previous and subsequent inattention.

It was as if he had used her presence as a mere excuse to come down to Rotherhithe for some purpose of his own. But what sort of purpose could that be? Certainly he looked the very personification of unthinking indolence as he lounged there on the green-and-buff sofa, sipping his coffee at an impossible angle and dividing

33

his attentions between Aunt Cassandra and the old Dowager Marchioness of Wildergrise.

Presently, when Deirdre reached the end of her song, no doubt he would come over to the pianoforte and request that she honor the company with another piece. Then, of course, he would retire once more to do anything else but listen. Had he dined at Rotherhithe today merely in order to annoy her?

Mr. Oakton, although delegated to play backgammon with his mother, was listening far more attentively than anyone else in the drawing room. Indeed, he must know better than Deirdre herself what songs she was honoring the company with. Why did not the viscount take his brother's place at the backgammon table? Aunt Cassandra would be perfectly well able to entertain Lady Wildergrise alone; before the gentlemen joined them, she had entertained both the marchioness and the countess with perfect ease. And Bevil had often enough, on past occasions, left his betrothed and his brother to keep each other company—why not this evening? Had it anything to do, perhaps, with the smallness of the present party? How Deirdre longed to know what had passed between the two young gentlemen as they sat over their brandy in the rather unusually short time before they joined the ladies!

She reached the end of the song and, surprisingly, Bevil did not request another. Half resigned, Deirdre waited a few moments at the instrument, playing random snatches and expecting he was only absent in his mind, and would be at her again so soon as he realized she was no longer singing. Mr. Oakton would not be the one to importune her—*he* could sense when she would prefer not to sing.

Eventually, glancing from the backgammon table to the sofa, she saw that her aunt was engaging the viscount in the most animated conversation in which he had indulged all evening. Dear Aunt Cassie! She was diverting his attention! Deirdre slipped from the bench and made her escape before Bevil could disengage himself from Lady Cassandra.

Deirdre moved toward the backgammon table, stopping at what she hoped was a respectful distance to watch the game. Oh, it was almost over. Mr. Oakton had let his mother win—she was sure of it. Perhaps to shorten the game?

"You must let me allow you a chance for your revenge, George," said Lady Rotherhithe, with an upward glance at Deirdre that made the girl retreat.

"I fear not, Mother." He glanced at the elegant old silver clock on the mantelpiece, compared the time with his own simple, tasteful gold pocket watch. "If I am to stop this evening with the Wingates and help young Tom with his Latin, I'm afraid I must leave you now."

"The time for morning calls and tutoring," said her ladyship severely, "is in the morning."

"True, Mother, but the lad had a good deal of work in the morning."

"You spend entirely too much time and worry on these common parishioners of yours, George. It is good for neither your health nor your breeding. After your brother is married and settled, I trust you will treat your family with equal courtesy to what you lavish at present upon your rustic scholars."

From earlier conversations with him, carefully treasured up in her diary and her memory, Deirdre knew that Mr. Oakton considered charity not only to take precedence over what elegant society considered etiquette, but sometimes even to demand that a clergyman, like a doctor, bend the latter forms. He did not, however, take the opportunity to admonish his mother with a platitude, as the Reverend Mr. Bamfyld of Steddinghill was so fond of doing. He merely addressed her ladyship a few words of apology. Deirdre did not overhear them distinctly.

There was a sharp ache in her nose and cheekbones, and telltale moisture gathering in her eyes; and she felt awkward and conspicuous here in an open space of the room. Blinking hard, she glanced about for cover. Return to the sofa to beg another cup of tea after her vocal exertions was impossible—the viscount sat beside Aunt Cassandra on the sofa. In desperation, Deirdre moved to the fireplace and began scrupulously to study a gold candlestick on the mantel. By the time Mr. Oakton reached her to make his *adieux,* she had recovered well

35

enough to control her emotions, even when, after kissing her hand, he glanced up with what seemed to her a momentarily unguarded look of affection.

Then he was gone! He had not stopped to supper—she might not see him again until Sunday. For the rest of the evening she was at the mercy of the viscount, her betrothed, with only Aunt Cassandra as buffer.

"Still rather too early to sup," drawled the viscount. "I tell you what, Mater—you should make up a card table."

"Mercy, Bevil, what are you thinking of? Here are five of us present."

"Lord, I never play with ladies when I can avoid it. I'll have my entertainment looking on, to study the curious ways of four lovely dames engrossed in the mysteries of quadrille."

"Come, then," said Aunt Cassandra. "Lady Muriel shall be the Queen of Diamonds, Lady Agnes the Queen of Clubs, Deirdre of Hearts, and myself of Spades; and we will see whether we cannot convince you that you might not like to play with us sometimes, after all."

For all Lady Cassandra's efforts, it was, as Deirdre had foreseen from the moment of Mr. Oakton's departure, an extraordinarily dreary evening. Bevil hovered around the table, looking over all their shoulders in turn, but over Deirdre's longest, and over the others, it seemed, only to chuckle and wink and throw sly glances to her as if to say "You could win this fish easily if you saw what I see," or "You're quite ruined now—pity I can't tell you how to save something from the wreckage." Of course she played miserably, to his obvious though unspoken delight. And after he tired at last of wandering round the table, he drew up a chair and planted himself close beside his future wife. There he would perhaps have sat the rest of the evening, laughing over her shoulder, but for Aunt Cassie. In answer to Deirdre's look of trapped appeal, Lady Cassandra remarked, "Lord Bevil, I fear I must beg you to break your rule after all and take my place for a moment."

It was rather better to have the viscount across the table from her than studying her play from behind; and, although Deirdre still played very badly, Bevil was now himself trapped into making good his air of superiority and concentrating on his own play; old Lady Agnes, dull in other respects, retained a shrewdness at quadrille, and cards were a minor passion with Lady Muriel, so for a while Deirdre's time passed slightly less painfully. When Lady Cassandra, after a prolonged absence, reentered the drawing room and quietly satisfied herself that Bevil was more or less entrenched in the game, she moved to the pianoforte and tranquilly began to play, leaving him caught at the card table until supper.

Supper was no better than quadrille. With the most irreproachable table manners, the viscount somehow contrived to take his food in a way indefinably offensive to his fiancée. Deirdre herself could eat very little, only a few bites of chicken and a small dish of custard.

Early as it was when their carriage was called, Bevil now made a veiled display of yawning, as if he waited with them only for politeness' sake. This although it was well know, even to Deirdre, that he habitually kept very late hours indeed in town, often, according to rumor, remaining up all night. Really, it seemed to her that his behavior the entire evening had been aimed at no other end than to make himself odious to his unhappy bride-to-be! By the time he handed up the two ladies into their carriage, it was all Deirdre could do to blink back her tears.

The cool evening air and the bouncing of the carriage behind the smooth-trotting ponies restored her somewhat, until she remembered that in less than two months she would no longer be able to escape his company with such comparative ease. What must it be, then, to ride back from a dinner party with him instead of Aunt Cassie? Or to remain in the same house with him after their own guests would be gone? To endure his possessive teasings or his supercilious neglect of her when he was actually her husband? To be . . . alone with him in his chamber or hers . . .

In a few days, if he avoided her company for that length of time, she might be able again to think more calmly of these prospects—but for now . . . And when she would be his wife and no longer able to escape from him except for a rare, stray fortnight now and then? Other wives, she had always understood, frequently wished their husbands with them in the evening, and grew annoyed when they stopped away from home too long. What would it be to be a wife who actually *hoped* for her husband to stop away from home for days and nights on end?

No, she could not bear it. She glanced toward her aunt. Lady Cassandra was sitting quietly, gazing out at the moonlit scene. Was she actually smiling a little? Deirdre, in her own misery, could not imagine what her aunt could find in the evening to make her smile; and that strange, preoccupied half-smile kept the younger woman from speaking at once, forced her to screw up her courage and remind herself of all the reason she had to be sure of her aunt's sympathy.

To break off her engagement now—would not it devastate her mother? Shock society? Bar her from the circles into which Uncle Crump and Aunt Cassandra had introduced her? Mark her as a silly, wayward girl with no provident eye to her own future? Was it even possible that she *could* break off a match with a member of the nobility? Yet she had heard of other women who broke engagements—not many, true, but a few, here and there. Had not Aunt Cassandra herself refused one or two men who offered for her, between the tragic loss of her own true love and her marriage with Uncle Crump? although Deirdre was not sure whether Aunt Cassandra had actually entered into any formal engagement with these men, or merely refused them at once when they offered . . . Still, Aunt Cassie would at least know whether it were possible, and if so, how it could be accomplished.

They were nearing Ploverchase Hill, almost halfway back to Derwent. If Deirdre meant to ask, she had best speak soon. "Aunt Cassie," she began timidly, "is it possible for . . . for a young woman to break off an—"

"Hold!" The heavy voice cut in on them from without. "Stand, and deliver!"

6

Yes, thought Lady Cassandra approvingly, he has chosen
his ground well. A short gallop to northwest and up, and
he is on the hill and in one of the copses, very convenient
to the path between the villages. And from a certain ring
to his words, more theatrical and less businesslike than
she remembered from his stopping her brother's carriage
two years before, she understood that he had entered
into the spirit of the evening, that he would play his role
to the hilt.

But Deirdre—Cassandra's heart misgave her a little
when she turned to her niece. Deirdre had started to say
something; Cassandra had tried to listen, so as to be able
to make some intelligible reply at need; but at the highwayman's interrupting shout, the girl had shrunk abject-
ly back against the cushions.

"Don't be afraid, dear," whispered Lady Cassandra,
leaning over and taking her hand as the carriage came to
a stop. "We have money enough with us to satisfy him."

Although trembling slightly, Deirdre remained utterly
silent. Almost as if she were more resigned than frightened? Cassandra's misgivings grew. She would have felt
easier if her niece exhibited nerves and flutters, but this
silent acceptance . . . Now the moment had arrived, she
suddenly wondered if she had done wrong to arrange
this. What had Deirdre been about to ask her? Something about breaking off the match? The brooch of
paste diamonds, Charles's gift, lay snug in a pocket of
Lady Cassandra's gown, ready to be pinned to her bodice

39

in a moment as a last-minute signal to Sir Roderic that the game should be called off.

But she reminded herself that her captain would be gentle and gallant, and that the joy of being rescued by George Oakton would more than repay Deirdre for the passing fears. Had Cassandra not foreseen that the girl must of course be frightened—would not that be a necessary part of the evening's adventure? Had she not, in sober judgment and after months of observing her niece, formed her careful opinion that Deirdre's constitution was not only capable of surviving the thrill, but of treasuring it up afterwards?

And what must Sir Roderic have thought of a woman who would change her mind and back away from her carefully laid plans at the last moment, for no more reason than an ungrounded and vague uneasiness? To have called him this distance, discommoded his own affairs to enlist his particular aid, and then call him off for no good reason—she would have deserved the name of a fickle, undecided female, unsettled in purpose and unsympathetic to her friends.

These were the thoughts of a few seconds. Outside, they could hear the highwayman relieving Thomas of his purse (which Cassandra had given her loyal coachman beforehand, along with instructions for his behavior during the robbery). "Does not Thomas have a pistol?" whispered Deirdre, speaking at last, her face very close to her aunt's ear.

"These robbers rarely mean bodily harm unless opposed," Cassandra whispered in reply, hugging the child. "Give me your purse, dear—we will give them to him at once."

Deirdre fumbled for her purse and put it into the older woman's hand. A light little thing, containing only a few sixpences for the countess's card table. What might Deirdre have thought had she known the very substantial amount her aunt had carried along to a quiet dinner party?

Her purse delivered, the girl sank back, quivering, in Lady Cassandra's arms. After a moment of hesitation, her ladyship decided it would do no harm to confide, "I have even been abducted by one of them once, and come to no harm whatever."

"Aunt! You never—"

"I tell no one."

"Held for ransom? Oh, Aunt Cassie, suppose—"

"Hush, Deirdre, hush. All will be well."

Sir Roderic had made Thomas climb down and lie on the ground, and now he was coming to the carriage window. He had brought one of the carriage lanterns, which he flashed in on them. Lady Cassandra doubted he did not usually look over his victims by lantern light when he struck after dark—it would give them too memorable a glimpse of his own gray eyes and high forehead, besides encumbering his left hand. No doubt tonight he was looking for the sparkle of paste diamonds at her throat, and not finding them. Lady Cassandra nodded very slightly. There was no danger of her niece seeing the nod; Deirdre's eyes were fixed on the masked apparition.

"My ladies," said the captain sociably. "My very lovely ladies."

Cassandra held out both their purses to him. "As you see, sir, we wear no jewels save our cameos, to which you are welcome."

"I see two jewels far fairer than any cameo, *mesdames*. As I cannot take both, my difficulty lies in the selection."

"Oh, Aunt Cassie!" murmured Deirdre, her arm clutching more tightly around the older woman.

It is not yet too late to give him a new signal, thought Lady Cassandra. Not to abandon the abduction—having said so much, he will not change his avowed intent. But at some small hint he would take me instead.

And what would have been the use of that? To leave Deirdre, terrified at her aunt's abduction, to the loyal but justifiably confused care of a coachman who expected a much different charade and had not been prepared for this turn of events. Who would be the only gainer? Cassandra herself. No, it would be unpardonably selfish—she had already had her adventure with him, had already sounded him and could entrust Deirdre to him with confidence for a few hours. Deirdre would never have such another opportunity.

"You had best be content with the coin, sir," said

Cassandra coldly, for appearance' sake. "The heavier your prize, the more encumbered your escape."

"The sole consideration which prevents me from taking both. But even one such beauty is well worth the risk."

"A grave risk. This is not a desert, sir. Help will come at any moment." Meant to sound like a defiant warning, this was actually a hint that he should not prolong the pretense of making a choice. Deirdre was trembling with a suspense that served no useful purpose in her adventure, and at any moment Cassandra's more self-centered temptation might overpower her.

"Many thanks, my lady." He touched his pistol—which they had arranged must be charged with powder only—to the side of his forehead in a salute. "I will take the quieter."

"Oh, Aunt!" Deirdre clung tighter yet.

Sir Roderic reached through the window and set the lantern on the carriage seat before opening the door. "The younger and the one of fewer words, then. I must caution you, my child, not to scream like that again."

"Be content with a lock of her hair, sir," said Lady Cassandra. "Ransom will be paid as fully as for the child herself."

"Perhaps, and perhaps not. But who would be content with a corner of the canvas when he might gaze at it in its entirety, even for a single night?"

The women remained locked in each other's arms, huddling against the far side of the seat, so that he had at last to dismount from his well-trained horse and enter the carriage with them. He took Lady Cassandra's wrist in order to drag them out together. After a brief, conspiratorial pressure, he held it loosely, allowing her to twist her hand and return his signal with a tap of her fingertips before pretending to be dragged forth against her will.

She had a delicate task, for Deirdre was struggling in earnest not to be dragged. For a moment, between the captain's mock force and Deirdre's desperate leverage, Lady Cassandra felt as if the entire labor would fall to herself. She jerked her wrist almost free of Sir Roderic's grasp. To her relief, he took the hint, gripped her more firmly, and exerted himself. The next several seconds, although they resulted in sore arm muscles for Lady Cassandra, gave her the satisfaction of a realistic struggle and drawing-forth.

The next moment, when he had got them outside, was still harder. Dropping Cassandra's wrist, he took Deirdre's—and Cassandra's conscience pricked her again at the girl's struggles, at the way she still clung to her aunt. "Do as he says, dear!" exclaimed her ladyship, managing to add in the girl's ear, "Wait your chance—help will come."

Then, to her relief, Sir Roderic broke her hold on Deirdre and pulled the young woman some feet away. "Quiet now, child," he admonished, "or I may be forced to put a ball into your companion."

"Oh, Aunt!"

"Do as he says, Deirdre—for now. Don't worry—he daren't harm us. The hue and cry will be on his heels in moments. Sir, you have not named the ransom nor told me where to direct it."

"When I escape your rustic hue and cry, I'll send a message." He swept Lady Cassandra a hasty bow, then picked up Deirdre in both arms and lifted her to the horse's back, vaulting up himself the instant after and clamping one arm about her waist. "You will not try to jump, sweet lady," Cassandra heard him tell her gently. "You might injure yourself." The horse jumped into a canter, probably at a pressure from the rider's knees.

He could have started his mare into a gallop equally well. Yet he did not gallop even after a few moments of the gentler, slower gait. Lady Cassandra listened to the sound of the canter fading away in the direction of Ploverchase Hill, and nodded. She had told him Deirdre was a poor horsewoman; even though he held her secure, he would not risk her falling, jumping, or being unduly frightened by the speed of a gallop.

Yes, the child was in safe custody. By the time Mr. Oakton rescued her, she would probably be glad to see her captor escape arrest. Lady Cassandra's earlier misgivings dissolved in a twinge of envy.

"Now on to Tiptree, mum?" asked Thomas, who had risen from the ground and approached his mistress.

"Now on to Tiptree, Thomas. And remember, I have been exceedingly shaken by this calamity, and must be taken to Mr. Bellew's house at once."

7

Marie Cluzot flung down her mending for the dozenth time, rose, and walked to the window of her small upper room. *"Par mon marteau!* Where is he, then? Is he to come this night, or is he not?" Opening the shutter a crack, she peered out at the dark street winding up toward the gaggle of houses that formed the tiny village of Little Tiptree. Such a tiny little village, not worth two words in its name, no, not even when one of the words was to tell how tiny it was. The chambermaid pouted at the scene— no life, no movement, no bustle, only an old watchman who now and then came tottering on his feeble old legs, swaying beneath the weight of his feeble old lantern, staggering to the Grain and Grape to drink away the rest of his watch and confide to Mr. Perry that all was well. As why should the old one not drink and loaf instead of making his silly rounds? Was there ever any excitement here? *Ciel!* If they ever should come to Little Tiptree, the robbers and the highwaymen, they would die of the boredom. But why did Bevil not come?

Ah, well! It was early yet. The time did not pass so slowly at one of those brave dinner parties for the *aristos,* as here in a chambermaid's room where one mended sheets and stockings to occupy one's evening. Bevil made the great pretense that he was bored beyond endurance at their quiet gatherings, playing quadrille with his *maman* for sixpences, and pretending to flatter his fiancée—but Marie knew better. No, he was not bored. To him the hour was early yet, and to herself the hour merely seemed late
44

because it was truly boring—a boredom Bevil knew nothing about at all—to sit and mend stockings, with one's small bundle tied waiting beneath one's bed.

But it was better to mend the stockings than to sit doing nothing at the window, or to sit with one's hand in one's lap and one's gaze on the old, scratched clock that still kept good time because it was meant to tell a servant when she should go down to her work. No, it was not for Mr. and Mrs. Perry she mended these sheets and stockings, it was to keep herself a little busy, to make the minutes pass not quite so slowly.

Read she could not—Molière and Chateaubriand, they had quite lost their charms this evening, and as for these authors *anglais*—bah! She did not even keep them in her room. To write a letter would have been something; but to whom could she write it? "My dear Monsieur Perry, I have eloped to be married with Monsieur the Viscount Fencourt, you must hire a new maid to make your beds and tease your guests." *Mon Dieu!* Would they not see for themselves quickly enough that she had run off? And as for the who, best to say nothing until it were made very sure and she could return as my lady the Viscountess Fencourt, and bespeak a dish of coffee from Mrs. Perry in the common room downstairs. *Non, non,* not the common room. A private parlor she would have, like the great lady she would be. But if something should go wrong and she not return the Viscountess Fencourt, best no one should know what had been her plans. They were private affairs, her plans, and the fewer knew of them the easier to change them and make new. Even if she had known anyone beyond these little villages, to whom she might direct a letter, how would Mr. Perry post it for her when she had run off and left him with no one to make the beds and clean the rooms and do the mending in the evening, except the fat, lazy Jenny?

But why did Bevil not come? Did he think she would wait forever for him? Bah! She would run off alone and go to London, and then let him find his own way out of this marriage he had made believe to arrange with his English chit!

Or was it herself, Marie, *la Comtesse d'Azalaine,* to

whom he was lying? Ah, *mon bel ami*, the days are gone when lovers stabbed their rivals at the altar (and you and your chit would not be worth the grief in any case), but we will find some polite, some exquisite revenge when we have found another noble English gentleman and are the Marchioness of Wambly or the Duchess of Twiddleham! To lie to a chambermaid—that would not be so much, little more than to lie to an English miss. For Marie was fair-minded even in her annoyance, and did they not lie continually to women, these brave gentlemen? But to lie to *la Comtesse d'Azalaine*—that was serious—ah, very serious, *ma mie*. I might have had you torn apart by horses in the old times, if you were a peasant and I truly the *comtesse*. And what is even worse —to keep me in expectation for all these hours, mending stockings and looking up at the ugly clock and listening to the boring quiet outside—this is what will be unforgivable, this is what I will find some sweet vengeance to repay you for!

What was that? A clattering in the street? No, it could not be Bevil. He would not announce to all the world his intention, by clattering up with a carriage and pair in this way—not unless he was very, very drunk. They would come back again to Little Tiptree in his large carriage with four matched white horses, when she would stop to drink coffee or chocolate at the Grain and Grape; but they would slip out tonight quietly, as riders, with her behind him on this newest mare of his. So, the noise outside was someone else, some gentry coming late to the inn.

This was not Marie's worry, no. Her work began early in the morning, before the cock with his *cocorico! cocorico!* Almost never did Mr. Perry demand that Marie rise out of bed for a late traveler. Almost never did the late travelers come here, and when they came, there were enough downstairs with Monsieur and Madame, Jenny and Will. But that they should come was some small excitement, some refreshment during her long wait. Marie hopped from her chair, blew out the candle so that she could see outside and not be seen, and opened the shutter several inches.

Yes, the carriage was nearly to the inn already. Two

horses—her ears were good; again she had known the number from the sound. But were they not stopping? He seemed in wonderful haste, this fat coachman. He was not yet even slowing his team. He must pull them up short at the very last moment, and that was not good for the horses. Only young rakehells like Bevil drove their teams so, to make the big display—good, fat, respectable coachmen did not.

Was it possible he would not stop at the Grain and Grape? *Vraiment!* He was passing by without a turn of his head. Where was this carriage going, then? The carriage of an *aristo*—Marie had glimpsed the fine blazon on its side, shining a little in the lantern light as the coach sped past. Whose blazon it was she did not know —impossible to see it clearly in the night and at such speed, even if she had been able already to learn all these English arms. But where were they driving in so much haste? There was no other inn or carriagehouse in Little Tiptree. To some private house? What families lived in Little Tiptree to whom an *aristo* would be hurrying so late at night? *Non, non,* the *aristos,* they would go to the abbey or the castle, not come here.

Perhaps they had learned of her elopement? They meant to stop them, Bevil and herself? Ah, that would show he was serious to her and meant to come. But no— why would these meddlers, coming into Tiptree, not stop at once at the Grain and Grape and accost her? She wished they had done so; she was in a mood to have snapped her fingers with pleasure in some sleek English goddam's face. Perhaps they knew Bevil would elope with someone from this village, but did not know with whom or from what house? No. Even in such a case, the Grain and Grape must be the first place they would stop and make their questions. And when one investigated such an affair, one came gently and softly—one did not begin by clattering down the quiet street at something after ten o'clock in the evening.

Unless Bevil had already left Rotherhithe Castle, and these people had learned of it and were hurrying to meet him and keep him from the inn? And why then would they take a carriage, and not ride on the horses' backs, as he was riding, for speed and liberty from the roads—that

47

would be stupidness. No, whoever these persons were, their trouble did not concern Marie's own affair.

Still, she owed them the great debt, these unknowns. They had diverted her for several minutes of this long, long evening. Returning to her small fireplace, she poked up her fire, added coals with a prodigal hand, and relit her candle. Then she sat and picked up the stockings again with a sigh.

He had promised her to come by midnight, for they should be many hours on their way to Gretta Green before she was missed before dawn and he was missed very late in the morning. Well! She would wait for him until half-past twelve. Then she would go to bed, and if he so truly meant to bring her away, he must come another night. It would be a small test of his devotion, that—far less than he deserved; but there were no lions here for him to fight, no rivers that she herself could not have swum with ease. Perhaps, for his penance and proof of devotion, she should demand he take her at once, before they were yet married, to his parents and introduce her as his affianced bride? *Bien sur*, the earl his papa would then find ways to stop the marriage—ah, but their expressions, their shock, their *bouleversement*—it would be worth the price, almost!

8

Thomas, meanwhile, whipped Beauty and Teazle on for another quarter mile before drawing up at Wantage, the residence of Mr. Bellew, the apothecary. After jumping down to ring, he returned at once to hand her ladyship down from the coach. She leaned heavily on his arm, walking as if in a daze; she had decided, despite her captain's opinion, that a fit of the vapors would best answer her purpose. No one but her brother, a hired coach boy, and Thomas himself (who had come with her from her father's household to continue in her service) had witnessed her behavior two years previously on the occasion of her own kidnapping by Sir Roderic; nobody of her acquaintance in Little Tiptree or Ploverchase, Rotherhithe, or even Derwent Abbey could know how she would react in a crisis. Certainly Mr. Bellew could not know. She had met him only two or three times before, once at a ball given by a local gentleman and once when he came to attend Lord Roger's gout. Moreover, experience had shown her that calm women received very little attention and sympathy during times of crisis, while vapory and hysterical women received a great deal. And how often had she the opportunity of indulging her theatrical bent to such a degree as this?

Mr. Bellew's housekeeper opened the door. She had been some years with her bachelor master, and had clearly learnt to take a situation in hand at once. "Lord bless us!" she remarked—not, Cassandra perceived, that she was unduly alarmed, having seen other folk in sorry case brought round to the apothecary's house; but that strong expressions were a means of comforting the stricken. "Here, here, then!"

She took Lady Cassandra from the coachman's arms and herself supported her to the parlor, where she settled her on a small sofa and provided her with brandy and a vinaigrette. Thomas had followed; Mrs. Epworthy now directed him to make up the fire; she would send Jacky in with more coals, summon the master from his study, and then come back with some nice hot tea for the poor lady.

Left alone with the coachman for a few moments, Cassandra opened her eyes to find her faithful servant peering down at her anxiously, as if half afraid that she were not, after all, pretending. Dear old Thomas! If she had caused him concern, knowing the scheme as he did beforehand, no doubt she had really succeeded in hoodwinking Mr. Bellew's housekeeper, for all the latter's experience.

Lady Cassandra solemnly winked up at Thomas. She dared say nothing aloud, for Mr. Bellew or Jacky might

49

arrive at any moment; but the wink was enough. Thomas beamed, fully reassured, and went back to the fireplace.

Mrs. Epworthy had, of course, closed the door to prevent drafts. Thus, a fresh draft as well as the sound which accompanied the opening of the door alerted Lady Cassandra. Moaning, she held the vinaigrette to her nose, careful to sniff very lightly.

"Dear lady!"

The apothecary strode quickly to her side, clicking his tongue. Thomas, seeing what was needed, placed a chair beside the sofa, and Mr. Bellew sat, taking Cassandra's wrist. This was the supreme test, whether she could deceive a medical man of twenty years' practice. She let her arm go completely limp; and she inhaled deeply at the vinaigrette, which actually did make her giddy for a few moments.

He laid his hand on her forehead, then pulled down the skin below her left eye. She rolled her eyes upward and let the lids droop, hoping that was the expected reaction in one on the verge of a faint.

"Some kind of shock, apparently," he remarked, seemingly convinced of the reality of her condition, although a trifle perplexed as to its exact nature. "What happened? Some accident?"

"Highwayman," said Thomas.

"Mr. Oakton!" exclaimed Lady Cassandra. She had been so caught up in her performance she had almost forgot its purpose.

"Mr. Oakton? Good Lord, man, has—"

"Bring Mr. Oakton!" her ladyship amended. "Needed —save her—"

"There, there, dear Lady Darnham. Calm yourself . . . rest. All will be well. Rest now." The apothecary patted her hand reassuringly, then left her side to ask Thomas in an undertone (which, however, she managed to overhear) what had happened?

This was not at all to Lady Cassandra's liking. She had thought to enjoy a circle of attention, but now found that the attention paid her was of the sort given a sick child, excluding her from rational debate of the situation. If she were not to be shunted into a completely

50

passive and patronized role, it was high time to make at least a partial recovery. Not *too* quickly, however, lest she arouse suspicion. Thomas was well rehearsed in the tale, and she let him tell the apothecary, in tones just audible to her, how the highwayman had carried off young Miss Chevington and left orders that the nearest clergyman be summoned to deliver the ransom. Before the coachman finished, Cassandra had eased herself upright into a sitting position on the sofa and relegated the vinaigrette to her lap, although she still held her head bent forward a little, with one hand to her forehead.

Mr. Bellew was most satisfyingly scandalized at the tale. He was trying, as it seemed, to take command of the situation; but the shock of such an outrage in this quiet neighborhood prevented his being decisive. "Good God!" Cassandra heard once, quite loudly, and then in a lower voice, clearly remembering his patient, "Here? Damme, they're everywhere!"

"Aye, m'lud," answered Thomas.

"And you stood by and permitted him to take the young lady, man?"

"What else could he have done?" said Lady Cassandra, unwilling to see her loyal servant censured even for the sake of charade.

"My most dear ladyship!" The apothecary hurried back to her side. "Rest and put all worry from your mind. We will see to everything—"

"I most certainly shall *not* put all worry from my mind. What! While my niece is being held to ransom? No!" as Mr. Bellew attempted to push her back into a reclining position. "Indeed, I feel very much stronger now."

"Nevertheless, dear lady, rest and quiet—ah! Here's Mrs. Epworthy now. Mrs. Epworthy, if you will just stay with her ladyship—"

"You are not going off to browbeat my coachman!" said Lady Cassandra. "What would you have had him do? He could not have fired at once without alarming the horses, and he could not fire afterwards without being shot himself in return. How would that have helped us?"

"Here, what's all this to-do?" The housekeeper set

down her tea tray as if to guard against dropping it on being informed.

"A highway robber has stopped us and stolen my niece, Miss Chevington, to hold her to ransom," said Lady Cassandra at once.

Mrs. Bellew, so self-controlled in face of simple, accidental complaints, forgot matronly reserve and explained, "Good Lord! What, here in Tiptree?"

Mr. Bellew began again at Thomas. "But surely you might have —"

"Might have what?" said Cassandra. "The robber had him on the ground and his pistol taken away before ever he approached us in the coach."

"Please, your ladyship, please calm yourself and rest. Here, let me give you a powder—"

"No, I will not take a sleeping powder!" Her ladyship was suddenly alarmed. "I tell you, we had no idea but that he meant only to take our money—"

"There, there, of course not," said Mrs. Epworthy. "Here, drink some tea at least. Tsk, tsk! Here in Tiptree!"

Cassandra took the cup and sniffed at it suspiciously, wishing she had watched it poured.

"But what's to be done?" the apothecary was saying. "A very mild preparation, Lady Darnham. Only to calm your nerves, nothing more."

"I do not wish my nerves to be calmed. My niece is in danger and I am as calm as I wish to be under the circumstances."

"It's good, plain tea, your ladyship. I never put things in until I know the master's judgment. Here, I'll drink a dish of it myself. Does your ladyship take sugar?"

"No, thank you, nothing." Lady Cassandra sipped cautiously, satisfying herself that the only flavor was that of tea. "I must have my wits about me when I speak with Mr. Oakton."

"Please, Lady Darnham, you'll do serious damage to your nerves. Leave the matter entirely in our hands. If you'll only take a little powder, it will help you to feel much more calm . . ."

Good Heavens! thought Cassandra, Sir Roderic was right—it was a grave mistake to have the vapors. "I will

52

not take anything until I have talked with Mr. Oakton," she capitulated. "Send your boy for him at once."

"What?" Mr. Bellew stared at her for a second, then took a few steps between sofa and fireplace, industriously hemming. "Send Jacky?"

"Send a child of ten years out, with highwaymen loose in the neighborhood?" said Mrs. Epworthy.

"Dear Mrs. Epworthy, what on earth would the bandit wish with Jacky? Why, he himself told us to summon the clergyman. What purpose would he have to stop the messenger? Assuming he has even so much as lingered in the immediate neighborhood."

"How should he know Jacky's business?" Apparently satisfied that she had made her point, the housekeeper poured her tea into her saucer.

"Exactly!" said the apothecary. "No; no, far better raise the hue and cry here in Tiptree at once."

"I beg you will not rouse the village," said Lady Cassandra, wondering if she ought to have shrieked a negative and deciding that a shriek would only have brought on more talk of powders. "This man has Deirdre in his power—what might he do with her were he to panic on hearing the constabulary raised?"

"Leave the child and run," said Mrs. Epworthy.

"Yes, yes, safest for her," concurred Mr. Bellew. "We'll just send Jacky round to Randall's, and—"

"You have not seen the highwayman," said Cassandra, "and he struck me as a desperate rogue." (Forgive me, Captain, she thought.) "I say we must first have Deirdre back safe before we provoke him to . . . desperate measures."

"That's right, sir," Thomas corroborated. "I wouldn't like to hear his threats again."

"But . . . but consider, Lady Darnham, in such a case . . ." The apothecary floundered, clearly trying to put the case delicately.

"Best have her back soon or not at all," said the housekeeper, more bluntly.

"Nonsense!" Lady Cassandra forgot her weakened condition and rose. "I hope you do not think me a fool! I do not believe he dare threaten her honor while he hopes

53

for the ransom tonight. But in any case—in *any* case—I prefer my niece returned alive."

"Dear Lady Darnham! Do rest—you must not excite yourself! If you would only take a very small preparation and permit us to handle—"

Cassandra sat again. "I am no more excited than the situation warrants. The safest way to recover Miss Chevington is to maintain secrecy and follow the scoundrel's instructions."

"Time enough to raise the country and take him when Miss is safe back," said Thomas.

"Exactly! Thomas must return at once to Derwent Abbey and bring back my jewels and money for the ransom, while Jacky goes for Mr. Oakton—"

"I will not send Jacky out with this rogue in the neighborhood," repeated Mr. Bellew.

"Good Mr. Bellew, do you suppose the abductor will remain hovering near the footpath?" cried Lady Cassandra, rising again. "Must I go myself for the vicar?"

She could hardly have caused more consternation had she fallen into a fit of screaming hysteria. Not only the apothecary, but also the housekeeper, rose to lay restraining hands on her shoulders. For a giddy moment Cassandra considered revealing the whole plot to them, at risk of—she knew not what.

Thomas came to her rescue. "I'll go for Mr. Oakton, m'lady."

"Ah!" said Mr. Bellew, as if it had been his own inspiration. "Yes, quite right, quite right. A very good plan. An excellent plan, your ladyship. Now, please, *please* do sit down and calm yourself."

"He can explain it all to Mr. Oakton at the vicarage," said Mrs. Epworthy, "and nobody will need to make these extra trips back and forth over the footpath at all."

Lady Cassandra looked at Thomas. The coachman's right eyelid twitched in a half wink.

She decided to argue no further. She did not at once see how Thomas was to get George Oakton onto the path over Ploverchase Hill, when it would naturally be expected he would go in the carriage and bring back the vicar, if he brought him to Little Tiptree at all, in the same way. And it must seem strange if Thomas did not assist Mr. Oakton in the rescue, thus robbing Mr. Oakton of some of his planned glory. With this in mind, Cassandra might have made another attempt to salvage her original scenario in all its glory, by insisting that Thomas must hurry on to Derwent and bring her money and jewels as quickly as possible.

But every good plan must be flexible enough to allow some little change, some improvisation. The apothecary and his housekeeper appeared capable of arguing their points for an hour, and Deirdre should be rescued soon; besides, it was hardly fair to keep Sir Roderic waiting longer than necessary. The faithful coachman had demonstrated already, in this unexpectedly cumbersome interview, that he understood the art of improvisation.

"Thank you, Thomas," said Lady Cassandra. "You had best go on straight to the abbey after explaining matters to Mr. Oakton."

"Trust me, m'lady." The coachman bowed respectfully to her and the rest of the group, then left. Yes, she would have to trust him. The success of the comedy was now out of her hands, and again she felt a sharp pang of envy for her niece. She had not foreseen it would be quite this dreary to face a long, idle wait so far from the scenes of action. Perhaps it was the lack of malleability of Mr. Bellew and his housekeeper which had taken the edge off her enthusiasm, to leave her feeling useless and bored when she might have been settling down in infinite satisfaction to picture the rescue and await the triumphant return of Mr. Oakton and Deirdre. Instead of the vicarious joys of following her play in imagination, she now faced a tedious period of warding off Mr. Bellew's relaxing preparations and his desires to raise the village.

She was very nearly tempted to submit to take some of his powder and doze away the interval. But she admonished herself for the thought. Arguing away his drugs and ideas for treating her would be the nearest thing to amusement she could hope for in the immediate future, while, were she asleep, he would have ample leisure to fret himself into alerting the village at once—and, although she did not greatly fear the efforts of such impromptu thief-takers as Little Tiptree and Ploverchase were likely to provide, still, their premature entrance would complicate matters. No doubt they must be summoned, for appearance' sake; but let it be only after Deirdre was safely rescued.

Lady Cassandra might, also, want to concoct a reasonable theory as to why the highwayman would have remained near the path when she had expressed her conviction a few minutes ago that he would not. And, considering the stimulating possibility that she might, after all, be needed again, she had best not be found muddled with powders.

Half fearing and half hoping for a new emergency that would upset what remained of her carefully wrought plan and call her into action again herself, she settled down to parry the apothecary's fears, solicitations, and fond attempts at soothing her nerves.

"And now it returns, this carriage!" thought Marie Cluzot, watching it for the second time that evening from her window beneath the eaves on the north side of the inn. "And again it passes without even a pause. *Sacre bleu!* What a business must it have?

This time she thought she could obtain a glimpse of the coach's interior before he disappeared from sight around the corner of the inn. The coach appeared empty. A plump old coachman was driving an empty carriage up and down the street of Little Tiptree? No, no—absurd! Perhaps Bevil had requested it of some friend as *fou*— mad—as himself, to carry her in comfort to his Gretta Green, and the driver did not know the directions? Ah, no, it was a pretty thought, but even if one were mad, this was not the way to carry out the elopement, by parading the carriage twice before the eyes of all the village who might hear and look from their windows. Bevil's rakehell friend would have sent the carriage first to Bevil, at some place near Rotherhithe, *sans doute,* but then milord would have drivon it himself.

Could it be, then, that it was hired to divert attention, to cover their departure? *Mon Dieu!* But why not? Who would think of a *pauvre* chambermaid, supposed to be asleep in her room under the eaves, when there was such a carriage to rattle back and forth and give them so much else to speak of and wonder about?

Ah, but was not she herself making much out of little? She had thought it was empty, yes—but who could see to know, in the night, with so little lantern light and so much darkness and shadow? And monsieur the apothecary, did he not reside in the direction where this carriage had gone? Merely some *aristo* taken sick at the abbey or the castle—

At the castle? At Rotherhithe? *Mon Dieu,* it could not be Bevil? Ah, *non . . .* some small accident to one who has been hunting the fox, and the viscount, he was not hunting the fox today. And if there is some confusion at the castle, that, no doubt, is why he comes so late.

Laughing at her own theories and alarms, the chambermaid and self-styled Comtesse d'Azalaine decided she might wait as long as one o'clock in the morning for her viscount.

9

Deirdre sat perfectly still. She was balancing between life and death, between the ground thudding past beneath and the highwayman's arm holding her in place on the horse's swaying back. Vaguely, she knew she ought to scream and struggle, but how could she struggle against the only thing that was keeping her from falling beneath those terrible flying hooves that thudded so fast and hard into the ground?

"A fate worse than death"—no, it could not possibly be worse than smashing down from this height, at this speed, to feel those dreadful hooves striking into one's body—one's face—but she feared the end of the ride too, dreaded the moment when he would stop his gigantic horse and pull her off, because then . . . No, the ride would never end, no matter that she was sick and giddy and would have fallen but for the terrible, iron arm clamped round her waist . . .

"Please, sir!" she managed at last. "If you could—only go more slowly . . ."

"Why, this is a mere canter, child. If we go more slowly we must endure a trot."

"But I—but I—"

She heard him chuck softly to the horse. The animal seemed to shudder, and next instant it was running almost as fast as before, and much, much more roughly, jolting her up and down. "Oh!" cried Deirdre, clutching tightly at the arm that held her. "Oh, I—" Despite her terror of falling, she snatched one hand from his arm and thrust it to her mouth.

"Here, here!" Slowing the horse to a walk, he obligingly loosened the pressure of his arm across her stomach. "I warned you you would not enjoy a trot."

"Thank you!—Don't let me go!" she added, snatching his arm again. The initial relief to her internal comfort when he loosened his grip was soon outweighed by her fear of falling without his support.

"My sweet young lady, I have not the smallest intention of letting you go. Nor of permitting you to be sick, neither. Now catch your stomach again quickly. We have considerable ground to cover tonight, and I would prefer to cover it at the gallop."

" . . . gallop? Oh, no! Oh, please, sir—"

"Silly girl," he chided—not, however, unkindly. "You've nothing to fear. Gunpowder is a lady herself and knows how to gallop with a lady on her back."

"But to go so fast—"

"How else are we to bring you safe out of the county, if not before your charming duenna raises the countryside?"

"You must not talk that way about Aunt Cassandra!"

"Aunt Cassandra?" He chuckled softly. "I took her for a very dragon of respectability, playing the stern watchdog over your harmless youthful pleasures. Is that not the usual relationship between fair young beauties and elderly dowagers?"

"Aunt Cassandra is not an elderly dowager! Perhaps she is almost thirty, but you would not think it."

58

"Would you not?" Again the strange, wry chuckle, as if he were amused at some secret game. "I swear, she tongue-lashed me like a true harpy."

"No, she did not." Was this the way one talked to a desperado who was abducting one? "She merely warned you not to take me, and now you have done it, she will have the constables after you directly."

"All the more reason, then, for the gallop. I trust you have recovered your interior, my lady?"

"No! Please—" She had been foolish to threaten him —why could she not think clearly? The first consideration was to persuade him not to ride at that terrible gallop. "I—I'm so very afraid . . . "

"Nonsense. I have never abducted a cooler victim."

It was not fair of him to make sport of her fright! But trying to think of what Aunt Cassie might do had helped clear her brain somewhat. There was another reason she must beg him not to gallop—the longer she could delay him in his escape, the likelier it was that help would find them. "Indeed, sir, I am terrified," she pled weakly, "and if you gallop I—I think I shall faint."

"Terror, my child, manifests itself in hysteria, screams, thrashing about, and suchlike. Now, you cannot sit quietly in my arm, informing me as a matter of polite conversation that you are terrified, and seriously expect me to believe you."

"You know nothing about it!" It was not, after all, as if she were lying to him. "If you wish me to scream and struggle, sir, put me on the ground where I will not fall off your beastly horse!"

"Come, come, sweetheart. Do you really want to struggle with me on the ground?"

She shivered, suddenly aware of a new menace in his voice—a terrible, veiled threat more nearly like the sort of tone one would expect from a highway robber. "N-no, I . . . but please don't gallop," was all she could immediately reply.

"Damme, I've half a mind to test you!" He did not stop and dismount with her, however. He made the horse go faster—not that dreadful trot, but a fairly gentle amble worse than the slow walk they had traveled for some minutes, but not nearly so bad as the canter. Deirdre plucked up hope both from the speed and the slowness of the gait. He must have decided to continue on to wherever he had planned, but to spare her the gallop en route. "Where . . . where are you taking me?" she ventured to ask after a moment.

"To find some secluded spot where we can try the experiment."

"The—the experiment?"

"Of course. The experiment. You claim you will demonstrate the usual symptoms of terror if I put you on the ground. Being a student of human nature, I am naturally eager to prove the event."

"Oh, no!" For the first time, her voice rose to a scream. At once he moved his hand to her mouth. At the same instant the horse seemed to break gait and lurch a little, and Deirdre, in panic at loss of the restraining hold round her waist, threw her arms up to clutch at the man behind her.

"Gently, gently, my dove. Scream once more and we gallop in earnest. Now then," he went on, removing his hand from her mouth to her waist again and holding his horse back to a walk, "you yourself have proposed the experiment, my lady, so kindly restrain your impatience until I find a suitable locale."

"You . . . are very quick to take suggestion, sir."

"Not at all. On the contrary, I am of a singularly complaisant nature, and only anxious to do all within my power to please my sweet companion."

"It was a silly suggestion. You'll be caught if you stop."

"Oho! Doubts, my lady? So may I be caught if we continue at a walk. Nevertheless, since I can hardly expect your sincere concern for my safety, you must permit me to take what chances I deem worth the risk."

Deirdre fell silent, cowed by the utter realization that he would do with her exactly as he pleased. He would not have seized on her foolish suggestion to be set on the ground had it not for some reason suited his own fancy. Did he not consider himself safe from immediate capture, he would hardly refrain from a gallop merely to coddle his captive.

With a sense of growing despair, she thought over the

futility of her efforts to persuade him. She would not speak again, she was merely amusing him when she spoke. Yes—he was amusing himself with her—toying with her. That was the only way to explain his behavior, for surely bandits could not actually treat their prisoners with such exaggerated gallantry as matter of course! No; she was very green, she knew it, but cousin Peter had taken her once to Newgate, to see the hangings and acquire a little town sophistication, and there had been nothing at all romantic about the poor criminals—at least half drunk and a few of them trying to shout out some dying speech, not at all like the gallows-speeches printed up for sale—only pitiable somehow.

But there was nothing pitiable in this one. He was strong and brazen and held her completely at his mercy. She shuddered, remembering that one of the wretches she had seen hanged had been a murderer. Might someone someday watch this man hanged for *her* murder, and think him pitiable? No—awful!—but what could she do? Was there nothing she could do except pray he did not mean to kill her? What victim of murder had not prayed that?

But then, assuming the best—assuming that she was not to be killed—what did he intend? To hold her to ransom . . . ah, but if that were all, why should he stop with her in a secluded spot, long before they reached his destination? Why not gallop at once to wherever he might mean to hide her, ignoring her sickness and terror of the speed? He would be capable of any cruelty—she was sure of that now—a tormentor behind a mask of false gallantry.

What could she do to save herself? She tried to think —break away somehow when he lifted her to the ground? Try again to persuade him? What words could she use to persuade a robber who spoke like an educated gentleman and twisted every conversation to his own purposes? He was stronger than her in everything— mind, will, determination, as well as physical power. He could force her to anything, and what *could* she do against him?

Perhaps if she submitted to him, he would not hurt

her much, after all. While if she resisted, or tried to escape, then he would kill her without mercy! No, she must not try to fight him, she must do whatever he said . . . but her mind and body recoiled at the prospect. No, better to struggle and be killed . . . or would he overpower her and hurt her at his pleasure and only kill her later? Better to spare herself whatever she could . . . but perhaps he was only teasing her, perhaps he did not really mean to stop?

"Ah," he said. "I think this will suit us very nicely, my dear."

Deirdre glanced round in surprise and dismay. All at once she realized that what she should have done, the only thing she could have done, was to mark their direction, note down in her mind every landmark she could glimpse in the moonlight. But it was so dark, for all the moon was nearly full . . . and she did not know the neighborhood at all well, only having been driven about between the abbey, Ploverchase, and Rotherhithe by the road. A few of the walks she might have recognized by day—especially that one she had once taken with George Oakton, in party with the viscount and Aunt Cassie, over the hill between the two villages—but certainly she would have been able to recognize nothing by night; and they must be far beyond the village by now.

He stopped his horse between some high bushes and a stand of trees. "There is . . . there is a fox-hunt today, sir," she said, only remembering after she said it that she had determined to protest no more and that, besides, it might have been better to say nothing to alert him, and hope some of the hunters happened by in time. "They may come up with you."

"I think not. I passed them earlier this evening on the other side of Bramblecombe. If any of them straggle back this way, they should repair either to the abbey or to the Graln and Grape, well before they penetrate to us here."

He jumped lightly from the saddle, leaving Deirdre alone for a moment on the horse's back. Vaguely she thought that she ought to seize the reins, shake off his arm, and ride away with all speed. Instead, she clung to the horse's mane, terrified lest the animal run away with her.

The highwayman put both hands about her waist and swung her down. For a few seconds she felt nothing but the dizzy, helpless swoop through darkness, followed by the perverse relief of having both feet again on solid ground. Then she noticed that his fingertips were pressing up very high toward her bosom.

She felt a blush, though she knew it could not be seen; and, hardly thinking, she seized his hands with her own.

"Ah, my lady! Spirit? Passion?"

He was standing behind her, his hands still clamped on her waist as if it were part of his wicked experiment to see what she would do with them. If she had not seized them, would he have released her by now? And, after releasing her waist, then what?

He would not let her run, surely. Nevertheless, could she escape before he expected it—could she take him somehow by surprise—he might know the area better than she, but surely he could not see so very well in the dark, no more than anyone else; and there seemed to be a great number of bushes and copses about . . .

She tried to pry up suddenly at his hands and realized at once the utter futility of it. He held her like a spring trap, his palms completely encircling her waist, fingers spreading a little between her hips and bodice, thumbs nearly touching like levers in the small of her back. She could never grapple with him hand-to-hand—both of her tiny hands together would scarcely cover *one* of his great fists.

He wore gloves, too—some sort of thin leather or doeskin—she could hardly hope to take an effective pinch in the back of his hand. But the spread of his fingers, as he stood there waiting, gave her a sudden inspiration. Seizing one of his little fingers in each of her fists, she jerked up and outward with all her strength and—wonder! He gave an exclamation of pain and his hands left her waist.

If only she had known in that instant what to do next! But, amazed at her moment of success, she stood perplexed by what to do with his fingers, while he recovered in half a second. Whipping one leg in front of her, he caught it around her skirt and both her legs, holding her fast; while at the same time balling his uncaught fingers into fists, he brought them back forcefully against her waist. "Now," he whispered, "let go my little fingers, darling, or I'll be forced to squeeze you in the manner of a North American bear."

The pressure of his huge, hard fists tight against her stomach was enough to throw her into panic, and she released her hold before she realized that his squeezing, uncomfortable as it was, had not yet become actually painful.

"First point to you, fair damsel," he remarked in a more conversational tone, although still softly. "As I predicted, you have not so far demonstrated the first sign of female hysteria; however, the experiment bids fair to prove all the more interesting."

"I am glad you find my behavior worth your study, sir," she managed to reply, trying to hold her voice steady.

"Very well worth my study indeed. I must thank you already for a highly educational evening. Allow me one small suggestion. Had you chosen either one of my little fingers, the right or the left, and concentrated your entire strength on it—so—you might very well have brought me to my knees."

He took her right little finger as he spoke, and tugged at it—very gently, he did not hurt her; he seemed at pains not to hurt her. Yet she felt her helplessness anew, and turned at once in the direction of his pull. Would she really have been able so to force him, had she known how to follow up her brief advantage?

"So," he continued, bringing her about to face him. "You might have had me on my knees, thus." But instead of forcing her down, as she feared for a few seconds, he knelt on one knee before her . . . without, however, loosening his hold on her finger.

Sometime during the ride, he had taken off the handkerchief from over his face, but in the darkness she could make out little of his features. She thought they were hard and strong; but she could hardly hope to know them again, by daylight, from those of a dozen other tall men she had seen.

"And . . . when I had you on your knees?" she faltered.

"You would have kicked me, of course. A well-aimed foot to my face, another, perhaps, to my ribs, an elbow brought down sharply on my neck . . . ah, yes, my lady, a few blows such as would not be beyond even your delicate arm, if placed neatly enough, and you might perhaps have made your escape at leisure." So saying, he slowly pulled down her finger, lowering her to his knee, where he thrust his other arm around her shoulders.

"If you please . . . to let go my finger," she said meekly, trembling as she sat there.

He released it, but at once gathered both her hands into his own, holding her palms together with just enough pressure to remind her he could have hurt her if he wished. "Having instructed you thus far, dear charmer, you must not think I mean to let you practice your new learning upon your teacher. No, you'll have to wait for the next rogue."

"I . . . pray there will never be another, sir,"

"Do you indeed?" His arm tightened around her shoulders, drawing her closer to his chest. His other hand moved inward, guiding her own hands to touch her dress over her heart. "Your wish might be taken in many ways, my child. Have you any idea, I wonder, how many ways?"

His voice had grown very gentle now, almost as she had imagined her father's voice might have been, had he not died before she could remember him. And he was holding her on his knee almost as she had used to imagine a father holding his daughter, for whatever conferences fathers made to their daughters . . . Not such jesting, good-natured sallies as those of her uncle and cousins, but the tender intimacy of—oh, how cruel this man was, to torment her like this!

"You must . . . you must instruct me, sir!" she said.

"It may be taken, then, thusly: *Primus*—that you hope no other rogue may ever take you from my tender embrace. *Secundus*—"

Despite her self, she half fell against his chest, sobbing aloud.

"Here, here," Almost immediately he released her hands, touched her cheek, stroked her hair. Vaguely she thought that he had contrived to draw off his glove; the fingers that brushed her cheek were leathery, but tufted with hair, and having the feel somehow of living flesh. As her sobs continued, he lifted her from his knee and laid her, quite gently, on the ground, keeping one hand still on her arm whilst with the other he placed some sort of rolled cloth beneath her head, for a pillow.

"No, we will hope there will be no other highway rogues for you, my dear. But should there be a brutal husband—"

"Oh, no!" Not the Viscount Fencourt—not even *he* would put her through such a nightmare—

"My dear, innocent child," her captor said sadly, "brutes are found in flowered silk as well as dirty linsey-woolsey. Better never marry at all than marry where you have cause to suspect."

There were stories . . . the viscount, she had heard, was a member of a thing called the Brimstone Club— and what did she know of the things he did when with his rakehell friends—they *were* called rakehells—what he might be capable of, besides mere cold possessiveness?

"Oh, George! George!" she sobbed, trying to turn her face to the rude pillow. The highwayman released her hands, allowing her to turn, and laying one hand on her uppermost shoulder, lightly, as if he meant to persuade her he was acting as a comforter rather than a gaoler.

"You are sure of your lover, child?"

"No—no!" She was sure of Mr. Oakton . . . but Mr. Oakton was not her lover. Bevil, Viscount Fencourt was her lover—she supposed he was her lover, because he was her betrothed—but . . . "Sir, you mean to . . . dishonor me, do you not?"

She had only a hazy image of what it would be, to be dishonored in the next few moments . . . but afterwards, surely the viscount would not marry her—nobody could tell Bevil's thoughts, but the earl and countess would not permit it even if he still felt inclined—no gentleman ever would marry her and she would live secluded forever and suddenly it seemed to her that she preferred to be here with this brigand than in some silken-sheeted bedchamber with the Viscount Fencourt.

"I . . . mean to study your behavior." For the first time she heard a catch in his voice. It could not mean that he was quite human, but . . . "As a student of natural philosophy," he went on, "I find you a most diverting specimen—"

"Sir!" She sat up, clutching his hand with both of hers. "Sir—whatever you mean to do—do it quickly!"

She felt the hand she held closing into a fist. His other arm came again around her shoulders. "A second point to you," he said at last. "I vow, you took me by surprise —you might have had my little finger again. I see I must guard you with greater watchfulness."

"What do you mean to do with me?"

"After studying you for a while, to carry you to a place of safety and comfort and hold you to ransom. Nothing more."

Would he toy with her like this forever? She bent forward and tried to bite his wrist.

At once the arm round her shoulders slipped upward, the hand lodging beneath her chin, drawing her head slowly but remorselessly back. "Excellent!" he said. "Biting—an excellent weapon, my lady, when used with the proper timing and discrimination. But you did not choose the proper time, you see . . . I could put your mouth to better use at once, but it need not come to your dishonor."

"Does it not . . . always come to that?"

"No, it need not. You are in some danger of it, I will not disguise from you. But I know several other dames in varying degrees of willingness; and you'll fetch a better ransom with your honor intact."

"It don't signify! I'll swear you dishonored me!"

When he did not reply at once to this outburst, she let herself fall against his chest—he had released her chin by now—and began to sob, loudly at first, then softly.

"Gods, child, you are a curious study!" he said. "Why?"

"Then—he will not—marry me!"

"George?"

"No! Lord—Lord Bevil!"

"This Lord Bevil, then, will be the brutish husband you have to fear. But your George might not have you, neither."

"Lord! Sir—will you stop tormenting—"

"Hush!" He suddenly pressed her close to him. She felt him stiffen, as if listening. Catching her breath, she listened with him. The sound was still faint, but growing louder.

"A horseman?" muttered her captor. "Coming at the gallop." Then he added in a very slightly louder voice, "Third point to you, lady. You warned me against stopping here."

She sat petrified, clinging to the hand that minutes ago had been beneath her chin. One of the hunters, gone astray! Or even someone out to search for her—no, they would not come searching singly. She had hoped for this . . . but had not imagined the wait before her rescuer actually reached them. "Is it—only one?" she faltered.

The hoofbeats had come much nearer in only a few seconds. "Only one," he replied. "An eager gallant, to outstrip his comrades. Well, lady? You have but to scream."

Scream? Her throat was entirely constricted—she thought she could not even swallow. He *wanted* her to scream! Else he would have his hand tight over her mouth—or her throat.

"Silence, lady? Am *I* to alert your preserver?"

Why did he want her to scream? To torture her—to clamp his great hand over her mouth at the last instant? Worse—for an excuse to murder her? Or so sure of himself he would kill the man who tried to help her?

"You wait too long, child! He will be past."

She could barely hear his voice for the hoofbeats. The rider was even now galloping past them, very close.

Without warning, her captor seized her bodice as if to rip it away. When she only clutched in silent despair at his hand, he threw her to the ground and wrenched her arm. Pain overcame terror and she screamed.

10

Several times that evening Sir Roderic had come dangerously near cursing Lady Cassandra in his heart. Romance! And so she imagined, because *she* might enjoy abduction by such a highwayman as himself, that every other woman must needs enjoy it as well? She was a fool—and he another, for agreeing to her harebrained scheme. He should have carried off Cassandra instead . . . aye, and given her such an object lesson as to make her think well before subjecting a young girl to an adventure like this again.

Meanwhile, having given his word, he had abducted the poor girl and was forced to carry the matter through. But damned if he had the confidence in his address that Lady Cassandra saw fit to repose in him. He had, of course, seduced at least his share of women, but he did not as a rule combine that occupation with the business of waylaying carriages, preferring safer surroundings and the time to work with calculation and reasonable mannerliness. Moreover, he had now to withhold himself from actually coming to the point. Cassandra expected it of him. She had, in effect, put him upon his honor. No doubt it would have taught her an excellent lesson were he to return her niece in tarnished condition after all . . . but, perversely, much as he railed inwardly at the woman, he no more considered betraying her serene trust in him than he would have considered reneging on a gambling debt, had he been a man to frequent the gaming tables. And yet it went against all instinct, all the rules of the present game as he had always played it, to dally with no intention of consummating the affair.

He had also learned to be a strict taskmaster with his late brother's children; he was hardly afraid to bully the young. But he disliked practicing the tricks of a harsh disciplinarian on this virtuous and terrified young girl. And how else was he to handle her? A combination of pseudogallantry and stern discipline— faugh! It would tax the powers of a Burleigh! All this, and he must keep her occupied for God knew how long until exactly the right moment (meanwhile restraining his own instincts); he must not terrify her too much, but he must not endue her with the notion that it was always pretty romance to be carried off by a highway rogue—Sir Roderic himself had so little liking for the common representatives of his trade that he inwardly deplored any sentiment which might hamper the commendable efforts of Bow Street and Newgate drop.

True, almost from the moment of pulling her from Cassandra, he had been agreeably surprised in Miss Chevington's behavior. It was easy to scent the girl's fear—she quivered like a captured rabbit in his hands —but she held herself with unexpected restraint for a delicately nurtured child barely out of the schoolroom. There was indeed a good deal of her aunt in her, waiting to be developed, he thought ... until he remembered that she was related to Lady Cassandra only by the latter's marriage, which made him wonder whence the incipient resemblance.

By the time he seized on the nonsense about trying an experiment in the study of human nature, he was in fact more than half interested in the foolish trial for its own sake as well as for a convenient excuse to stop in the prearranged vicinity of the footpath over Floverchase Hill. When she showed sufficient promise to seize him by the little fingers, his tutorial instincts came to the fore and he was perfectly sincere in his efforts to instruct her.

He would have liked to teach her more thoroughly

how to take care of herself; she had need of such learning, and the role of tutor was the only one in which he felt completely assured of his address with her. He had been prepared to take in hand a struggling, shrieking, vapory young female; and, perversely, the less hysterical was Miss Chevington's behavior, the less comfortable was he in his treatment of her. The better she seemed to control her fear, the clumsier seemed his own handling of the situation and the more was he inclined to curse Lady Cassandra for entangling him in this farce. Had he been a free agent, he might have seduced the girl very comfortably; instead, when at last her fortitude crumbled, he found himself in the unfamiliar role of comforting father, a role he had never adopted nor studied, even under more nearly normal circumstances, except in occasional idle reverie.

The hoofbeats came as a dintinct relief to him. Little as he relished permitting himself to be ignominiously routed by a country parson, it would spell the end of his role in the silly comedy, and he could return to his own concerns. He was somewhat surprised that this Mr. Oakton should come on horseback —from Cassandra's instructions he had gathered that the vicar habitually traveled the footpath by foot. But the cleric was a nobleman's younger son, presumably accustomed to the saddle from boyhood. Very likely, since his living was at his father's disposal, he had a saddle horse or two, and what more natural than that he should choose the fastest means of travel when his worshipful lady was endangered?

A scream or two from the girl, now, and Sir Roderic could feign panic and escape on Gunpowder, leaving the young pair to their happy reunion.

But the girl did not scream. He had anticipated that he would have considerable effort in keeping her silent until the right moment, and then have only to allow her free rein—he found he had the opposite problem, and no scheme ready to deal with it.

He hinted—she sat silent. He urged—she made no sound. Was she now too terrified to scream? Or was she actually enamored of him—had he played his part too gently? He changed at once into the role of ruffian. It was no part of his usual style to rip the clothes from a woman, but such an action must bring a scream.

When the first threads of her gown gave way and still she sat mute, clawing at his arm, he realized that not only might this effort prove futile, but that partial nudity might throw embarrassment between her and her rescuer—hardly the effect Cassandra wished. The horseman was passing beyond them—in seconds it would be too late. Desperate, Sir Roderic resorted to brutality.

Wrenching her arm showed lack of finesse. Cassandra might not pardon him—but at the moment he felt disinclined to pardon Cassandra. At least the pain would not embarrass the girl, and it served the purpose. She screamed, and the horse turned. A reckless horseman, by the sound of it, jerking his mount around in midgallop, on a narrow footpath, allowing scarcely a moment to slow the pace. Clearly a parson of the gallant school—the sort, indeed, one would expect to win a young maid's heart.

Miss Chevington was panting in pain and terror, her white face turned upward toward him. "Oh, sir—pray don't—"

She had no time to finish the plea. A crashing in the bushes between them and the road announced the horseman to be almost upon them. And coming too fast. The gallant young idiot would trample them both. "Hold, you bloody fool!" shouted Sir Roderic, hauling the girl to her feet and retreating with her against a tree.

The vicar reined short with a showy, foppish trick, making his horse rear up on its hind legs. "Have I interrupted a tête-à-tête? I acted under the impression that someone was in need of assistance."

Fop of a young cleric! The highwayman regretted not having come ahead of time to hear one of his services. A rare treat a sermon from such lips must be.

The girl had returned to her old pattern of quivering in silence. Sir Roderic disembarrassed himself of her, half-dropping and half-pushing her to one side, as he drew his pistol and fired. Loaded only with powder, it

72

could do no damage; but it gave the most succinct and unmistakable answer to the clergyman's question.

The girl screamed. The horse reared, the rider ejaculated " 'Sdeath!" and fired off a shot of his own.

The rescuer's pistol was loaded, and the cleric a surprisingly good shot, especially in the darkness. The ball thwacked into the tree behind Sir Roderic. More to the point, the highwayman's horse, who had merely snorted at her own master's shot, chose to take alarm at the strange pistol, shied, and bolted.

Cursing the animal, Sir Roderic reviewed his alternatives in an instant. It was already overlate to fall and pretend a wound—moreover, Mr. Oakton might decide to capture a supposedly senseless bandit at once, as well as rescue the victim. A duel with rapiers was tempting, but would only increase the danger of accident and prolong the voluntary ignominy of defeat and flight. Sir Roderic, deciding on the simplest and quickest course of action, retreated.

Hearing the vicar pursue him, shouting happily, for some distance, he went with speed. At length, when he had got into an area where the undergrowth was sufficiently thick to discourage equestrian access by moonlight, he went to earth in a tangle of thorn and listened to his pursuer abandon the chase.

Sir Roderic did not circle back at once. Eventually, he would return to the place. On recovering her horse sense, Gunpowder would seek her master at the place where she had deserted him, before proceeding to a wider search. He hoped that by then the vicar would have shown enough sense to take his lady away to some house of warmth and comfort. As for their immediate reunion, Sir Roderic had little interest in the effusions of young lovers.

11

Panting in fright and confusion, her thoughts a turmoil, Deirdre knelt clutching the tree. Was this a new brigand come to claim her from his rival? There seemed something familiar in his voice—but perhaps it had been only a familiar turn of mockery such as she had heard elsewhere and guessed to be a kind of fashion amongst blades. Perhaps she had been better off with the former highwayman? But had he not fired first? Then perhaps the new one was honest, a rescuer for her. Why, then, did she tremble at the prospect of his return to the place of rescue?

Someone must return for her, she was lost and alone in a strange wooded place . . . she thought it high land, like a rise or a hill, but she had been too preoccupied whilst riding here to notice even whether the horse was going uphill . . . she thought it had been—at least, she was sure it had not been going downhill. But she would not go to find out. She would not leave this tree, not until morning. Or until it became clear that her rescuer was not coming back for her. Her rescuer . . . yes, her savior. She could hardly be worse off with the now one than with the first. Then why did she dread his return?

Was she actually hoping the first captor would come back before the new one and take her away again? Impossible! Oh, George, George, if ever I come safely home with my life and . . . and my honor—I will speak to Aunt Cassie, we will cry off my engagement to

Bevil, no matter how it may look, no matter what Mother or society may say . . .

But meanwhile, Deirdre considered, with something like sensible calculation, should she not, after all, leave this tree and escape by herself before either of them . . . that was, before the original highwayman returned? No. What should she do, what way should she choose? Yet there must surely be a house somewhere near enough for her to reach . . . but in what direction?

She stood and tried to see a light somewhere in the distance, but she was surrounded by woods and bushes. Besides, the brigand would not have brought her to any place near respectable habitations. This whole neighborhood might be rampant with bandits and criminals! Yes, better—much better—to stay here for her preserver . . . or her first captor . . . rather than wander about lost and alone in a wilderness infested with rogues and footpads. Perhaps even wild beasts. Far in the distance, she seemed to hear a faint hallooing. She might have thought nothing of it had she been safe in bed at the abbey, but here alone at night in the desert, it had an eerie, wicked sound. She shuddered and shrank back against the trunk of the tree, wishing she knew how to climb as she had used to watch the little boys climb trees about Steddinghill.

Something approached, crashing through the dry grasses and bushes to break into the clearing quite near her. Gasping, she jumped round to the other side of the tree, then peeped out again at the beast which had come to tear her with tooth and claw. It was a horse, a dark horse standing riderless in the moonlight.

It shook its great head, then bent its neck and began to crop the grasses. With its head lowered and its back empty, it seemed dismembered somehow, headless and grotesque. Deirdre thought despairingly that if she jumped into its saddle, she might escape this place—she would surely reach a respectable house if she only rode far enough and fast enough. But to draw near the beast, clucking to it, gathering up its reins, then finally pulling herself up on its towering back . . . this was far less possible than climbing the tree. And even if she could have gained the saddle, suppose the horse ran away with her, or shook her off again?

She jumped back around the tree again as a second horse crashed into the clearing on the other side from the first. This animal carried a rider. He stopped his mount and seemed to turn his head, as if peering around. Almost at once he began to ride toward the first horse, clucking his tongue and making pleasant remarks to it. The first horse threw back its head, whinnied, and galloped off the way it had come.

"Damm!" said the newcomer. Surely Deirdre knew his voice? Yes! Though he had never used quite that exasperated tone in her presence.

She ought to have felt relief, and because she did not, felt a flicker of guilt instead. But perhaps, after all, it was not he, but only someone who sounded like him. Should she cry out to him, or slip away, trying not to make a sound? While she hesitated, it became too late. He turned again and saw her.

"Ah, so there you are! Well, miss, you've cost me a jolly quarter-hour of it. I trust you'll prove worth my efforts?"

"Bevil," she said. She felt dangerously near to fainting. The moonlit night seemed to be turning solid gray, before her eyes, and had it not been for the tree behind her she must have fallen. As it was, she felt herself slipping downward, the bark catching at the pale fabric of her gown. She tried to hold herself straight, but her legs would not be steady.

"Deirdre? My God, is it you, Miss Chevington?" He leapt from his horse and was beside her almost at once.

Lord! she thought as his arm went round her shoulders and she sank perforce upon his chest, now he will make love to me! The lace at his throat tickled a little.

"My sweet Miss Chevington, what brings you here?"

Was this a time for explanations? "Is this a time for explanations?" she said. "I think I am about to swoon away."

76

"That you won't, begad, until you kindly explain to me how it is I find you alone on Ploverchase Hill in the moonlight with a strange gentleman who proceeds to empty his pistol at me!"

Ploverchase Hill? Had she really been so near help the whole time? Oh, why had she not found the footpath and gone to right or left before the viscount returned? "It was a highwayman," she said, hearing a bit of—impatience?—in her voice.

"A highwayman? A gentleman of the road here in Ploverchase?"

"A highwayman. He abducted me from Aunt Cassandra's carriage."

"'Sblood!" The viscount threw back his head and laughed. "Had I known the fellow as a highwayman, I would not have chased him. I thought you was cherishing a lover on the sly!"

She had never heard him laugh so before: hearty peals rather than his usual soft, sniggering chuckles. "You did not know me, I think," she said.

"No more I did not! I took you for some rustic beauty at tête-à-tête with her local swain. I would have made my apologies and left you alone at once, had the fellow not opened fire on me."

"Left us? After hearing my scream?"

He shrugged. "What's a friendly scream between lovers on a lonely hill?"

"You take the matter very lightly, my lord. Had you not happened by, I think . . . I think I would very soon have been unfit to be your wife." And that, she felt tempted to add aloud, would have made me very happy.

"Not unlikely, if the fellow really was a ruffian. Which, in its turn, is not unlikely, seeing he fired without so much as a challenge. Meanwhile, what are we to do with you?"

Deirdre wondered if she were safe from . . . that . . . with the viscount. She had heard that betrothed persons sometimes took liberties, and a man like Lord Bevil, so possessive—heavens! If he should do it tonight, there would be an end to all hope of crying off the engagement. "You will bring me at once safe to

Derwent Abbey," she said with as much dignity as she could muster, trying to push herself away from his chest. To her relief, he let her push away quite easily.

"To the abbey? Impossible—it's more than an hour's ride, my girl."

She would not tell him it seemed little exertion enough for his fiancée under such circumstances. "Then you will take me back to Rotherhithe. That should not be above half an hour, and a message can be sent from there that I am safe."

"Lord, miss, you don't know the time I've just had getting away from the old pile! If I was to go home again tonight, with you in tow and some tale of highwaymen, devil if they'd let me slip 'em again for a se'ennight."

"And what is so important that it keeps you from home at a time like this?" Lord, was she actually daring to begin a quarrel with him? Somewhere in the back of her mind the idea was forming that here might be the start of a reasonable pretext for breaking their betrothal. "I begin to think you are waiting for a carriage to waylay yourself, my lord."

"What, here on the hill? Gad, girl, d'you take me for a fool? What carriage would come trundling between Ploverchase and Little Tiptree?"

"Then you have a . . ." She hesitated to make such a bold accusation, but if she were to quarrel, she must be fearless. "You yourself have a *rendez-vous* here with some country beauty."

"Damn!" He checked himself. "Maidens who go about with strange highwaymen by night are in a poor position to bandy accusations like that, my dear."

Ah! She must have struck home. "Since my presence is obviously an embarrassment to you, my lord, and since you cannot afford the time to bring me to safety, I pray you will stand aside and permit me to walk. The village, if I remember, is nearly at the foot of the hill."

"Walk? Lord, girl, you mean to stroll quietly down to Little Tiptree with a highwayman about?"

"No, I do not mean to go to Little Tiptree. I mean to go to Ploverchase." To the vicarage, where she
78

would find his brother, Mr. George Oakton. She must be facing in the wrong direction. "I think you have just told me that highwaymen are unheard of in this neighborhood, my lord." Turning her back on him, she took two steps.

He caught her shoulder. "Damme, if this don't prove the fellow was a lover of yours—"

"He was not!" She spun round in a fury, knocking away Bevil's hand. "He was the wickedest brute imaginable! But I would prefer even his company to yours!"

"So-ho! You would, would you?" Catching her wrists, he laughed his familiar, sniggering chuckle.

"Yes! Alongside of you, he was a gentleman!"

"Begad! Had I known what opinion you had of me—"

"You would have done less to earn it?" As her anger wore itself out against his obvious amusement, she began to be a little appalled at what she was saying. But it was too late to go back; and she determined to say enough to cut through even his indifference and make it impossible for him to marry her. "I am sorry you find it humorous, my lord," she went on coldly—for now he was laughing in great guffaws—"*I* have found it exceedingly trying."

"Trying! And I suppose you've found *me* trying, also? Jove, Deirdre, had I known you were such a spitfire as this, I swear I might have loved you, after all! I took you for a milk-and-water namby."

He caught her to him and forced his lips down on hers. For a moment she was in a panic. Then she remembered her highwayman's lesson. Bevil's hands were no longer on her wrists, but around her back. Trying to pretend she was responding to his kiss, she groped up behind her, found one of his hands, patted her own over it softly until she had the little finger, then clutched and pulled hard.

He cried out and loosened both his arms; but somehow, instead of her forcing him to his knees, they ended in an utter tangle, with her still clutching his finger, trying to turn her back to him, whilst he limped around with her in a circle. After a few seconds of this,

79

he got his other arm round her waist and squeezed viciously, making it difficult for her to breathe.

"Here!" he panted. "Truce, wench!"

"Wench?" She twisted his finger more sharply, and tried to kick. He cried out again and returned the kick.

"Lady, if you will! Truce, my lady!"

"Let me go, then!"

"At count of three. One . . . two . . . three!"

He let her go and she, rather surprised, loosed his finger. The viscount sat on the ground. Deirdre was tempted to sit likewise, but did not quite dare. So they rested for a few minutes, panting and looking at each other in the moonlight.

"By God!" he swore softly at last. "I've half a mind to marry you, after all!"

"After all?" For an instant she seemed unable to think. Then she turned and began running, towards which village she cared not.

He was up in a moment and catching her arm again. "You're running away from the footpath, little fool! Have you no sense of direction? No—don't turn on me again, I beg you! I swear I will play the gentleman for at least ten minutes."

"But you will not let me go?"

"Not with your highwayman—whom I now almost believe to have been really the brigand you claim—still lurking about, No, it shall not be said that I left my betrothed alone at night to the mercy of lawless brigands." He stood musing, his free hand to his face. She thought, by the soft sound, that he was tapping his fingerpads against his cheek. *"Allons.* The Grain and Grape it will be."

"The Grain and Grape?"

"A comparatively excellent establishment in Tiptree."

"I would prefer you returned me to Ploverchase."

"You presume too much on my temporary good manners, milady. The Tiptree Inn is grander than any comparable house in the sister village. Indeed, I fail to remember any comparable establishment in the sister village at all."

Deirdre remembered once stopping for tea at the

Grain and Grape, though she had not immediately recollected the name. It had been that same, beautiful morning when she and Mr. Oakton, Aunt Cassie, and Bevil had taken the walk over the hill from the vicarage and back.

"I am sure, my lord, that Mr. Oakton will provide me succor."

He tsked. "To stop unchaperoned at a respectable vicarage and compromise a handsome young churchman—what can you be thinking of, my love? No, sweet child, it's off at once with you to the Grain and Grape before my ten minutes of playing the gentleman are up."

She made one last attempt. "You never scrupled before to leave me to your brother's entertaining."

"That was generally under my own watchful eye—if sometimes at a slight distance—and before I knew you capable of allowing yourself to be abducted by strange highwaymen. *Allons*, my darling, up!" He propelled her towards his horse and cupped his hands to give her a mounting step.

She drew back. "Oh, please, Bevil—couldn't I walk?"

"Walk? Could I permit a rescued damsel to arrive at the place of succor walking on her own dainty feet beside her knight's steed?"

"Please, Bevil, it's so very near."

He stroked his horse's neck. "Well, my Calpie, you must instruct me sometime in how to tame spitfires. It seems you have the way of it. Very good, sweet Miss Chevington, you've cost me a deal of time already, but since you ask it so politely, we shall walk, side by side. Will you accept the honor of leading Calpie?"—offering Deirdre the reins, from which she shrank. "No? Very well, then. *En avant!*" Looping the reins over his right arm and putting his left about Deirdre's waist, he stepped off smartly.

The footpath was only a few yards distant through the copse, and the path was all downhill; the highwayman had brought her to the wide, gentle summit of Ploverchase Hill. She found it far preferable to walk than to endure another ride, held almost on the horse's neck in front of the saddle, with the ground spinning past at a dizzy rate beneath the animal's heavy hooves. Still, comparatively easy as it was to walk, this new journey was purgatory to Deirdre.

The viscount was mercifully silent for much of the way, as if abstracted; but he kept his arm about her waist, loosening his hold a little whenever he subjected her to a stray quip of what he clearly thought witty conversation, but tightening it again when he went off into reverie. She dared not try too strenuously or too obviously to break free, lest he decide to force her up on his horse and gallop downhill after all; moreover, whenever she attempted, cautiously, to pull away a bit, his arm at once drew tighter yet. His absent-minded squeezing from time to time, the too-frequent straying of his fingers upwards or downwards, were pure agony. She dug into his hand with her elbow, trying to show him how violently averse she was to his casual pinches and ticklings. His response was a fondle very high indeed, and she realized in despair that he must have taken her displeasure as a bit of flirtation. She resolved to do nothing at all further for the moment, but to be ready and, if his fondling should grow too unbearably bold, to strike down sharply with her elbow in hopes of causing him pain, and at risk of striking her own ribs or hip.

How different this terrible walk from that earlier one, by daylight, down this same path with Mr. Oakton!—George, she called him fondly in her private thoughts. How lovely to have been walking again with him now, by moonlight . . . how pleasant to have been feeling his hand instead of his older brother's between her hip and breast . . . Deirdre blushed (quite uselessly, in the dark and with her present company), but there it was. Or how pleasant to be sitting by this time in George's parlor, sipping a little tea or cordial, and being comforted by him after her fright ho would commiserate her, he would be decently shocked and grieved, properly indignant at the outlaw—he would see the country roused, and return to solace her with his conversation . . . with his mere presence. Not like the viscount, who seemed to treat the whole matter as

82

a jest, and a rather tiresome jest at that. Were not his attentions even more perfunctory, albeit more offensively personal, than hitherto? And how very dog-in-the-mangerish of him, suddenly to refuse taking her to the vicarage, on some silly pretext that her presence there would compromise his brother . . . and then, himself, to tickle and pinch her beyond all bounds . . . if truth were known, his noble lordship, so tender for her reputation, was outraging propriety even more than had her highwayman. No, not quite—for a moment she had forgot those last horrible few seconds when he seemed about to rip her gown . . . a baffling affair, all around.

She was not, of course, sorry to rescued. It would have been wanton to prefer a brigand's company even to the viscount's, and she did not think Bevil meant her injury. He was too preoccupied for that this evening. Not even a rakehell nobleman like Viscount Fencourt could behave so absently as this if he meant to ravish a girl . . . and his own fiancée, too—no, surely he would go no further than this odious wiggling of his fingers at her ribs. Besides, they were now able to see a few lights below. Not many; most of the villagers kept early hours, and it must now be quite late indeed; but that large building almost directly ahead, with one small light in an upper window, and considerable light reflecting out from a ground-floor window onto the road in front, and with the dark shapes of sizable outbuildings around—was that not the inn?

No, he would try nothing, this near to help. There was another party at the inn, too, departing . . . no, arriving. Two or three horsemen. Searchers for her? No, their shouts were far too happy. They must not even have heard of the trouble. Fox-hunters gone astray, then, separated from the rest of the field and out very late. Oh, why could not they have gone a few hundred yards farther astray and been the ones to rescue her? Why could not anyone have rescued her, instead of the viscount?

And why were they pausing here, on the slope overlooking the inn?

12

They were pausing because the viscount's own confusion increased tenfold at sight of the hunters dismounting and going into the Grain and Grape. These chance and unexpected late guests somehow brought home to him the awkwardness of his situation, arriving to elope with his mistress, and bringing his fiancée along on his arm. He should have stowed the chit with George in Ploverchase, and the matter would have been solved to everybody's satisfaction. He would probably have thought of it himself in a moment . . . but when she said it first, when she frankly avowed to his very face her preference for his churchman brother, he had been understandably angered. What if he *had* been throwing them together, dabbling in a bit of matchmaking for his own amusement, with some vague ideas of softening the blow for his betrothed by providing her a new lover to mend her broken heart with all due gradualness? She should not have been already preferring the new suitor while the old, so far as she knew, was still otherwise unattached! Damned unseemly of the chit, and she deserved to be punished.

Still, having her on his arm made things awkward.

He had thought, when first he yielded to the impulse of humbling her, that it would be no complicated matter to bring her into the Grain and Grape, quietly bespeak a private room for her, and leave her there whilst he proceeded upstairs to Marie's garret. With the arrival of the hunters, it no longer seemed quite so convenient. They had apparently bespoken the common room, to judge by the light; and he would have a hard time of it to slip Deirdre past without any of them noticing or without old Perry blabbing to them about the young lady just installed in a private room.

But to bring her and abandon her would cast no auspicious light on either of their reputations. Hers it would leave in worse case than had she spent the rest of the night alone with the vicar; while as for his—there were certain manners a man should not adopt toward his own gently nurtured fiancée. Not that Bevil, Viscount Fencort, was overly tender about Deirdre's troubles, nor that he would not again be snapping his fingers at general opinion and thus winning it back to his favor within a month. His own set would approve his action at once, whoever the fellow had been with Deirdre, and whether his lordship were acting as a lover unexpectedly encumbered with rescuing a superfluous maiden at an inconvenient time, or as an outraged party chastising his faithless intended. But, dash it! Today's hunting party had been largely made up of such stodgy relics of past generations—Harkendell, Darnham, the earl himself, a smattering of local dignitaries full of fawning and self-importance—as would applaud the rescue but think it devilish queer if the rescuer did not sit the rest of the evening calming his lady's fears in company. Let them get wind of this evening's episode, and devil if he would be likely to find the chance to slip up to Marie. Riding out the earl's displeasure and the censures of the antiquated set with his bride already on his arm would be one thing. Eloping with her immediately, past the assortment of the governor's cronies drinking in the common room, would be another. Explanations would be difficult, at the least: "Excuse me, gentlemen, while I leave you for a few minutes toasting my betrothed and go up to collect the sweet French filly in the garret."

Briefly, the viscount considered bringing Deirdre in boldly, with her tale of highwaymen, enjoying the excitement, basking in his own role as hero of the adventure, and later explaining it all to Marie and

85

setting the elopement for a few evenings later. He calculated the chances of her accepting his apologies and found them almost nil. She had led him a pretty chase, had *la petite comtesse de chambre,* but there was too much mischief in her temper—he sensed that she did not take their quarrels seriously enough for him to be assured of winning her around every time, and tonight might well be the occasion for a final rupture.

Well, then, was the Cluzot-d'Azalaine worth it? Were there not other mermaids in the sea? Quickly, in his mind's eye, Bevil tallied up Marie's charms: the quick black eyes, smooth downy skin, luscious full lips, and remarkably responsive French tongue. True, it could be a stinging tongue as well, but what a saucy good-tempered one in its stings! Her nose was too straight, her chin might have been too sharp were it not softened by the plump throat just beneath, the delicate hint of a double chin. Had she been thinner, he might have worried seriously that her sauciness would develop into the temper of a virago; but with her ripe young body bulging so enticingly above and below her waistline—her heartiness so clear both toward the pleasures of table and those of bed—her self-will showed exactly the right degree of spirit and no more. The perfect mare, begad, for the Viscount Fencourt to manage to their mutual enjoyment. He had spent some years developing his natural appreciation of the fair sex, and rare plums like the Cluzot-d'Azalaine, whatever her rather ludicrous pretensions to blue blood, were not so common as a man might think.

Moreover, his wedding date was approaching; and should he miss his chance with Marie, it was not likely he could find another suitable partner for an elopement in time. In that case, he would have to scramble for excuses, postponements, or an outright break. The highwayman-lover might provide an excuse, but not before the earl and his compeers had made a great botheration and prying into the affair. Bevil might even find himself trapped in the ruse of his own connivance, yoked at the altar to the Chevington chit.

Which might almost be worth it, for the turn it would give the chambermaid-countess! Savoring Marie's outrage in imagination, Bevil glanced down at Deirdre for a rapid comparison. Marie's black hair and black eyes were not really so much preferable to Deirdre's gold and blue; indeed, the Chevington's coloring frequently met the greater praise amongst connoisseurs. He had noticed, too, that Deirdre's face had much the same downy softness as Marie's, the fine silky layer that shone like an aura in the right light. Deirdre's nose, also, had the fetching tilt which was one of Marie's most serious lacks. But for size, the Chevington was a shrimp, with hardly enough flesh even on her bosom to make a decent pillow. Her soft soprano voice was well enough in its way, but poor beside the French maid's firm contralto. And her temper . . . impossible! He had never seen Deirdre anything but meek and mousy until tonight; and now, when at last she showed some spirit, it was serious and intense, hopelessly lacking in any touch of humor.

Could he have had Deirdre as viscountess to decorate his residences, and Marie as mistress in a cozy love nest, he would have been well satisfied. But, while he might manage the first part of such an arrangement, he knew the d'Azalaine too well to presume she would stand for it. Taken a page from the book of the Boleyn, had Marie, to snare herself a husband by forbearance rather than the other trick—clever of the wench, since the other trick worked only on milksops inclined to respectability, not on men like Fencourt. Seeing her viscount married and her own chance of title, town house, and social standing gone in that quarter, the d'Azalaine was not only capable of snubbing Bevil cold and carrying out her threats to find another nobleman, but damn likely to do it.

No, there was nothing for it but to stow Deirdre somewhere in the Grain and Grape and slip off with Marie to Gretna Green as planned. But how arrange it? Between fanfaring Deirdre into the common room and then slipping away somehow from a half a dozen of the earl's busybody hunters, or presenting the chit to the chambermaid and making a clean breast of it

87

at once to Marie, he rapidly decided his chances were much the better with the second scheme.

"My lord," said Miss Chevington coldly, "are we to stand here in the dew all night? Is that the inn, or is it not?"

Her long mousiness broken at last, Miss Chevington was showing a definitely shrewish streak. Yes, he had made the right decision, not to trade his French pseudo*comtesse* for Deirdre. Damn it if he did not begin to regret having taken her from her highwayman! "It is, as you've so shrewdly observed, the Grain and Grape," he replied, searching for an excuse to keep her quiet, "but you're hardly in a state, m'dear, to appear before the august company that just went in."

"What?"

"Half a dozen venerable elders halfway in their cups, and you with your hair falling down and your bodice torn half off? Child, you'd shock 'em into evil thoughts, and that might kill them."

She groped at the top of her dress. "It is *not* torn half off, it is only torn a very little!"

Aye, this was the way to manage her. "Trust me, love, their lascivious old minds will supply the rest."

Had there been light enough, he was confident he would have seen her blush. "It is not my fault, sir! I'm sure they, at least, will believe me and raise the countryside."

"Come, love, is that what you really want? To raise the countryside for some poor devil who was carried off by your beauty?" It was certainly not what Bevil wished—to have to dodge through a local hue and cry with his French turtledove.

"You seem to have a misapprehension, sir, of who was carried off by whom. I'm sure the old gentlemen inside will understand it more perfectly. If you will stand aside, I shall walk down to the inn myself."

She actually did take two steps forward. He caught her arm. "Not without me, you won't, my girl."

"With you or without you, my lord. Thank Heaven I have still the use of my legs."

"You'll walk in there alone with your dress torn and
88

expect them to believe you escaped by yourself from this rogue of yours with your honor intact?"

"I shall tell them exactly who rescued me—though I cannot tell them *why*—and leave them to wonder why you were so ungallant as to let me find my own way to the door."

"A pretty picture you'll make of it."

"Let go my arm, Lord Fencourt."

"I'm only trying to keep you from folly, dear heart. The best way to win their respect and commiseration will be to appear before 'em in a decent *toilette*."

"Will you let go my arm, Bevil, or must I scream for help?"

"Damn it, girl, you're my affianced, I can't go parading you to the world looking like a trollop!"

She turned to him with what she might have intended for a withering stare (if the light had been brighter) and spoke more slowly. "You seem singularly unable to comprehend, my lord, that the circumstances are extraordinary and may well excuse some slight disarray in my appearance. As for my being your affianced, I would be only too happy to change a situation so obviously distasteful to both of us."

"Would you? Would you indeed, begad?" A sudden inspiration, flashing through his brain, mitigated the anger he would ordinarily have felt at her insult. He had already determined to make a clean breast of the muddle to Marie—why not simplify the situation still more and make a clean breast of it to Deirdre as well? "Look here, then, old girl, we can solve the problem very neatly all round. Come up with me to yonder garret and let me present you to my mistress!"

13

She drew back as if stung—indeed, she felt almost as if a wasp had darted somehow up the back of her neck and driven its barb into her brain. "My—lord!" It took her a moment to catch her breath. "Let me be sure I understand you. You are proposing to bring me face to face for a rendezvous with one of your paramours?"

"Don't go putting on a show of prudery, sweetheart." He sounded annoyed and a little nonplussed. "It ain't as if your own affair with that supposed highwayman was entirely above suspicion."

"What you are pleased to call my 'affair' was thrust upon me—"

"Thrust upon you, hey?" She must have made a bad choice of words, for now he chuckled. "I'm sure it was, and no doubt entirely through no choice of your own. Now come along, my dear, outraged little lady. You ought to love Marie. I'm about to elope with her and free you from your odious engagement."

In another moment she might have reconciled herself to his brazen proposal of introducing her to his mistress. After all, she had always known he must have many such, and intend to keep them or get new ones after his marriage; and she had somewhere heard that women of that class were frequently good-hearted and friendly to a wonderful degree. But to hear him calmly announce his intentions of running off with this . . . this *courtizan* and leaving his betrothed, almost at the foot of the altar, as an object of ridicule! For a moment she forgot her own desire to be free of the man in her shock at his method of freeing her.

"Well, what is it now?" he was demanding. "I'd swear, a man would think you weren't happy about it."

"*Happy* about it? *Happy* to be told to my face I am to be jilted on the eve of my wedding for a—a harlot?"

"In the first place, the Cluzot-d'Azalaine is not a harlot. She's a botherish respectable emigrée countess whom I am going to rescue from the fallen condition of chambermaid. Secondly, no blame will accrue to you in the matter unless you choose to make yourself ridiculous over it. On the contrary, everybody will pity you and execrate me to your heart's content. I shouldn't be astonished if you became such a nine days' wonder of sympathetic interest as to net yourself a marquess or duke out of the business—"

"I don't want a duke—"

"Lord! You're not going to tell me you never meant any of it? You're not going to protest that you're in love with me after all?" When he began this speech he sounded vexed, but at the end of it he chuckled. No doubt his vanity was soothed by the notion that he might actually have snared her heart—did not men of his sort delight to think of themselves as heart-breakers?

"Let me reassure you," she said, gathering control of herself. "I have not the smallest atom of love for you." Tell him she wished for his brother she would not. "I meant I did not wish any nobleman or gentleman of *your* stamp, my lord!"

"Tut! Has a bit of a temper, has it?"

"For a moment," she went on, ignoring the jibe, "the remedy you proposed seemed almost worse than the complaint. But now I perceive that no operation, no matter how rude and violent, can be too painful or too quickly performed if it has the blessed effect of freeing me forever from your odious attentions." She spoke slowly and distinctly, choosing her words with care and hoping to make it clear to him that she meant every one of them. "So lead on, my lord!"

" 'And damn'd be him that first cries, "Hold, enough!" ' "

His quip made no kind of sense to her—certainly its

connection with what she had just said was totally obscure. But perhaps he was quoting literature. She seemed to recall having read something like it on a dull rainy morning in her childhood at the dear old Willows. She would try to remember the phrase and ask Aunt Cassie about it later; and, with this end in view, she kept repeating it to herself as she followed Lord Fencourt down the hill towards the side of the inn and the lighted upper window.

Once below it, he threw a pebble. It missed the window, clicking ineffectually on the lower wall. He tried again, with no better success.

Deirdre giggled. "The glaziers will have little to fear from you at this rate, my lord."

"It's the damned shadows!" He turned his face briefly towards her, then mounted his horse. For a moment she thought he was about to gallop away in disgust and leave her to her own devices. The prospect would have been welcome but for a nagging doubt he had implanted in her conscience, as to how the gentlemen in the common room really would react to her disheveled appearance.

But, instead of riding off, he climbed higher, balancing like an acrobat, with his feet on top of his saddle. Much as she disliked him, Deirdre held her breath for him as, from this precarious stance, he aimed a whole handful of pebbles at once at the elusive window.

Again they missed, beginning a chatter like rain on the wall—but the horse shied at the movement, and the viscount lost his balance and tumbled to the ground. "Calpie!" he cried, catching at the air—no, he was catching at the horse's reins—"Hold her, Deirdre, damn it!" he went on in a slightly lower tone. "No—never mind, I have her. Blasted mare, Calpurnia! Do you think my old Roxy would have pulled that trick?"

"Are you questioning me or your horse, my lord?" said Deirdre. His fall had put her into a somewhat better humor.

"What is it that is going on down there?" The new voice came from above. Looking up, Deirdre saw the lighted window was open at last, and a dark head protruding from it.

"Marie, *mon chou*—"

"Bevil? Is it you? *Mon Dieu,* you will wake the entire house! Is this the way you English make the elopement, by bringing out all the world to see?"

"*Ma mie,*" his lordship pointed out with ruffled dignity, "at the moment you also are guilty of your share of the fracas."

"You were to creep around by the servants' door and silent up the back stairs like the little mouse."

" 'But hark!' ' he rejoined obscurely. " 'What light through yonder window breaks?'' "

"Breaks? It is to break your foolish head, *ma mie,* I will drop out the chamber pot on it!"

Deirdre could hardly repress a chuckle. She felt an unexpected liking for this French mistress of the viscount's.

"Dash it, Marie, don't you know the common room's full of fox-hunters?"

"Ah? And how should I know it? Their noises they have not yet come up to me so high, like yours, and it must be that I dozed when they came, here waiting for you so long."

"Well, they're here, take my word on it."

"Very good, then William will be serving them, or the fat Jenny."

"Yes, but I can't very well dodge through the servants' door now, can I? It is the east, and—"

"Ah, yes, yes, yes! The other plan, and your silly watchwords. Two minutes, then." Marie's head disappeared. Deirdre giggled. Decidedly, she liked this Frenchwoman . . . and also envied her saucy tongue and the freedom with which she laughed at the viscount. Yes, Deirdre quite approved the match. Doubtless, once the shock of being so played with and misused had turned into indignation, she would have approved any match that secured her forever from the danger of marrying Bevil herself; but much as she might in the abstract welcome her rival, she had not expected also to like her. She did not like Marie quite enough to commiserate with her on her fate—the woman was, after all, a chambermaid and French, and almost certainly of loose morals and soaring ambition —in short, a foreign adventuress who had chosen to

93

prey on Bevil and probably deserved him. But for so singling out the Viscount Fencourt, of all noblemen, and for the wedded life she would be able to lead him, Deirdre loved her.

A crude rope ladder, made of old sheets with knotted handholds, tumbled down from the window and remained swaying, a flimsy white strand against the wall. "At last," muttered the viscount. "And high time, too! Now, then, my darling dear, up you go."

"What?" said Deirdre.

"Up you go."

Deirdre stared at the improvised ladder. "Bevil, are you mad? I can't—"

"What is going on?" Marie called down. "Bevil, who is it you have there with you?"

"Only my fiancée, chère Marie. You'll adore her."

"Your fiancée? The fine English lady? Par mon marteau! Bevil, if you make the sport with me—"

"He makes the sport with everyone, madame," Deirdre interjected, deciding it was no time to be over-scrupulous about addressing a chambermaid as "madame." "But it happens we are only victims of chance."

The Frenchwoman's chuckle, though muffled by the distance, was still audible. "Ah, and is that you, lady? She has a good voice, and I think, my Bevil, you may be the silly goose. Come up, then, my sweet lady, and you will explain it all to me—we will not listen to Bevil, for he does not always tell the truth."

The viscount swore softly and propelled Deirdre towards the dangling rope. "Be very sure the end is tight," he called up maliciously. "She's on her way."

Deirdre put her right hand on a knot above level with her neck, and reached her left to one above her head. It had always seemed a simple matter, in books and romances, for a prisoner to escape by such a ladder. It was almost the first thing one did on being imprisoned, after slyly enlarging the window opening, to tear and knot one's sheets. She had read of it and accepted it without even considering, as if the ability to climb up and down ladders of knotted sheets were a born instinct in the race, at least in prisoners and lovers. Perhaps that was the difficulty: She was neither.

"I cannot do it."

"What do you mean, you cannot do it?"

"I cannot do it, Lord Fencourt."

"Oh, lud! Do you mean to say you can't even climb up a simple rope ladder, you silly chit?"

"That is precisely what I mean to say, my lord," she replied coldly. "I will walk round to the door and take my chances with the drinking gentlemen."

"That you won't!" He seized her wrist.

Having had a bit too much of gentlemen seizing her that evening, she pulled back fiercely. "You need not be afraid I shall tell them of your tricks here! I want nothing more than for you to elope and marry someone else."

"You do not trust your own affianced, Bevil?" the chambermaid called down, sounding vastly amused. "But she has the fine idea, that one—let her go round and make—what do you call it?—the *divertissement.*"

"And have the whole lot about our ears combing the entire place for highwaymen?"

"Suppose *you* try to climb up a sheet ladder in skirts, then!" said Deirdre.

"Oh, if that's all the matter—" He put his hand to the material at her waist.

"Bevil!" she half-screamed, as the cloth began to give.

"Bevil!" added Marie. "Naughty, wicked nobleman! We will both scream, and then what will they do with you?"

"The devil!" He unwillingly let go Deirdre's gown. "She'd do it, too! Now what are you tittering at?"

Despite her surcharged emotions—or perhaps because they had been surcharged so often within the last hours—Deirdre was now giggling uncontrollably at the silliest trifle. "Oh, my lord, I just realized—'Bevil' rhymes with 'devil'!"

"Ah! She is right, you see," cried the chambermaid. "Come, Bevil who rhymes with devil! First you will climb up, and then we will pull her up together, you and I. I have greatly the desire to meet this dear English lady who is so clever."

"Let down a bit more rope, then," he conceded after swearing a little more, not quite so softly.

"But why, my Bevil-devil?"

"If we're going to pull her up, I want to secure her now."

"My lord!" Not even the highwayman had offered to bind Deirdre.

Marie seemed to have something of the same impression of the viscount's proposed impropriety. "You do not trust your own fiancée, *ma mie?* You fear she will run away when you are up the ladder? Or become a little mouse and chew the sheet?"

"No, damme, you silly females! If we're to haul her up, she must be tied to the end of the sheet sooner or later, and I want to be sure the job's done right."

"Ah, we have made him to be annoyed, *le pauvre.* One moment, then." Marie's head disappeared from the window. A few minutes later, a ball of heavy worsted dropped down at their feet, causing his lordship's horse to shy and snort. "The sheet I cannot let down even one more foot," the maid explained cheerfully, looking out again. "Perhaps you will make it do with the yarn, no? It is very thick, that yarn."

Bearing it almost silently, the viscount began to loop lengths of worsted together to make a reasonably stout cord. Deirdre, who had seen the force of his argument once it was stated, submitted meekly to have the improvised sling fastened about her waist and knotted tight to the sheet ladder. Secretly, she saw no reason she could not have made as secure a job of it herself after Lord Fencourt had climbed up; but she began to fear that a little more of their teasing and he would ride away in a dudgeon, leaving both her and Marie to disentangle themselves from the situation.

That they could have done so, and done so very nicely as far as the needs of the moment went, Deirdre had little doubt. She herself was the outraged innocent, with no cause for shame (no matter what Bevil might insinuate), whilst Marie seemed very capable and quick-witted. But though the chambermaid might laugh to see her lover ride away angry, if he did so now he might also leave his formal engagement unbroken and raise great difficulties about it being broken in some more regular way—Deirdre would not put it past him to insist on marrying her merely to torment her, if he were sufficiently piqued.

In effect, being tied to the end of the sheet ladder as he climbed up, she was serving as his anchor; and it jerked her about and squeezed out her breath from time to time. But she had a good deal of satisfaction in observing that, after all his words, he himself had considerable difficulty in making the ascent.

14

Sir Roderic, judging that more than sufficient time had elapsed for the young lovers to gain a place of warmth and comfort, returned to the scene of the late rescue. His mare had not yet come back. He would wait half an hour for her, if he did not hear the hue and cry in the meantime. He was in some need of refreshment himself, and on Gunpowder's back he could make the Royal Oak in Tamiston within an hour. If Gunpowder did not return to where she had deserted her master, he thought he might walk down to the Grain and Grape. Refuge there would have its perils. By the time he arrived, the tale of Miss Chevington's abduction would almost certainly be current at the neighborhood's only inn. But he had not spoken in the hearing of the vicar, and he doubted even Deirdre had not been able to study his features in the dark. If he walked in boldly, masquerading as a second victim of his own, with a tale of having been robbed of his horse by a fleeing footpad, he had a very tolerable chance. Putting his story together with that of Deirdre and Mr. Oakton, the rustics would accept Sir Roderic as a late traveler waylaid by the same rogue who had kidnapped the young lady. They might even find and return him Gunpowder in their search for the highwayman. He had carried off more desperate ruses than this with success.

He settled himself on the grass, his back against a tree, relaxing his large limbs but ready to spring up and melt into the shadows if need arose. An owl hooted, off to the south; some small night creatures foraged with little rustling sounds just within the edge of the woods. Most of the stars of Cassiopeia's Chair could be seen above the treetops. Sir Roderic had no quarrel with the night in itself. Night hunters like the owl, being animals, made their kills quick and practical, leaving inanimate nature to resume its tranquility with little pother. It was not unpleasant to sit alone in a hillside copse in the autumnal dark. It was, however, damp; and Sir Roderic would consider a roaring fire, steaming supper, and bottle of good wine as an excellent trade for the moonlight beauties of the wooded hillside.

Hurrying footsteps became audible. Some new party on his way over the hill. For a few seconds Sir Roderic sat in more or less idle meditation on the identity of the rustic and probable nature of his errand. Most likely it would be connected with his own evening's work.

Little Tiptree lay to the west of the hill, Ploverchase village to the east. The new footsteps were coming from the east. Sir Roderic, in Oakton's place, would have returned with Deirdre to the quiet vicarage in Ploverchase. The runner, then, might well be on his way to alert Little Tiptree.

Having reached this hypothesis between the time he first heard the footsteps and the time they drew abreast of the clearing, Sir Roderic decided to seize the opportunity thus offered, without waiting longer for his errant horse. Groaning loudly, he got to his feet, leaning against the tree like a man just recovering his wits after some heavy shock.

He was prepared, if necessary, to stagger towards the path and call out for help, but his first groan was sufficient. The footsteps halted; the runner paused, obviously listening, no doubt wondering if he had indeed heard what he thought. Sir Roderic was about to groan again and begin rubbing the back of his head, when a voice from the path called, "Miss Chevington?"

Miss Chevington? If a man's groan could be mistaken for possible evidence of a young girl's presence here, then the newcomer must know that the girl had been kidnapped, but not that she had been rescued.

Sir Roderic decided the safest means of ascertaining the situation would be to continue in the role of his own latest victim. "Here!" he called weakly.

The newcomer crashed through the bushes and began to shine a lantern round the clearing. In his other hand, Sir Roderic noted, he carried a pistol, barrel pointed up but no doubt ready to be lowered and aimed at the first menace. "Miss Chevington?" the newcomer inquired again; but, failing to discover her by the beam of his lantern, he approached Sir Roderic at once. "What is it, man? You're hurt?"

"A blow from behind." So much was necessary to explain the groan and the apparent state of temporary incapacitation; but best to leave the story vague and fluid until he could learn what, precisely, was believed in the villages.

"Have you seen a young lady?"

"I have seen no one, but I doubt it was not a lady who dealt me the blow."

"Have you any idea what direction the rogue took, then?"

"None. Nor from what direction, other than behind, he came at me. But there's a young lady missing?"

"Abducted. A highway rogue. Can you walk?"

The young man contained his obvious disappointment reasonably well. He had sense enough, even in his agitation, to attempt precautions; still, his immediate trust in a stranger met under such circumstances was little short of touching. "I can walk," said Sir Roderic.

The newcomer cast his lantern beam about the clearing once more. "I think someone may have broken through over there, not long ago."

"Not unlikely, but from which direction?"

"If it were daylight . . ." The newcomer sighed and pocketed his pistol. "It's fortunate I was going to Wantage," he said, apparently deciding to adhere to his original plan. "Bellew can examine your head."

Bellew was the apothecary to whom Cassandra had planned on being taken, to whose house she had calculated on summoning Oakton as a pretext for bringing him over the hill. Damnation! thought Sir Roderic, I have let the girl be rescued by the wrong man. The truth was now so obvious as to need further verification only for the sake of form. "Bellew being a medical man?"

"A tolerable apothecary—the best, at least, within twelve miles." The young man offered his arm; Sir Roderic shrugged away the support.

"Set your pace."

Obeying, the younger man set his pace, a rapid stride that bespoke his anxiety.

"You have not honored me with your name," remarked Sir Roderic, matching his stride.

"Oakton, sir. George Oakton. At your service."

Sir Roderic nodded to himself, unsurprised. "A man of the cloth?"

"You seem to have the advantage of me."

"You have some little fame beyond the limits of Ploverchase and Rotherhithe." But who the devil was that puppy who had rescued the girl by mistake?

"Ah," said Oakton, "you'll have heard of the earl. Or of my older brother. Who is not, perhaps, quite so black as painted," added the vicar, as if sensible of some obligation to his family.

"The latest follies of the future Earl of Rotherhithe fail to engage my interest."

Sir Roderic's immediate problem was whether and how much to confide in Oakton. The boy deserved to know that his light o' love might be in danger; but that much he supposed already. He did not know that she might be in more serious danger now than when in the hands of her original abductor—nor, Sir Roderic reflected, did he himself know so much. He knew that he himself was faithful to his own resolutions; and he suspected that the popinjay who had rescued Miss Chevington by mistake was a rattle-souled collector of women's honor; but the world in general would probably consider appearances more against the highwayman than the gallant.

The longer he put off informing Oakton and taking useful action, the greater possibility of Mistress Chevington's undoing. But how the devil break such information to the vicar without imparting Sir Roderic's own part in the business? An infernal mess indeed: Delay was dangerous, haste impossible.

Still, mused Sir Roderic, it is barely conceivable that I have misjudged the popinjay. It is vaguely possible he has carried the maiden safe to Bellew, or the Grain and Grape, or some other respectable house. In which case my revelations would be superfluous as well as dangerous to myself. In which case, also, the whole escapade will have served no purpose; but let the girl be found safe and whole, and Cassandra may plot whatever new match-breaking and matchmaking schemes she pleases, without my help.

"You were coming from Tiptree?" asked Oakton.

"From London. To Endercombe." London was the truth, and Endercombe a reasonable fleshing-out of the tale.

"A longish trip for one day."

"And a short one for two. But it seems I must break my journey after all, within a few hours of my destination."

"You have business in Endercombe?"

"I am not aware it is a place to which one travels for pleasure."

"There used to be decent shooting thereabouts. . . . Your business is pressing?"

"Comparatively."

"You might be able to hire a horse at the Grain and Grape. Or from old Tom Pearse."

"If I hire a horse tonight, it will be to help search for this unfortunate young lady."

Oakton paused, the lantern trembling slightly in his grasp. "Sir, that is—that is decent of you. May I take your hand, Mr. . . .?"

"Marblehead." The pseudonym was out almost without thinking—preoccupied with the novel sensations of not being as fully in command of the situation as usual, Sir Roderic had neglected to consider whether to use his real name when occasion arose. "As for my helping find your young lady, any man who would not do so does not deserve the name of a man."

"I know one or two who would not bestir themselves for a stranger of either sex, Mr. Marblehead, when they had their own business in hand."

Sir Roderic guessed Oakton was thinking of his elder brother. He also noticed that, even with Miss Chevington's actual fiancé in his mind, the vicar did not disclaim the reference to "your young lady." He briefly shook hands, noting with approval the steadiness which must have cost Oakton some effort. Unwilling to appear overly altruistic, Sir Roderic remarked, "Before you credit me with any great measure of selflessness, you should perhaps bear in mind that I have lost a rather valuable mare. Which may be carrying your lady farther away as we stand here exchanging civilities."

15

Oakton resumed his pace immediately; indeed, he began to walk even faster than before. While Sir Roderic had no difficulty in matching his stride, he was unsure which of them was setting the pace and which exerting himself to keep up with it.

Speed was admirable under the circumstances; but further probing must also be some use, if only to ascertain more fully what Oakton knew or believed of the situation. "I think you said you were going first to the house of this apothecary Bellew?"

"Yes."

"An original plan, to start the hue and cry from the house of a medical man. Have you no constables?"

"A better one in Ploverchase than Tiptree—although neither of them, I fear, inspire much confidence. But there must be no uproar, not yet."

"And why not?"

"A question of ransom. It seems the villain left instructions with Miss Chevington's aunt. I—I am apparently to act as messenger or go-between."

An admirable device to keep matters quiet—if the rescue had gone as it should. As the abductor, Sir Roderic blessed Cassandra for her precautions; but he had now taken the role of honest gentleman, and counseled accordingly. "Honorable ransom may have been a trick of feudal times. In our day, it's hardly likely a common brigand would abduct a young woman with no other thought than holding her to ransom."

"Good God!" But Oakton's tone suggested it was no

new idea to him—rather, a fear of his own which he had been trying to bury and was appalled at hearing echoed in the mouth of a disinterested party. "Then— it is your opinion, Mr. Marblehead, that the ransom instructions may be a ploy to give him time to escape the country?"

"It is my opinion that is a definite possibility. He may hope at last to obtain his ransom, but I doubt he would not linger in the neighborhood to wait for it tonight. If he suggested any such arrangement, I would be almost assured of a trick to gain time." What, precisely, Sir Roderic mused, has Lady Cassandra put into my mouth concerning these ransom arrangements?

"I . . . know nothing of where he may have arranged to be paid the ransom, but Thomas—Lady Darnham's coachman—has driven for it at once. That . . . suggests the bloody scoundrel only means to gain time?"

The use of the adjective by a hitherto mild-spoken clergyman did not escape Sir Roderic. "It has a bad look."

Oakton began to exclaim something still more forceful, controlled himself with an effort, and after a moment spoke in a carefully rational voice, although with a vibrato of guarded emotion. "I know only what Thomas told me of the business. The scoundrel waylaid them below this hill, between the villages. He forced the coachman to lie on the ground, seized Miss Chevington, and left some kind of private instructions with Lady Darnham. Apparently these instructions concern me. I do not know what or how the wretch knows of me to involve me, but perhaps he merely asked for the nearest clergyman. Thomas offered to drive me back to Wantage—that is Mr. Bellew's home in Tiptree—on his way to Derwent Abbey for Lady Darnham's jewels. I judged it would be equally fast for me to come dircetly over the hill rather than the roundabout way by the road, and the coach would make better time if Thomas did not have to curve again into Tiptree. It was a hasty decision. It may have been ill-judged."

"Better a hasty decision than all action deferred

104

until too late." Sir Roderic had listened with great interest to the vicar's account of the abduction. He observed, also, that the coachman had been able to leave Oakton with the impression that coming alone over Ploverchase Hill was the vicar's own idea. Cassandra's confidence in her servant had not been misplaced.

Reaching the downward slope, they emerged from the trees and came within sight of Little Tiptree. More exactly, within sight of a large building with outbuildings, unmistakably the inn, by its size, shape, and the sign visible in the light from the common room; and of a few more lights here and there amongst the houses beyond. Most of the village had retired early.

"We'd best stop at the Grain and Grape and raise the alarm, then," said Oakton somewhat bitterly.

"How far beyond the inn is the apothecary's house?"

"Perhaps a hundred yards."

Sir Roderic made his decision both as disinterested stranger and as a principal player in the comedy. "Having come so far, better first learn what communications the scoundrel left with this Lady—Darnham, is it?" If the dandy had taken Miss Chevington with evil intentions, he now had such a start of them that a few additional minutes before raising the alarm could make little difference; and Cassandra deserved, at least, to learn of the development privately.

As they descended the hill, however, Sir Roderic listened sharply to the sounds issuing from the common room. Had he heard aught to suggest rejoicing over a rescued maiden, he was ready to steer Oakton to the inn first, after all. But, satisfied the noises betokened only a group of hunters drinking after their day in the saddle, with as yet no suspicion of the night's drama, the two men proceeded round by the side, rather than risk being hailed from the front by some roisterer.

One upper window near the back of the building was lighted, and from the corner of his eye Sir Roderic thought he glimpsed the end of something thin and white disappearing into it. At that moment he stumbled over a half brick, no doubt rolled there earlier by some promising village lad aiming it at the feet of a horse; and by the time he looked again, the thing had disappeared and the window was demure, with its curtains and unsullied sill.

Sir Roderic was not given to hallucination; and if the window had suddenly been shuttered, he would have been inclined to investigate at once. On the grounds of a mere tail of cord or cloth, however, which might or might not have been a trick of the moonlight, he declined to check their progress to Wantage and Lady Cassandra, resting content merely to file the impression in his mind.

16

Lady Cassandra had drunk, thus far, three and a half cups of tea, more to soothe the nerves of Mr. Bellew and his housekeeper than her own. She had managed to ward off a fresh pot being brewed, had successfully parried all the apothecary's suggestions of powders, and had endured the efforts of the good pair to make her quiet and comfortable.

Their attempts to calm her consisted of Mr. Bellew's pacing the parlor in a fret, when he was not disappearing into the back regions of his house for up to a quarter hour at a time; whilst Mrs. Epworthy sat beside Cassandra dispensing condolences with a practiced motherliness that was meant to be reassuring, and offering every few minutes to make another pot of tea. Cassandra amused herself largely by timing the housekeeper's remarks and offers, watching the clock on the mantel to see how often each reoccurred. Thus far, "Just let us call up Simmons and Mayhew"—the constables—"my lady, and we'll have the child back safe before morning," had come about twice as often as "Another dish or two of nice, hot tea will do us all the good in the world," whilst some statement to the effect "Whoever heard the like here in Tiptree?" came more often than either. Cassandra was tempted sometimes to remark on another result additional dishes of tea would have.

She could have calmed her own nerves much more nicely if she were left to herself, the fire, and one of the books blinking in their shelves on the far side of the room. Since they clearly included a few rows of standard titles bound to order for the display, she would no doubt find some author worthy of perusal amongst them. Or a game of draughts or piquet, or possibly backgammon—she doubted Mrs. Epworthy did not play chess—would have helped considerably to ease the wait. Alas, it would have seemed callous in Cassandra to suggest such expedients. Mrs. Epworthy might with propriety have suggested them. A hand or two at piquet would have been as valid a proposal on her part as another pot of tea. But clearly the apothecary and his housekeeper were accustomed to deal only with emergencies of a far different sort than the present.

Mr. Bellew was away on one of his private journeys to library, study, or wherever he wandered in his agitation, when the bell rang. Thus, after Mrs. Epworthy jumped up with a flutter of reassurances and went to the door, Lady Cassandra was left for a few blessed moments alone. Happy anticipation, long stifled by the apprehensions and anxieties of her hosts, now reasserted itself. She heard voices in the vestibule, very low, but obviously more than one; and she leaned back on the cushions with a sigh of content, beginning to plan her congratulations to the vicar.

Soon, however, she began to suspect something amiss. That deep voice which had just interjected a few words, almost loudly enough for her to hear them —that was not Thomas. It sounded . . . it sounded like her captain. And surely she ought by now to have

107

heard Deirdre's voice, if only in an exclamation of excited relief?

She had no time to listen more intently, for the apothecary reappeared, carrying a medical book closed on one finger, and exclaiming about the doorbell. His questions as to what new catastrophes were ensuing made it impossible for Cassandra to give the murmuring voices any useful attention. She stood. "Perhaps we had best go and see."

"No, no! That is to say, my lady, I shall go, you must stay and rest—you must not disturb yourself." Predictably, he hurried to her side in order to push her back down into the cushions.

Of a mood to resist, she dodged his hands and took a few steps away from the divan, intending to proceed at once to the vestibule. Fortunately, her determination was forestalled. Before she could reach the door—which Mrs. Epworthy had left ajar—or the solicitous apothecary could prevent her from so doing, it opened and the housekeeper returned through it in a state of disapproving perplexity, followed by the newcomers. Even before Mr. Oakton was quite through the door, Cassandra saw behind him the high forehead, silvering dark hair, and broad shoulders of Sir Roderic.

To the great relief of Mr. Bellew, who did not suspect her real motivation, she returned to the divan and sat. Appearances were disturbing, but she still had no actual proof that her plan had gone so very far amiss. What purpose the captain could have had in allowing himself to be taken by the vicar was beyond her for the moment; but he remained, after all, in many ways an inscrutable man. Even when it became obvious that Deirdre was not going to appear in the apothecary's parlor with the rest of them, Lady Cassandra did not quite despair. Perhaps, for some reason she could more profitably wait to hear than attempt to guess, they had found it advisable to leave her niece in the care of someone else. Knowing Mr. Bellew better than she herself had, the vicar might well have been unwilling to subject Deirdre to the apothecary's flutters. But had she been really hurt, through some mischance, of course they would have brought her to

108

Wantage no matter what might be Mr. Bellew's behavior in nonmedical crises. Moreover, Sir Roderic was neither carrying himself like a prisoner—though Cassandra could not imagine him carrying himself like a prisoner even were he flanked by Bow Street runners —nor did Mr. Oakton appear to regard him as such.

All these thoughts went through her head almost simultaneously, in a very few seconds. Of one thing only was she reasonably sure: her captain had shown not the least recognition of her. So, until she knew what had happened, she must not appear to know him, either. It did not chafe her to have to follow his lead —it was, rather, a challenge, they two in secret conspiracy against the others, treading as carefully as if they were clandestine lovers.

It was the chance for which she had been hoping— and, in all conscience, trying not to hope—the chance to reinsert herself into the drama. If only she were assured of Deirdre's safety, she almost thought she could have relished this moment infinitely, preferring even to draw it out than to have burst into a commonplace and tame explanation requiring no activity on her part.

"Lady Cassandra!" said the vicar, with no more attention to formalities than the situation warranted. "I understand the scoundrel directed you to send for me?"

Yes, but what else did he understand? She realized he expected to hear details of ransom arrangements; but he was to have rescued Deirdre on his way and so have made such arrangements unnecessary; therefore, she had not planned them. Clearly she had left a gaping hole in her scenario. Deirdre had *not* been rescued; Oakton believed her still in the highwayman's clutches; and the man who should have had her safe until the vicar arrived was now standing with them in Bellew's parlor, looking at Cassandra with a raised eyebrow, as much as to say, "I am supposed to know nothing of the business. You must manufacture my words for yourself, but do it quickly. There is no time to be lost."

To waste effort devising ransom arrangements now

would be mere foolishness. What she must do was be rid of the apothecary and his housekeeper. There was no comfortable explanation forthcoming, after all. Lady Cassandra must know at once what Sir Roderic had to communicate; and, failing a few moments with him alone, George Oakton must be taken into their confidence. But not Mr. Bellew and Mrs. Epworthy!

"What I have to tell you," she said, "is for your ears alone." An excessively gothick remark, but had she not created a situation more befitting gothick romance than modern life?

"You're quite private here, my lady," Mr. Bellew assured her. "Quite, quite private. It won't get beyond this room until the villain is caught."

"His directions were very specific on this head," insisted Cassandra, even while thinking, Oh, Lord! How am I to keep Sir Roderic here this way?

"Now, who on earth's to tell him?" asked Mrs. Epworthy.

Sir Roderic leaned back against the doorpost. "If you intend to follow this rogue's instructions, you would be well advised to do so to the letter. By all means, let us leave Mr. Oakton five minutes alone with her ladyship."

In effect, despite their continuing reluctance, he herded the apothecary and housekeeper from the room, pausing, himself, in the doorway to give Cassandra a slight nod. She breathed a little more easily. If she could not yet learn from him what had happened, at least she could be assured that neither apothecary nor housekeeper would listen at the door.

If the vicar saw Sir Roderic's nod, he seemed entirely unsuspecting of its significance. Even as the door closed, he approached the divan. "Then it's your opinion we can have her back most safely by following his instructions?"

Cassandra rose and poked up the fire, which the housekeeper had poked up only a few minutes ago. "Mr. Oakton," she said, "you are going to be very angry with me, but I beg you will save your just rage for a few hours, until we have Deirdre back safe."

"My lady," he protested, coming nearer the fireplace, "I can hardly blame you for this—"

"You must blame me entirely." She would have liked to swear him to secrecy before confessing all, but decided to trust his own natural discretion instead. In any event, her niece's safe recovery was more important than her own reputation. Returning the poker to its stand, she turned and faced Mr. George Oakton. "This was to have been a romantic play. The gentleman who enacted the highwayman is a trusted personal friend of mine, and you were to have been the hero of the piece."

She rather wished she had not turned to face him. The explanation might have been easier if she were not able to see his expression. "You were to have found them on your way over Ploverchase Hill," she went on, "and rescued Deirdre whilst my friend made his escape."

"Good God!" said the vicar.

"I only beg you will not blame Thomas, who has acted entirely under my instructions throughout all this."

For a moment she thought the young man would stagger backwards and sit on the first piece of furniture available; but with some visible effort he retained his stance. "But why?"

"If you cannot guess why, Mr. Oakton, perhaps the charade would have served no purpose, after all." She wondered at her sudden impatience. If he could not be immediately practical, he might at least have railed at her. "Since my pretty plan has obviously miscarried, the first question is how to undo the mischief. *Then* you may ask 'why,' if you have been unable to guess."

"This friend," he said after a pause. "You had good reason to trust him?"

"Implicitly."

"Could he have mistaken the place?"

"No."

"Could he have—forgive me, my lady—could he have been . . . less than worthy of your trust?"

"He could not. Depend on it, whatever has gone amiss, it is not the gentleman's fault."

Oakton began to pace between the wall and the divan. "Who is he?"

"You do not know him."

"Forgive me again, but—can we be so perfectly sure he has not made off with Miss Chevington himself?"

Cassandra wondered how long Oakton would require to connect his acquaintance of the footpath with her unnamed friend. She would not, without consulting Sir Roderic, clarify his identity herself; nor could she explain her assurance without making the revelation. Simply repeating her trust without stating the reason would only waste yet more time. "Suppose it were my friend. How would your efforts differ from what they would be if you knew it had been a stranger to us both?"

"If there is any possibility—even the least—that your friend has himself taken her—I do not say with . . . evil intentions, my lady; he may be simply prolonging this—this rather strange practical joke—then perhaps you may be able to guess where he might have taken her."

Lady Cassandra sat in an armchair near the fireplace and rested her forehead on her hand. If she had some clue, some idea as to where Deirdre might be, she would now have a pretext for sending Mr. Oakton thither.

"If he has not taken her, he may be in danger himself," the vicar went on.

She had been on the verge of making this suggestion, but, knowing him to be safe, had balked at such a palpable untruth—a lie which, moreover, if it became necessary to reveal Sir Roderic as the original abductor, must damage Cassandra's credibility with the vicar. It now occurred to her that her captain was not safe, after all. Lying wounded on a hillside or bound in the power of some new brigand he was not; but, thanks to her, he was in peril of arrest, prison, even the gallows. That these were dangers he often courted in his own daily affairs was one thing; that this time he was courting them in *her* affair was another. "Yes," she said. "They may both be in danger." She must consult with Sir Roderic, and soon!. "How far," she went on, lifting her head to look again at Mr. Oakton, "how far do you think we may trust the gentleman whom you met on the hill?"

The vicar shrugged. "If this were an ordinary case of kidnapping, as I first thought, I would see no reason not to trust him as far as any honest gentleman. Indeed, as another victim of the highwayman—the fellow seems to have stolen his horse—I would have relied on his help. But as a stranger . . ." His voice trailed off as he gazed

112

at Lady Cassandra. "I do not think I had mentioned where I met with Mr. Marblehead."

So that was the name he had given. At least she had learned he was guarding his incognito. Now she must try to cover her slip. "I assumed you must have met him on your way."

"You assume a great many things, my lady." Under the circumstances, it was a very mild reproof, and she accepted it without comment. "I've already told Mr. Marblehead all that I then understood of the affair," Oakton went on.

"And could he cast any light on it?"

"None. However, I would trust his goodwill and judgment, were it not for—"

"Then let us call him in at once," said Cassandra decisively.

"We must first decide what to tell him."

"Tell him! Why, we shall tell him the truth, of course."

"Would it be wise, Lady Darnham, to publish your part in this to a stranger?"

"You are incredible," she said. "I had credited you with some regard for my niece, yet here you stand prattling of my reputation whilst Deirdre is in some danger through my contrivances. I do not care a fig for my own reputation when Deirdre's safety is in the balance with it, Mr. Oakton. If we wish Mr. Marblehead's help, we must give him a true picture." Ah, she continued in her thoughts, if you knew how little I deserve that look of admiration you are bestowing on me!

"I'll call him in, then," said Oakton.

"And have Mr. Bellew and Mrs. Epworthy listening at the door?"

His look of admiration dissolved before this apparent inconsistency. "If we are going to put Miss Chevington's safety above all other considerations, why not have them in as well?"

"I find I care at least a fig for my reputation, after all," said Cassandra with what she supposed was a wan smile. "A stranger would have little reason to gossip afterwards. A casual acquaintance like the apothecary or his house-keeper, much. Does Mr. Bellew keep a carriage?"

17

Mr. Bellew kept a light carriage; and, though at first adamant against his patient's leaving his roof, was at length persuaded that there would be little peril to either her or his equipage in allowing Messrs. Oakton and Marblehead to return her, jointly to Derwent Abbey. Cassandra suspected that a good part of the apothecary's unwillingness to lose his patient lay in the idea, that as long as he had her to care for, he could hardly be expected to take a more active part in helping hunt down a dangerous criminal. She quieted his social conscience as well as she could by assuring him that the new plan might enable her to meet her coachman, already on his way back with her jewels, thus expediting the ransom; by allowing him to arm both gentlemen with his own fowling pieces; and by instructing him that if he had heard nothing from them within three quarters of an hour, he should go and rouse the constabulary.

At last the carriage was readied and they had a measure of privacy. Yet not quite as much as she could have desired. Acutely aware that Oakton, who was driving, could hear most of their conference, and unwilling—despite her resolution of perfect truth and candor —to compromise Sir Roderic, she found herself confessing the situation to him as if he were indeed a stranger, speaking in the third person of her friend who had played the highwayman, and asking for his "conjectures," rather than his "knowledge," of what might have gone wrong.

"It is possible," he said gravely, "that this friend of yours did not know Mr. Oakton and so allowed Miss Chevington to be rescued by the wrong man. Knowing the circumstances, I would be easier if we had alerted the constables at once."

"You should have expressed your opinion more strongly at once," she replied, thinking that, even in the character of casual stranger, he had left the decisions and subterfuges entirely too much to her lead in the apothecary's house.

"Our local constables mean well," interjected Mr. Oakton from his place in front, "but I could not with an easy mind entrust Miss Chevington's safe recovery to them alone." By now well away from any houses, he drew the horses to a stop and turned in his seat. "Forgive me if I draw a hasty conclusion, but if Mr. Marblehead and your obliging, trusted friend are one and the same, we can save time by speaking more directly."

Sir Roderic gave a low chuckle. "How long have you suspected, Oakton?"

"Almost from the moment of Lady Darnham's confession to me."

"I had not thought we were quite so transparent," said Cassandra.

"You are not. Your excellent performances were all that kept me in doubt so long. But the coincidence of a second stranger on Ploverchase Hill within the hour was a little too great."

"Can you listen while you drive?" said Sir Roderic.

Oakton started the horses again at a walk. Sir Roderic described succinctly what little he could tell them of the unknown horseman who had been where the vicar should have been. Darkness had prevented his seeing the young man's features, or even the color of his mount, except that it had not been white or gray; but he gave particulars of voice and manner of speaking which, added to the trick of making the horse rear up, firing off a pistol with a fair degree of accuracy, and giving chase to the supposed desperado with more the apparent attitude of a schoolboy hunting a fox than a grown man trying to run down a criminal, sent a peculiar shiver—half of relief, half of new foreboding—through Cassandra's flesh. She kept silent, however, waiting to see whether the vicar's unaided conjecture would match her own.

"That sounds very much like my brother," said Oakton grimly, echoing Cassandra's thought.

"When last I heard, the Viscount Fencourt was in town," observed Sir Roderic.

"He had just come down today, supposedly to pay his respects to Miss Chevington. Were you aware they are engaged?"

"I was aware of it. But had I encountered our jack-a-dandy in London, could you have told him from a hundred other fops by my description?"

"By your mimicking voice, I think I could," replied the vicar. "Besides, you did not meet him in London. The chances against another such town dandy suddenly appearing on the hill tonight, and without having been seen in either village earlier today, are even greater than the chances against a sober stranger passing through on late business the same evening of this affair. You remember Ockham's Razor, of course?"

"I do," said Sir Roderic.

"Briefly stated, Lady Cassandra," the vicar began to explain, "the term 'Ockham's Razor' refers to the principle that for purposes of explanation, things not known to exist should not be presumed as existing—"

"I am intimate with the Law of Parsimony," she responded with some impatience. "It provides a good test by which to compare two or more theories, but it is not the Eleventh Commandment. As for your brother, the description seemed to me, also, to fit him singularly; but I awaited your opinion, as a person more closely acquainted with Lord Bevil than myself, thank God!"

"Yes, you would thank God all the more for that if you had grown up in the shadow of his bullying," said Oakton.

"The way to deal with a bully, even in nursery or school," remarked Sir Roderic, "is to stand up to him

116

and bully him in return. I speak from experience."

Cassandra could not resist teasing a little. "I expect you began as the bully, Captain?" Then she grew grave again. "Assuming it was your brother who took Deirdre, Mr. Oakton, is she now more safe, or less so, than if it were some stranger?" At first, the mere probability that it was not a stranger had given her a measure of relief; but, on reviewing what she knew of Fencourt's character, and the privileges, moreover, to which he might already consider himself entitled . . .

"They are engaged," said Oakton bitterly. "The marriage is to take place in less than a month. Her reputation, at least, is safe, if not her feelings."

"There is no possibility he may choose to break the match?" said Sir Roderic. "Especially if he has his way with her beforehand?"

"He is marrying her for convenience and to please our parents. I can think of no other reason. He is hardly passionate for her favors. Or, if he is, he hides it remarkably well."

"Oh, God!" exclaimed Cassandra. "He would not force her now, anonymously, and then, pretending to be the injured party, use it as an excuse to cast her off?"

"Then I would marry her myself," replied the vicar. "What I would do to him, I . . . dare not say."

"If, as a man of the cloth, you would feel it improper in you to thrash him," remarked Sir Roderic, "I would be happy to claim that pleasure. But might not there be theological objection to your union with a woman your brother had enjoyed?"

"We must find them quickly!" interjected Cassandra.

Oakton was already responding to the other man's remark. "In such a case, I would risk the objection and hold ourselves blameless man and wife in the sight of Heaven."

"But your bishop might not think so liberally of the matter," said Sir Roderic. "So we must, as her ladyship remarks, find them both quickly and privately— and if there is cause for scandal, we must keep it from going beyond your families."

"I could believe my brother capable of almost anything," said Oakton, "but we must not assume the worse. Even Bevil may have some hidden sense of honor. He might already have escorted her safely home."

It was a pretty suggestion. Cassandra thought it overly hopeful, but it should not be passed off without some examination. "To Derwent, or to Rotherhithe?"

"Or some point between?" suggested Sir Roderic. "Perhaps your own residence, Oakton?"

The vicar hesitated. Cassandra wondered if his thoughts echoed hers: the times Bevil had gratified an apparent whim to throw his younger brother and his fiancée together, whether to tease or to experiment. "The vicarage would have been closest," said Oakton at last. "For that reason he may equally have chosen it or avoided it, as the fantasy took him."

"If he carried her to Derwent," said Cassandra, "Thomas will be able to tell us of it, whether he saw them there or encountered them on the way."

"Assuming Fencourt galloped there by the road," commented Sir Roderic.

"If he had the sensibility to restore her to her friends," said Cassandra, "surely he would also have had the consideration to take her by the road rather than subject her to riding over rough country?"

"He might," said Sir Roderic, "have thought it more romantic to cut across fields and leap hedges. Is Fencourt a rogue of the romantic or the hard-headed stamp, Oakton?"

"I gave up trying to outguess my brother long ago, but it seems to me more probable he would take her to Rotherhithe than to Derwent, whether by the road or the woods."

"You must turn and drive back to Ploverchase," said Cassandra decisively. "If they are not at the vicarage, you can proceed directly to the castle. Mr. Marblehead and I will wait here for Thomas's return."

"What, leave you in the middle of the road?"

"It is not likely to rain, and the dirt will not dissolve me. If Mr. Marblehead had his horse, I would send
118

him at once to search for them across country, and wait alone for Thomas."

Sir Roderic chuckled. "You shock Mr. Oakton's sense of propriety, m'lady. Ride back with him and trust me to meet Thomas alone."

She hesitated a moment, annoyed at Oakton's protectiveness, yet more than half convinced Fencourt would far more likely have carried Deirdre to his brother's home or his parents' than to the abbey. Why, then, had she proposed so unthinkingly to wait with the captain? "Very well, then. I will ride back to the vicarage. We shall use that as a place of rendezvous."

"Or, more likely, as a point at which to leave messages for one another, said Sir Roderic.

Apparently satisfied with the revised plan, the vicar put the team into a canter and then a gallop, arriving in a very few minutes at the crossroads. Stopping to put Mr. Marblehead down on the Abbey Road to await Lady Darnham's coachman, Oakton turned his horses eastward and sped back toward Ploverchase village. Cassandra, holding herself with some difficulty on the rather threadbare seat cushions, had a few minutes of lonely leisure to reflect upon the situation brought about by her machinations.

She knew by the vicar's speed, now that a definite course of action had been decided on, and by the tone of voice when he had pledged himself to redeem Deirdre's reputation, that if worst came to worst and Lord Fencourt proved as bad as the bleakest of her own fears, her niece's marriage with the vicar would be assured after all—but at what a price! If Fencourt were only slightly less depraved, then, in addition to the night's injury, Deirdre would be irreparably bound to the viscount with no honorable recourse to end the engagement. And even the best hope—that of Lord Bevil's returning her to some respectable habitati on unharmed—made of the entire evening's affair an utter fiasco, a wasted effort requiring a deal of explanation and perhaps even some danger to Sir Roderic, without bringing Deirdre an inch closer to breaking off the unsuitable match.

On the whole, Cassandra began to suspect she had

wanted to remain with the captain in order to escape the solitude that enabled her to meditate on all these gloom-ridden prospects. She would not, she resolved, be caught alone and unoccupied again until she knew Deirdre to be safe once more.

18

Deirdre did not enjoy being pulled up by a knotted cord to a garret window. The knotted sheet, which had seemed quite sturdy enough when Bevil was climbing up it, now seemed a thin and frail thing, constantly emitting short tearing sounds somewhere or other along its length. Nor did the yarn sling which had been so constraining when Bevil bound it around her waist now feel half secure enough, although it cut uncomfortably into her flesh even while threatening to break free of the sheet and dash her to bits on the ground below. Lifting her hands, she held tight to the nearest knots in the sheet rope. Why could she not have used them for handholds, as they had been meant, and climb up them? But she had not even strength enough to take any great degree of pressure from her waist by pulling up on the sheet with hands and arms. Besides all this, the increasing height gave her vertigo, and the swaying, seasickness. She could only close her eyes, prepare for doom, and determine that she was far more fitted to drawing rooms than to adventures.

To her surprise and relief, Bevil and his chambermaid eventually succeeded in pulling her to the window and helping her without mishap over the sill, the Frenchwoman meanwhile congratulating her on a swift and safe ascent. "So light you are—light as the little feather! Bevil, is she not light?"

"Almost blew away. Next time, damme, you can draw her up all by yourself if you think she's so infernally light."

"We have angered him again, *le pauvre*," said Marie, deftly unbinding her unexpected visitor. "Why are you in the black mood tonight, *ma mie*? It is me who should be in the evil mood. *Mon Dieu*, you have kept me here waiting for you, it is hours beyond the time!"

"I told you any time between midnight and four in the morning. I'm early."

"You told me you could come at eleven o'clock."

"I could not possibly have told you I'd be here at eleven! It's a lucky evening when the mater puts her bloody backgammon away by ten-thirty!"

"Then you were the silly goose to tell me you would come at eleven. Never mind him, my dear sweet English lady. I will get you a little glass of brandy and you will not look so white anymore."

The viscount waved his arms in the general direction of the roof. "Well, never mind what time I told you! I'm here now, ain't I?"

"But of course you are here. You are here very loudly."

"So the whole question is, are *you* ready?"

"I have been ready for many hours, my Bevil-devil."

"You are wearing that silly rhyme very thin," he said in a tone that was probably meant to be menacing but came out sullen. "And my patience with it. Are you coming?"

Ignoring him for the moment, the chambermaid produced a bottle and a plain glass tumbler from her wall cupboard. "Here it is, my lady, you see. Soon I will have the fine crystal carafe to pour from and the lovely thin goblets to drink from, but they would not be in place in this poor room, *non*? And besides, we could not take them with us to Gretta Green." Pouring the dark amber liquid and presenting the glass to Deirdre, she went on, "But it is the best, this brandy. Bevil would not dare to give me anything less. I would know it at once, me."

The tumbler was almost half filled with the strong beverage. Does she mean me to drink myself into a faint? thought Deirdre whimsically, taking a sip.

Lord Fencourt meanwhile went to the cupboard, pulled out a second glass, took the bottle from Marie, poured himself a drink, swallowed it, and thrust his glass back into her hand. "Now, if you're quite ready, my dear—"

"Ah, you see? Already the color comes back to her cheeks a little. Do not worry, dear English lady, you will find a lord much more *gentil* than Bevil who does not wish to rhyme with devil."

Deirdre nodded dreamily. From the beginning it had seemed unnecessary for her to take any part in the conversation here in Marie's bedroom; she had merely to rest and enjoy the Frenchwoman's dressing-down of Lord Fencourt. The brandy, too . . . She had determined, of course, to take only a few sips, but even those few sips, coming on top of her long excitement, her exertions, and her sudden comparative release from anxiety in a comfortable (if not precisely luxurious) refuge, took their pleasant toll almost at once.

"Damme, Marie, I've got my horse waiting below, and if you don't hurry—"

"Patience, patience, you silly Bevil, only a little patience. You have brought to me the pretty English lady, and we must not leave her uncomfortable. It does not befit the Comtesse d'Azalaine to leave her guest uncomfortable." Marie opened a dresser drawer and pulled out a white nightgown. "Turn your back now, you silly Bevil."

Deirdre, perceiving that the Frenchwoman meant to put her to bed, for which she was nothing loath, looked about for dressing screens and, finding none in the room, murmured, "Lord Fencourt can wait downstairs with his horse, can he not?"

Marie hesitated only a moment. In this mood of his, Bevil might take the notion to ride away and leave her, but — *eh bien!* Better to learn it at once if her hold on him was so slight. If he was the silly goose to ride away from her now and leave his pretty fiancée in her room for her to nurse—what a scandal she could make

122

of it for him, what a sweet picture of herself so patiently nursing the English lady! "Ah, yes, yes, yes!" she said. "She is the clever one, you see—very, very clever, this one. Bevil, you will wait outside and be sure your horse does not run away."

"And leave you up here dawdling forever?"

"But it will not be forever, you silly lord, only a few little minutes."

"And just how do you think you're going to climb down the sheet without my help?"

Marie giggled. "I watched you when you climbed up the sheet, and I would prefer you to be at the bottom and catch me if I fall than if we should fall both together, and so much heavier, to the ground."

"I had proposed to lower you in the same way we lifted Miss Chevington."

"And I say no, I will make the climb, me, myself. Now go! It is you who are being forever, *n'est-ce pas?*"

He grumbled a few oaths. She thought they were stronger than those English expressions already at her command, and made up her mind to learn them as soon as possbile. But he climbed over the windowsill. She watched him down to the ground where his horse waited and where they became two shadows, close together. No, she did not think he would leave her. She hurried back to her unexpected guest, who was already fumbling weakly with her buttons, and took over the task.

"Are you really a countess?" asked the English girl. She was so small and thin, her face so pale, like a little child's.

"But yes, of course—*la Comtesse d'Azalaine.* Have I not told you already? I lower myself to marry your *vicomte,* you see, but—*eh bien!* It does not matter. One must make the little sacrifices for love, yes?"

"I wish you much joy of him, then, your ladyship."

Marie's heart made a great bound. So easy would it be, then, to receive her chosen title? Perhaps she did not need Bevil at all. Perhaps she could have entered the English society clad in only her borrowed title? But—ah, *non,* this was a sweet, dear innocent, Bevil's

123

little English lady. Also, one needed much more money to live *comme il faut;* and a real title, with a document of marriage which none could question, would be so much safer than a borrowed title with no papers. And then, she had grown fond of her *vicomte* with his silly ways.

"It is not my best nightgown, this one," Marie apologized as she slipped it over Miss Chevington's head. "It has the little hole mended here, in the sleeve. But, *eh bien!*" She shrugged delicately. "It was a long time before I could decide, between this one and my best, which of them was my best, to pack it up."

"It is perfectly all right." Miss Chevington sipped a little more brandy.

"It is something large for you, but it will be comfortable, *n'est-ce pas?*" Marie turned down the bed with practiced hands. Soon she would never need to do such work again, so she did it this once more with a flourish of benevolent sentiment. It was a pity she had not the time to fill the warming pan, but she did have her own brick, growing hot in her tiny fireplace because it had been easier to leave it in its usual spot than move it elsewhere this evening. Wrapping it deftly in the towel, she slipped it between the sheets near the foot of the bed. "You do not like our Viscount Fencourt, you?"

"I wish him at Jericho. No, that is not quite fair, he did save me from the highwayman."

"Ah, yes?" Marie had intended hearing the explanation from Bevil, why he had brought his fiancée for her to nurse a little; but she was very glad to coax it from Miss Chevington first. Thus she learned how a highwayman had carried Bevil's pretty English lady away from her own aunt and carriage, and how the *vicomte* came just in time to chase him away and rescue her. "But it is strange, no?" remarked the chambermaid. "How this so strong highwayman should run from our little Bevil?"

"I suppose Lord Fencourt can . . . appear . . . quite terrifying to a . . . guilty conscience." Miss Chevington yawned. She spoke with many pauses, not of doubt, but of drowsiness. "And he did . . . fire off his pistol."

"Eh bien!" Bevil would tell his own version, and it would be very interesting. Meanwhile, it was time to hurry, before the English girl fell asleep there, sitting on the edge of the bed. "Pardon me so very, very much, I should wish to see you so cozy in bed and blow out the candle, but you must pull up the sheet after us, you see."

Miss Chevington yawned again. "Of course. I would not do anything to stop your eloping . . . for the world."

Marie's cloak and little traveling bag were waiting ready, the one on and the other beside her chair. She swung the cloak about her shoulders, caught up the bag, and stopped to give Miss Chevington a kiss on the forehead. "You will come to the window and make sure he has waited?"

"Of course." The English girl rose and walked with Marie to the window, stumbling a little in the large nightgown. "How would you have got . . . the rope up again . . . if I were not here?"

"We must have left it to dangle, poor rope of sheets, like a ghost in the wind. But it would not have mattered so much—they would have seen it and come up to find the empty room. Now if they see it, they will come up and wake you with their noise. No. You must rest and sleep, and then when you wake the words will come, how you will explain what has happened; and then we will be so far they will not catch us again."

Monsieur Perry and his wife, tall thin William from the stables and fat Jenny who served the beer and sometimes made up a bed late at night—how they would stare to find Mademoiselle Chevington in Marie's room! And then how they would scrape to her and bow to her and run about the old Grain and Grape to send word to her high relations where they must come and find her! Perhaps the chambermaid's conscience should have smote her at leaving the delicate English lady here for the night, but what would you have? It did not have satin sheets, the bed; but it had linen that was mended very well (Marie had smuggled up other sheets, over the weeks, to make the rope

125

ladder), and it had also featherbed and pillows that she herself—Marie Cluzot d'Azalaine, soon to be the Viscountess Fencourt—had kept very fluffy for her own comfort. And Miss Chevington did not need to be clever, the darling—she would only need to tell them the truth in the morning. They would take care of her and not be able to catch the elopers; Marie would see to it that Bevil rode fast. And all would be so very amusing.

"I think he is still there," murmured Miss Chevington.

"Ah, yes, yes, yes." Peering down sharply, Marie made out the viscount's impatient form. She could hear his horse stamping a little, too. "You are ready, Bevil?"

"Ready to leave without you."

"Ah, *le pauvre!* I would not be so long if you did not bring to me your dear English lady."

"Are you coming down, or are we to remain here calling up and down at each other until someone hears us?"

"I throw down my bag to you, *ma mie.* Catch him carefully, do not let him break open." Marie tossed down her bag. Bevil tried to catch it, seemed almost to have it in his arms for a moment, then lost it, letting it tumble to the ground, where it struck with a plunk and made the horse shy. Giggling, Marie observed to her visitor, "But he did not catch it, you see," and then called down to Bevil, "And have you let it come open, my bag?"

"No, dammit, but if you don't come down yourself I'll break it open on your pretty little head."

Marie clucked her tongue reprovingly. "When I fall and lie there so white on the cold, hard ground with my head in many little pieces, you will be sorry to speak so to me, *mon bel ami.*"

"Don't talk so," whispered Miss Chevington.

Marie laughed and kissed her again, this time on the cheek. Then, whipping the sides of her cloak back from around her arms, she sat upon the windowsill, balanced there for a few minutes whilst she directed Bevil to "Hold it steady, the end of our sheet," and finally took the uppermost knot in both plump hands and swung her feet out into space, dangling for a moment until she found the cord with her legs.

She felt panic for a few moments, with a dizziness like a great blank wind in her stomach; but when she had twisted one leg around the sheet rope it was a little better. Bevil was holding the end very nicely, tight but not stretched; and it was better to hold fast and to climb down than to open one's hands and fall. And if she was too plump for the sheet—*eh bien,* one only died once. Better that she should climb down quickly than that he should laugh at her. She wished she could have practiced this climbing up and down sheets. Without practice, with determination—but, alas! with no *finesse*—now tangling and now untangling only to slide several feet much too fast—she scrambled, not too badly, down the sheet and landed in his arms, breathless but triumphant. "So, my cabbage! You do not leave me behind all broken in little pieces on the hard ground after all, you see."

"Hang me if I don't keep a tight rein on you from now on." Plucking her off the sheet ladder, to which she had still clutched in the victory of coming down it, he lifted her up onto his horse's back. She promptly made a half turn and thrust one leg over so as to sit astraddle.

"Marie!" he said in exasperation. "If you call yourself a countess, at least sit like a lady."

"When you give me a—what is the word?—sidesaddle, or a real, true pillion, *ma mie,* then I will ride like a lady."

"Damme, it hitches your skirts up to the knee!"

"And you do not like that, you?" She hitched her skirts a little higher yet, slightly above the knee, to gain even more freedom. "Who is to see except you, *mon coeur?* And you will sit in front of me and not see. I do not wish to slip from the horse's back when we gallop, and I have ridden to escape from the wicked Jacobins, me. My bag, where is it?"

He passed it up to her and then mounted. After slipping the bag strings over her right arm, she looped both arms around Bevil's waist, clasped her hands in front, and squeezed him, sighing in content. "You are so thin, *ma mie,* so nice and thin to lift up such a sausage as me."

"I'm compact. I daresay I weigh more than you, sweetheart, but I wear it pressed in, not fluffed up like one of your own nice, soft pillows." He tickled her with one elbow. She chuckled and pinched him in return.

"Then we must find how to fluff you up also, like another pillow. But now say the tender good-bye to your dear English lady and let us go."

He was in a much better mood now he was on his horse and ready to ride. "*Adieu,* sweet Mistress Chevington!" he called up, taking off his hat and waving it. "Convey my very best regards to both our families, and particularly to that indecently pious younger brother of mine."

"And the sheet!" added Marie, noticing that sweet Mistress Chevington seemed about to nod off to sleep with her head on the windowsill. "Do not forget to pull up the sheet, dear lady, and then off with you to the bed so you do not wake with the stiff neck!"

Miss Chevington nodded and began pulling up the sheet. That was well, then. Bevil turned his horse and started off at a trot. With Marie surreptitiously adding her kicks to his, they were soon in a nice, fast canter. This Gretta Green was ahead, and the length of England between for her to look at on the way; and when they stopped to rest, it would be someone else who made the beds and fluffed up the pillows at another inn for her while she, Marie Cluzot, soon to be the Viscountess Fencourt, had only to rest and be waited upon. Again she sighed, and hugged her *vicomte* tighter.

Deirdre, meanwhile, managed to pull the sheet about halfway up before it grew too heavy to haul another inch. Her eyes were closed oftener than they were open, her head was exceedingly heavy and her fingers very clumsy, whilst the rest of her body between head and hands seemed weightless and void. She was, in short, extremely tired and drowsy, with just enough wit to know what was the matter with her. Despite the Frenchwoman's warning, she must just lay
128

down her head on the sill and nap for five minutes . . .

It may have been five minutes, it may have been ten—a few more or less either way, but surely not many more than ten. She had not turned to look at the exact time before laying down her head to nap on the windowsill, but she remembered more or less the hour it was when she had last glanced at the clock while the chambermaid searched for a nightgown. However long she had dozed at the window, she was at least sufficiently refreshed to pull up the sheet a few more feet. Then a happy thought seized her. Blowing out the candle Marie had left on the table beside the window, Deirdre took the sheet in her fist and let it trail up after her as she walked to the bed and climbed in. That brought a good deal more of it up, but some of it still hung over the sill. Almost whimsically, the girl pulled it hand over fist whilst sitting in bed.

At last she saw the end of the sheet rope reach the window, balance on the sill for a moment, then—with one more jerk—slither down into the room and lie limp on the floor. What a frightful lot of spoilt sheet! she thought with a happy giggle. She was safe, she was comfortable, she was exhausted, and she could not be troubled just now to think of what explanations she would give in the morning. A vague memory crossed her mind that Aunt Cassie and George, if he knew of the abduction, and Uncle Crump, too, and the others would be worried about her; but when one knows oneself to be safe, it is always difficult to believe that one's family and friends do not know it also, by some process of sympathetic spirits. Deirdre sighed, blew out the candle beside the bed, and snuggled down between the sheets, caring not in the least that they were much mended.

19

Mr. Oakton kept but one manservant and a single maid, besides the local lad who groomed his horses but did not live in. For a young man brought up in the town and country homes of the Earl and Countess of Rotherhithe, and holding a living controlled by his own father, such austerity seemed little more nor less than an obstinate mortification of the flesh. Certainly the vicarage, having been improved at least once a generation, and most recently just before George Oakton's taking residence, would have admitted of a larger household. As it was, two or three of the upstairs rooms were covered in brown paper and the rest of the chambers kept almost starkly innocent of clutter. (This appeared at first somewhat puritan, but was actually meant to spare the housemaid too many complications of dusting.)

Once, in an expansive mood, Oakton had confided to Lady Cassandra that he was putting a certain amount of his income per quarter into an annuity for his future wife; or, if he unhappily remained unmarried, for some worthy charitable enterprise to be chosen at a later date. Indeed, his maid Susan was herself a recipient of his benevolence, having been a London waif to whom (acting counter to his mother's strenuous objections) he had offered the chance to escape an unwholesome occupation in the metropolis. Tim, the village lad who spent a good part of each day in the vicar's small stable, was a widow's son and very glad of the employment. Old Parker, the manservant, alone did not fall under the heading of one of Oakton's charitable impulses, since he had come with his young master to the vicarage from Rotherhithe by way of Oxford, where he had also attended the youth during his studies. Instead of being another beneficiary, Parker served as a sort of accomplice in welldoing, having trained both Susan, and to a lesser extent Tim, in their tasks.

Susan was now abed, not having been wakened when Lady Cassandra's coachman arrived an hour ago to summon Mr. Oakton. Parker, who had risen to admit Thomas, was alone waiting up; but for his reluctance to leave the young housemaid alone in the vicarage with a highwayman abroad in the neighborhood, the old servant would certainly have accompanied his master to Mr. Bellew's residence in the sister village.

Whatever developments Parker might have anticipated, as he kindled a small fire in the front parlor and alternately sat looking into it and rose with the poker in hand to make another round of the doors and windows, he had not expected Master George to bring back Lady Darnham to the vicarage. It was to his credit that Parker's only spoken comment on seeing her was a request to know what he might fetch to make her ladyship more comfortable.

"Nothing, thank you, Parker," replied her ladyship, glancing round. The only light in the parlor came from the fireplace and a single candle on the reading table; the room showed no sign of occupancy by unexpected guests—no brandy poured out into glasses, no boots or dirty tracks, none of the clutter which accompanied Fencourt when he came in from riding, and none of the bustle which accompanied efforts to calm a frightened young lady.

"You've had no one here since I left?" demanded Oakton, putting into a direct question what Cassandra could guess from a glance round.

"No one, sir."

"If he were bringing her here," said Oakton, "he would surely have been here long ago. Unless . . ."

He glanced at Lady Cassandra. Neither of them

would put into words the thoughts behind that "unless." If Bevil had chosen to take advantage of having Deirdre alone in such unlooked-for circumstances, he would not have brought her to the vicarage first, beneath old Parker's eye; but he might bring her here later, as the nearest place to deposit her after the damage was done.

"Lord bless us, why would the rascally knave bring her here?" said Parker, tapping the end of the fire iron against his palm, as much as to say that if the highwayman had dared show his face at the vicarage it was unlikely he would have much of it left to show when he appeared at the next assizes.

"We have reason to believe," said Oakton, "that Miss Chevington is with my elder brother."

"Lord bless us all! Master Bevil's turned highwayman?"

Cassandra glanced at Oakton. Instead of correcting his servant's misapprehension, the vicar continued, "Such being the case, we were in some dim hope he might bring her here."

Parker, who had returned the poker to its stand, began to light the tapers in a seven-branched candelabrum. "Well, I can hardly say I'm greatly surprised, Master George, except that he hasn't played some such trick before now. But, Lord! To chuse his own betrothed and so soon before the wedding, poor young miss!"

While the old servant's back was turned, Lady Cassandra caught the vicar's hand and pressed it firmly for a moment, to show him she understood and appreciated his ploy. He returned the pressure. It must have been the inspiration of the moment, or he would have consulted with her before.

As yet, no one but themselves and Thomas knew of Sir Roderic's part in the abduction. If the whole could be made to appear a prank of the young viscount's, no one would be prosecuted for it; and, if worst came to worst, poor Deirdre's reputation would not suffer quite so grievously if it were thought she had been made off with by the noble rake who married her within a matter of weeks afterwards, than if it were known she had been in the hands of two different men that night.

"Most likely he's taken her to the castle," Parker went on. "Perhaps I can show your ladyship upstairs?"

"You need not attempt to take me out of the way of unpleasant conjectures, Parker," said her ladyship. "You do not really think Lord Fencourt has taken my niece directly home to his father and mother."

Parker looked at Oakton. The vicar nodded. "You may speak your mind freely in front of Lady Darnham. She will not go into hysterics or faint away." He glanced shrewdly at her, as much as to comment upon how little right she had to be coddled from the consequences of her own doing. It was hardly generous of him, she thought; but he had some reason for annoyance . . . and perhaps, after all, it was merely her own conscience reading more censure into his glance than had been intended.

"Well, Master George," said the old servant, "it's my mind he's taken her to your old hunting lodge in Ploverchase Wood."

"What?" said Cassandra. The Earl of Rotherhithe had two hunting lodges in the vicinity, but one was in Bramblecombe, to the south, and the other in Rotherhithe Forest, to the east and north of the castle.

"Not a true hunting lodge," explained Oakton. "Rather, an old stone cot which Bevil and I found while exploring in our boyhood, and turned into our 'lodge' by mending the roof and adding a few makeshift rooms which we called 'wings' to either side. The inspiration was Bevil's—most of the labor was mine. Yes," he went on, "it would be entirely like Bevil."

He had taken up some visitor's card from the basket and twisted it into a pasteboard straw as he spoke. Now he suddenly pulled the twist in two. "Saddle Colly. If they are not at the 'lodge,' I shall ride on directly to the castle."

"You have two horses, have you not?" demanded Cassandra.

"I have, but they do not run together except in the traces. Tully has never worked well as a saddle horse."

133

"I shall chance that."

The vicar stared at her briefly. "You will stay here, your ladyship."

"You have never seen me ride!"

"Nor have you ever ridden Tully."

The old servant had already left to saddle Colly without waiting for the end of the argument. Cassandra sat on the nearest chair. One could keep one's voice steadier when sitting than when pacing about the room. "You do not mean to leave me here with nothing to do but wait on the edge of your Ockham's Razor?"

"I can make better speed alone, and I will not attempt to take the carriage through the woods. You do not know where to find our so-called lodge, and I do not intend to lose my time turning back to look for you, Lady Cassandra."

With a great interior effort, she again acknowledged to herself his right to be angry with her. "At least I do know the way to the castle. Let me take the carriage while you go to the lodge."

"I keep only one carriage, and Tully cannot draw it alone."

"Then I shall ride Tully."

"Lady Cassandra," he replied with a hint of exasperation, "I regret to say that, lacking the gift of prophecy, I have neglected to procure a sidesaddle."

"If Tully is a poor saddle horse to begin with, I much prefer managing him astride." She tried to read the vicar's expression. "Do I shock you, Mr. Oakton?"

"It is not a thing I would care to see my own future *belle-tante* do, riding up astride to shock my mother and father," he said after a pause. "But anything could perhaps be expected of Bevil's future aunt-in-law."

"Perhaps I should remind you that my own relationship to Miss Chevington is in legality and in friendship rather than by blood and birth." Lady Cassandra spoke quickly, only realizing when halfway through the sentence how far afield they were getting of the chief problem.

"In legality, perhaps," said Oakton. "At this moment, I have some difficulty calling it friendship."

Lady Cassandra started to her feet, understanding the emotions which led men to fight duels. Fortunately, she was a woman and Oakton a clergyman. Dueling would have been impossible; and, being a woman of sense, she saw almost at once how very foolish it would have been to shed each other's blood over such a justifiable pique of temper.

"George," she said softly. The circumstances were peculiar for addressing him the first time by his Christian name; but she judged they were right; and, when he replied with an attentive and not disrespectful gaze, she knew she had judged correctly. "I entirely deserve your disapprobation—you see how I confess it myself," she went on, crossing to him and taking his hand. "But I had meant it for her benefit and yours. Her feelings for Lord Fencourt are quite the reverse of love; nor do I think he values her, except, perhaps, as a pretty domestic trinket. I had designed this evening's adventure to be the initial means of breaking off the match and bringing about one far dearer to my niece's heart. If I have misread your sentiments towards Deirdre, tell me now, and let us proceed with a perfect understanding."

He held her hand firmly for a moment between both his own. "Your means are hopelessly romantic, Aunt Cassandra—if I may hope someday to call you aunt—and I doubt their respectability. But your reading of my sentiment for Miss Chevington is true."

She added her left hand to the clasp, making it a close knot of four hands in all. "Then let us undo the mischief and bring happiness out of chaos, with no further unkind words to one another."

After a pause, he said, "When we were boys, my brother used to pilfer cates and eat them immediately after dinner, though his stomach was still tight against his breeches. I fear . . . he is still capable of such childish behavior. We may already be too late."

"We may. But we must act as if we knew we would be in time. To despair when there is still hope would rob us of our energies. Did you not tell your congregation much the same in your own sermon last Sunday?"

"Did I?" He forced a smile. "I am never sure how many are listening and how many are merely remaining politely quiet."

"I was not quite as attentive as Deirdre, but I assure you I do listen to your homilies." With a last pressure, she released his hands, and he hers. "You may wrong your brother in your thoughts. Has it never seemed to you that he might almost have been using his engagement as a means of bringing her into a closer circle of acquaintance with you?"

"Yes, but was that consideration for us, or was it for his own amusement? You forget I have known Bevil for almost all of his life. I do not believe him capable of sympathizing with love as we lesser mortals understand the emotion. No; he has surely been playing with her for some purpose of his own—I have often hoped he meant to cry off at the last moment, in order to inconvenience everyone except himself, but— by God!" said Oakton unecclesiastically, "if he plays the villain tonight, my only hope is that he will play it completely and throw her off!"

Cassandra repressed a shudder. In such a case, could Deirdre bear even George Oakton's touch afterwards? "If that has happened," she said, "you must be very, very gentle with her."

"I could not be otherwise." He turned from the mantel and picked up his coat, which he had dropped on the sofa upon entering. "If Parker does not have Colly saddled by now, I shall buckle the cinch myself."

"I wish I could be there with you to find her," said Cassandra. "To help you . . . pick up the pieces. But if . . . You must not take it to heart, George, if she should not seem to feel towards you as she has. You must not try to do too much too quickly. Bring her to me as soon as possible."

He looked slightly perplexed, but bowed to her judgment. "I will entrust her to you, Aunt Cassandra."

"And to time. Now hurry."

"I will act," he said, "as if I knew I would arrive in time."

He left. Cassandra remained looking into the fire. It had not been poked for a while, and it was dying.

Time! So much depended on that invisible, uncontrollable, unrecallable element. Must she indeed wait here to count the minutes as they slowly escaped forever? The same hours that would bring her idleness as exquisite as torture were perhaps even now passing with brutal swiftness for her niece . . . a few hours of irreclaimable time lost from Cassandra's life—honor, respect, comfort, capacity for love, the joys and hopes of youth—all these, perhaps, lost from Deirdre's life, if not forever, at least for months, even years, of misery which must color the long remainder of her life with a somber hue. And this was to have been the romantic adventure to change Deirdre's life for the glowing best! One unforeseen slip—the possibility of which *should* have been foreseen—in the plot that had seemed so firm and so—adaptable, but had proven so frail . . .

Cassandra covered her face with her hands for a moment. Why must I be forever attempting to tease life into new romantic patterns? she thought. Why could I not have sought out a prosaic, sensible way—interviews with his lordship and her ladyship, a talk with their son, merely the support of Darnham and myself to stand behind Deirdre if she wished to break the match. Her mother must have seen reason, when given a true estimation of the matter. At worst, a closing of relations between Rotherhithe and Darnham House could have done Lord D. and myself little material harm; and for such clergymen as George, there should be other livings to be found, other patrons besides his father. Why could I not have left the child in peace to learn to draw what comfortable romance is to be found naturally in lives like ours? It is all very well to play Quixote with only my own life and honor, but to endanger my niece like this is beyond excuse!

Lady Cassandra uncovered her eyes, got the poker from its stand, and poked up the fire. The activity helped her shake off for a moment the worst devils of self-accusation and think more determinedly again. It had been bad enough waiting idle at Wantage with Mr. Bellew and his housekeeper to divert her, when she had had no reason to suspect her plan was going astray. It would be absolutely intolerable to wait here idle and alone except for the shrewd old manservant Parker, whilst she knew her niece to be every moment in unknown danger.

No, she must be active, purposively active.

It had, indeed, seemed likeliest from the first moment of Parker's suggestion that Bevil had taken Deirdre to this make-believe hunting lodge. Therefore, George's action must be the most purposeful; moreover, in the event his lordship had for once behaved honorably and returned with Deirdre to Rotherhithe, all was already well, and the vicar would shortly find them there. Nevertheless, there remained the chance that the viscount had made for some other place entirely; and the more ground covered, the better likelihood of finding them.

Lady Cassandra extricated one candle from the seven-branched candelabrum and began to explore the vicarage.

Ten minutes later the old manservant, returning from the stable, was shocked to find her ladyship in his young master's room, industriously rummaging through his wardrobe.

"Leave me, Parker," said Lady Darnham. Already she had laid out a pair of old riding breeches, worn no more than twice since Master George was ordained; a buff coat in much the same condition; and a newish shirt; and she was now shamelessly and rather curiously examining smallclothes.

"If your ladyship would care to come down to the sitting room," said Parker, with difficulty retaining a respectful composure, "I will have tea ready in five minutes."

"I have drunk an ocean of tea too much already this evening. But if you can have a stirrup cup ready in three minutes, I will take that."

"Perhaps your ladyship would prefer to wait in the library. It will take only a minute to lay the fire there—"

"No," said her ladyship, "we have no time for a stirrup cup. Go at once and saddle Tully."

Octavius Parker stepped inside and closed the door. There were occasions when firmness was, ultimately,
138

the greatest respect a man could show his betters. Her ladyship would thank him when she recovered her senses. "'My lady," he said with a careful admixture of apology and resolution, "what you appear to be thinking of is unbecoming madness."

"Parker," she replied, "if you do not go at once and saddle Tully, I shall be forced to change clothes in front of you."

There was no dressing screen. There had been one, left from the time of the last incumbent, but, being old and sadly bedraggled, it had been thrown away, and in the bachelor residence there had seemed no need to replace it. Even had there been a screen, Parker had some doubts, from the calm manner in which she began to undo her buttons, that Lady Darnham would have used it. Short of laying hands on her ladyship, there was nothing for it but ignominious retreat.

Briefly he considered waking Susan and sending in the maid to expostulate with Lady Darnham. Aside from the advantage of being of the same sex as her ladyship, however, what powers of persuasion did an unlettered girl from the streets of London have to succeed where he had failed? More likely her ladyship would reduce the girl to a wretched sense of incompetence, and he would spend the rest of the evening comforting her for her failure. Better to let Susan sleep.

Nevertheless, Parker refused to go saddle Tully. Stubbornly, he brought the things from the kitchen and began to prepare toast and tea as he waited. Unable he might be to stop her ladyship's impropriety with the master's wardrobe, but he was determined to let her get no farther than the parlor.

20

Fortunately, Lady Cassandra and George Oakton were much of a height. She found his breeches loose in the waist, and snug, though not dangerously so, in the hips; but, all in all, his old clothes fitted her tolerably well. There was no necessity, she decided, for such a drastic step as cutting her hair; she could more quickly and easily catch it up in a bun at the back of her neck than find shears to clip it. Clipping, moreover, would have forced her into the fashion of bobbed hair, which she had always resisted. Should the question arise, she would brazen it out and declare boldly that she had donned the scandalous attire for convenience rather than disguise.

Her greatest problem were the riding boots, which were too large for her feet. She tried unsuccessfully to pad them with handkerchiefs; but, even when tied round her foot, the improvised pads of cloth would not stay in place whilst she pushed her foot down the long neck of the boot, nor, with the top of the boot almost at her knee, could she reach down to make adjustments. She must either settle for short boots, her own slippers, or the risk of blisters. She chose, after a few seconds' deliberation, the risk of blisters on her toes rather than sores on her inner calves.

For all her difficulties, she noticed with satisfaction that it was little more than five minutes from Parker's intrusion to the time she walked out the dressing-room door.

Parker was still in the parlor, fussing about with a

tea service. Lady Cassandra was distinctly annoyed.

"I could not find a riding crop," she said, striding into the middle of the room.

"There's only the one, and the young master took it."

"Then I must make do with something else. You have been remarkably quick to have saddled Tully in this amount of time."

"If your ladyship will pardon the observation, you could hardly make Tully carry you where you wished, with or without a crop."

"In that case, I shall let him carry me where *he* wishes. Random as this search must be, it should make little difference."

Parker made an infinitesimal adjustment to a cushioned armchair by the fire. "The kettle is just on the boil now. If your ladyship would care to sit . . ."

Lady Cassandra laughed. "Does the world mean to drown me in tea tonight? Where is the stirrup cup? At least you might have prepared that."

Ignoring her comments, the servant placed a footstool. "I am sure your ladyship will find this to your liking."

Unsure whether to be angered or amused, she walked across the room to the decanter of brandy on the beaufet. She seemed to be swaggering a little, but she could not tell whether this was due to the heady effect of masculine attire, or to the way her feet slipped in the riding boots. She unstoppered the decanter and poured herself a brandy. Half turning, she saw that Parker had put a piece of bread on a toasting fork and was holding it at the fire, meanwhile keeping as wary an eye on her as she on him.

She tossed the brandy down successfully and started for the door. The old servant rose and blocked her way. In spite of her increasing anger, she could not but admire the fine mixture of deference and determination in his manner. Had the apothecary been more of Parker's stamp, he might have ended by persuading her to take a drug. All the more reason to escape the vicarage quickly.

"Beg your ladyship's pardon, but if I could suggest a little bite—"

"Thank you, Parker." By moving quickly, she plucked the toasting fork from his hand. "With a bit of something tied round the prongs, this should do reasonably well for a riding crop." She made a deft circle round him as she spoke. There was now little way, short of actual scuffling, that he could prevent her from reaching the door; nevertheless, she wasted no time in getting there.

Safely in the doorway at last, she took pity on him and turned back for a moment to say, "Next time, Parker, when you wish to block a person's way, take your stand in the doorway itself rather than in the center of the room."

"Has your ladyship any message to leave in case of inquiries?" said Parker stiffly, turning a formula of propriety into a complete condemnation of everything he found improper in her conduct.

"Yes. Should a tall gentleman with square jaw, gray eyes, salt-and-pepper hair, and several capes to his greatcoat come seeking me, be completely truthful, tell him all you have told Mr. Oakton and myself in regard to his lordship's lodge in Ploverchase Wood—with directions thither, if you have them—and inform him that I may be anywhere at all in the neighborhood on an unmanageable mount."

Taking a bite of toast from the toasting fork, she proceeded at once to the front door. She had, somehow, little heart to savor her triumph over the old retainer—if triumph it had indeed been. The toast was very dry in her mouth; after the one bite, she tossed the rest of the slice on the ground for the birds and hurried on to the stable.

Since Parker had not obliged her, she must saddle Tully herself. It had been years since, as a hoydenish child, she had saddled her own mounts in her father's large stables; and now, in the vicar's much smaller one, she took time to look the tack over well. She had some choice of passable bits and bridles; the best saddle remaining was an old one, in some need of saddlesoap, although the girth seemed reasonably safe.

She smoothed out the padding as best she could, then brushed Tully's back preparatory to receiving the saddle.

Tully's faults as a mount seemed, so far as she could yet judge, to proceed from lassitude rather than mettle. The horse stamped once or twice, switched his tail now and then, and looked back at her with sleepy curiosity while she adjusted the cinch. "Well, my fine fellow," she told him, "we must just hope the night air and the call of the chase will put a little spark into you."

"Nothing sparks this one except another horse beside him in the traces, your ladyship."

Lady Cassandra turned her head and saw that Parker had come into the stable.

"If he will not trot," she said, "then we will ambulate."

"Your ladyship will be fortunate to ambulate out of the village."

Cassandra tossed the old servant the toasting fork. "Strap some leather round the tines, Parker."

"If you hope to get speed from Tully, my lady, you had best use it uncushioned."

"Any horse that runs in the traces can be made at least to trot under other circumstances."

Parker stepped forward and extended his right hand. A pair of pointed spurs, glinting with newness, covered his palm. "A birthday gift from Lord Bevil to the young master two years ago Martinmas. Master George has never used them because they seem over-sharp for Colly."

Cassandra gazed at the old retainer. Disapproval was still writ large in his face, but it had been joined by something else: an acceptance of the situation, even a grudging acknowledgment that her action might, conceivably, be justifiable. She took the spurs from his hand. "Thank you, Parker. I shall use them with utmost care."

"Your ladyship might also find this useful." Reaching into his waistcoat pocket, he brought out four lumps of coarse sugar and gave them her.

Pocketing the sugar, she bent to strap on the spurs.

143

The last time she had worn spurs on both heels was in her teens, taking stolen early-morning rides astride, on a gentleman's saddle, one of her mother's oldest gowns hitching up around her knees.

Parker, meanwhile, giving Tully yet another lump of sugar, was slipping on the bridle, which she had selected and hung ready on a post. By the time she rose, he had the horse ready to lead out.

"Parker," said Lady Cassandra, "when we bring back Miss Chevington, you shall ply us with all the tea and toast you wish.'

The old servant shrugged, but did not demur when she took his hand for a brief clasp. They proceeded outside, where he gave her a leg up (she slightly nervous lest she scrape him with the unaccustomed spur on her right heel), solemnly handed her the toasting fork, and smacked the horse soundly on the rump to encourage his forward motion.

When Cassandra added the encouragement of both spurs to Parker's swatting, Tully, with a snort of surprise, broke into a jog; and she was away. Away not at any exhilarating speed, but, at least, away.

She very quickly felt the warning signs that the horse was ready to stop at the first opportunity; but by knee pressure and other measures she was able to cajole him almost to the middle of town before applying the spurs and toasting-fork switch. If Tully's reaction at Parker's slaps had been surprise, his reaction on being spurred was surely blank astonishment. He stopped dead, as if to puzzle out what was going on; and it required a second and third application of the spurs to encourage him to amble ahead.

Up until now, Lady Cassandra had been so much involved in the details of changing her attire, getting past the old retainer's disapproval, and encouraging Tully's cooperation, that she had spared little thought as to where, exactly, she would go. It was almost a surprise to notice herself riding, as if by instinct, south toward the Rotherhithe-Derwent road rather than north toward Ploverchase Wood. Of course, George was already searching the woods. Cassandra realized her instinct had directed her, before she was quite aware of it, to the place where Sir Roderic might still be awaiting Thomas's return from the abbey.

Why was she headed towards her highwayman, perhaps to wait with him for some time in an inactivity almost as useless as if she were waiting at the vicarage? To keep him informed of his fellow searchers' movements. By the time she reached Sir Roderic, George would have either found his brother and Deirdre at their childhood "lodge," or not found them and gone on from there; and Cassandra's lack of knowledge as to which was the case could scarcely benefit Sir Roderic. To consult with him? Her own action he might disapprove as strongly as had Oakton and Parker. To search with him? How could she, hobbled to this turtle of a mount, materially aid his search.

Ah, but if Sir Roderic should be the one to find Deirdre, how could the girl know to trust him, if not by her aunt's presence? Clearly, then, it was much better after all that Cassandra accompany her captain than it would have been had she gone with George. Then, too, Cassandra could spare Sir Roderic a useless return to the vicarage for news.

The wisdom of her route justified, Lady Cassandra proceeded with all the haste she could coax and bully from her mount. When they met Thomas with the carriage, they could change the saddle to Teazle's back and put Tully in the traces alongside Beauty.

But did not Sir Roderic lack a horse? They might, after all, be forced to search in the carriage.

Meanwhile, so total had been the destruction of her original scheme that she had mentally to retrace Thomas's probable movements since he left the apothecary's house. He had gone to the vicarage, sent George over the hill, and then, not knowing Bevil had been over the hill before George, the coachman would have proceeded to Derwent Abbey. By now the abbey would believe Deirdre to have been abducted for ransom—but that could not be helped. Perhaps, especially if the fox-hunters had arrived home, others would even now be out searching; that would do no harm. It would be best if Cassandra or George could find Deirdre first;

145

but if she were found by Darnham, or even Lord Roger, that would be preferable to her continued captivity, with Bevil as captor. In the meantime, faithful Thomas would be driving back to Tiptree with his mistress's jewels, as if for the ransom, secure in the belief that neither he nor they were longer needed except as protective coloration.

Would Thomas have yet had time to reach the abbey and be on his return? Might he, indeed, have already met Sir Roderic? Cassandra attempted a mental tally of the minutes which must have passed since her coachman set out from Ploverchase. She concluded that he could probably not have reached Sir Roderic yet, but very well might reach him before she herself could arrive on the supremely sluggish Tully.

She blessed the moon, wondering what she should do if it went down or were hidden by heavy clouds before she had come to the end of her search. An old line ran through her head: "The moon doth shine as bright as day." The simile was singularly ridiculous; the darkest day was far better illuminated than the brightest night. At least, however, the moon did give her light to stay on the road.

She found no one at the crossroads leading from Ploverchase; and for a moment she thought Thomas must have arrived and consulted with Sir Roderic, and the two then separated and gone their unknown ways. Yet where else could Thomas go, with the carriage, except along the road? He would have had much less reason for turning up toward Tiptree than for continuing on to Ploverchase and the vicarage, for as far as he knew she was still at Mr. Bellew's. And had he been coming to Ploverchase, she would have met him on the road.

Peering farther, she made out the shadowy figure of a single horseman. It was on her tongue to call his name, but she hesitated. He might swear by the ability of his mare to find him again, and the mare had seemingly justified his confidence; but suppose Cassandra were mistaken and it were not he?

For a moment the fear of a true desperado flashed through her head; but one highwayman whom she
146

herself had called in for a specific task did not mean the countryside about here must at once be cluttered with true outlaws. It might well be a straggling hunter, separated from the rest of the field. If there should be danger here, however, by some strange freak, then best she should know it while still at a little distance from him. "Mr. Marblehead!" she called, remembering to use his incognito.

Without replying, the horseman turned and rode toward her at a trot. She might as well have waited until she reached him, after all. Until she was sure of his identity she could make no move; and should he turn out a bad-intentioned stranger, she could neither depend on Tully in a chase, nor on having time enough to slip from Tully's back and hide in the hedges. She had neither knife nor pistol. She had, however, the toasting fork, which she gripped resolutely, and the sharp spurs on her heels.

Another few moments rendered such thoughts superfluous. Reining up close to her, the horseman remarked, "I expected some such action from you," and she instantly recognized her captain's voice.

"You might have answered me at once, Mr. Marblehead. I could not be sure you were not some dangerous scoundrel—the more so as we left you unmounted."

"Rest assured that I am only your own tame criminal." He slapped his mare's neck with a genial sound. "When driven from her master, Gunpowder has a pleasant trick of wandering calmly about until her path crosses mine once more. And, as I have been assured more than once this evening, highway robbers are a rarity in this sylvan neighborhood."

"Nevertheless, an honest stranger would have answered my call."

"An honest *stranger*, perhaps. I am none. And, although you have my anonym, I do not have yours."

"What makes you suppose I'm using an assumed name, Captain?"

"The light is not good," said he. "If I did not know your voice, I should think myself confronting a young man."

Lady Cassandra shifted in the saddle, uncertain whether to be complimented or annoyed. "I am dressed for convenience, not disguise."

The two horses were putting their heads together. Sir Roderic pulled Gunpowder's head away. "I see. Nevertheless, we cannot stop to explain all this to anyone who might overhear me address an apparent stripling as 'my lady.' How if I call you Cass?"

"How if you avoid addressing me? I think I am old enough, sir, to merit better than 'stripling.'"

"I might have guessed," said he, with a slight bow, "that you alone of all your sex would take the decrease in presumed age as uncomplimentary."

"Alone of all my sex, indeed? You presume on us, Captain. Whereas you are willing enough to credit your own sex with as many individual differences as it has members, you believe ours to be all of an uniformity, and each woman's character interchangeable with that of any of her sisters."

"Yours, at least, I do not presume to be interchangeable with any other's, female or male. On the subject of the remainder of your sex, Jerome and Donne both observe—"

"Ah, if you choose to borrow the opinions of authorities, of course you must have the weight of the argument. We have had few authoresses, and even fewer whom you will allow on your shelves unless, like Castilian Teresa, you can catch them denigrating their own sex somehow." She answered lightly, for she saw what they were doing: indulging in a verbal fence in order to ease the dull anxiety of their wait.

He shrugged. "What would you have of us? Admit that our opinions may be unevenly formed—still, men of honor, having at most one or two living exemplars of the fair sex for intimate study, have no other source of information than the classics chosen by our ancestors. Whereas men of less than honor . . ." He left the sentence incomplete, no doubt seeing too late its application to Bevil, Lord Fencourt.

Rather than leave the unfinished thought to fester in the air between them, she seized it boldly and finished it. "Whereas men of dishonor study us at our
148

worst and weakest, eh? And which are you, my captain?"

"Both, my dear Cass. And in the first capacity, I have been honorably intimate with two strong-hearted women only."

"Then I see I must write my own treatise for your study."

"You'll need to clothe your authorship with a man's name, if you wish a general hearing. I doubt I would not have confessed so much to you already if you were not in masculine attire."

"You mistake my treatise. Its topic shall be philosophy, history, or perhaps humane understanding —with the defense of my sex tucked into corners here and there, as the famous classic authors tuck in their censures of us. But a truce to this, Captain," she added more soberly. "You do not ask what progress we've made."

"Do you need to ask whether your coachman has yet come? Finding they were not at the vicarage, Oakton went to search elsewhere, while you came here prepared for a long evening's riding. If there were any other news, you would have told me before now."

Beneath her, Tully shifted his weight from right legs to left. She rebalanced herself to compensate. "I did not bring a pocket watch, but as nearly as I can calculate without one, our wait should not be much longer." She sighed. "Captain, let us talk nonsense for a little while longer. Of all Cyrano's methods for reaching the moon, which would you judge likeliest of success?"

"First," he replied with all due gravity, "we should settle what we are to do with the moon upon reaching it."

For no reason except, perhaps, proximity, she felt strongly tempted to move her horse closer to his. "Can you ask, Captain? We should, of course, send up missionaries at once, to convert the benighted natives to our own superior religion and civilization."

"Thereby creating in them our vices and miseries also, eh?"

"Who knows but that they have their own vices and
149

miseries already? Or that theirs are so very different from ours?" She resisted the temptation to move closer; it would hardly be prudent to risk tangling their stirrups, or allow their horses the chance for an equine tête-à-tête.

"As well as their own corresponding virtues, belike. Well, how can we say but they are even now planning to missionarize us?" He pulled his reins, ostensibly to turn his horse for a better angle to see the moon; but she noticed that his maneuver put slightly more distance between their mounts.

With some effort, she brought her own refractory steed round also. She meant at the same time to increase the distance a little further yet; but Tully, perversely, sidled closer again, using up Sir Roderic's gain. Lady Cassandra did not glance at him; he did not make the unspoken comment of moving Gunpowder away once more. They sat and talked nonsense about the moon.

21

A few miles away, in an old stone cottage in Plover-chase Wood, another couple were looking up at the moon through the half-fallen roof. They, however, were making no effort to keep their distance. Quite the contrary. The horse was tethered at the other end of what might once have been the parlor, and they themselves were lying side by side on a cloak spread over an ancient pile of mossy hay.

"You are the wicked nobleman," said Marie, "to bring me here. I have always said it."

"Yes, and you love me for it, don't you, sweet-heart?"

"For being so wicked? No, I do not love you for being so wicked. I love you because you have a title and a clean face and you wear clean clothes, *ma mie.*"

"And ain't all that a mark of depravity, little cabbage?" He put his left arm around her shoulders.

"Ah, no! It is the disguise you wicked noblemen wear to make us poor young women think you are good and honest."

They had only to turn on their sides to be lying face to face; and neither of them quite knew his or her own mind. He was not sure why he had insisted on stop-ping here for a while—his mare Calpie hardly needed a rest, the night was trickling away quarter hour by quarter hour, and this time he was fully convinced of his intention to wed the wench even if he succeeded in bedding her first; but habit was strong, and seeing the old place in the moonlight had been too great a temptation for him to resist. She, for her part, sensed that she was probably sure of him—but, *mon Dieu!* one should not take the risks. She would tease him a little here, play his silly game up to a certain point and no further; she would inflame him just a little more and then he would take her all the more quickly to the place where people were married very easily . . . In the meantime, she realized this was a very dangerous double game she played, for in teasing him she teased herself also, and so had the work of holding them both off. But, *ciel!* For what else were such nights and such ruined cottages? Could one . . . no, two . . . enjoy such delicate danger after marriage?

He moved closer, lying almost against her. "How can you tell the good men from the bad, then, sweetheart?"

"It is in the flesh, my Bevil who rhymes with devil."

"In the flesh, *ma mie?*"

"There!" She poked two fingers suddenly and sharply into his waist.

"Agh!" He sat up, rubbing his belly with both hands.

"There, you see? Yes, you are wicked—there is the proof."

"The hell it is!"

"A good gentleman would not have let me come so close," she explained contentedly.

"A sensible gentleman wouldn't, you mean." Bending back down, he pinioned her arms. "A sensible gentleman wouldn't let you go around with your hands free."

"Ah, Bevil, *non, non, non!* Ah, you are not wise, *ma mie!*"

"The hell I ain't!" He poked her sharply in the waist. But to get this vengeance he had to let go one of her hands, and even while gasping, she reached up and caught the ruffle at his neck.

"Now, *mon petit,* you must be wise or I will tear off your lace that is so fine."

"Damn!" he cried in something akin to real horror. Then, recovering himself, "If you tear it, love, you'll mend it for me."

She gave the lace a playful tug. "Ah, but I mend nothing for you until we are well married, you see."

There was one way to save his lace, and that was by going down instead of pulling up. "All right, then, truce," said he, sinking towards her.

It was a long kiss, and for a while they both forgot that she retained her hold on the lace ruffle, her fist a small lump between their upper chests.

"Now then," he murmured at last, "let go my lace, little sweetheart."

"Ah, *non!* It is a truce, but a good general does not give up what he has won before the truce."

"Deuce take it, you have to leave me decent. How could I marry you with my best Brussels lace torn?"

"Then you must also leave me with my wedding dress not torn, eh, *mon* Bevil?" Gently she tugged him down for another kiss.

"What is that?" she murmured languidly when next he raised his face from hers.

"Don't you know the English word for it yet, m'dear?"

"No, no, not that. The sound. It comes to this house."

He shrugged. "Fox. Deer. Nothing to bother us, *petite.*" Engaged in a secret maneuver to recapture his lace, he was working his left hand towards her fist; and to cover the action and divert her attention, he found it necessary to kiss her again. Had they been able to spare the concentration to listen to them, the approaching noises might have sounded remarkably like those a horseman would make riding up, dismounting and entering the ruined cottage . . .

A determined hand clamped down on the viscount's shoulder and plucked him bodily from off Marie. Before he could gain his balance, a second hand smashed into his chin and sent him staggering back against the wall. Marie screamed.

"What the hell—?" said his lordship. "Damme, I'll have satisfaction—"

"Don't go for your sword, Bevil. Or your pistol. I'm unarmed, and I will not offer you a duel, but by God, if you have hurt her, I'll—"

"George? Is that you? 'Sdeath, brother, you've torn my best Brussels lace!"

"Lace? *Lace!* By Heaven, you shallow-brained fop, I'll tear more than your damn lace!" Quivering with emotions the full strength of which he had not realized until now, the younger brother advanced toward the elder.

The girl rose and scrambled between them. *"Non, non, non!* Ah, what is it that you do?"

The vicar stopped. "Madam?" he said in a voice of total surprise.

"You are the Mr. George Oakton? My Bevil, what is it your brother does? Ah, you *chien,* is this your trick so that you will not take me to your Gretta Green?"

Lord Fencourt finished inspecting the damage to his lace—no easy task by moonlight and feel—and tucked it up as best he could. "M'dear, if you suspect any collusion, pray absolve me! I've not the least idea what brings my pious brother on a midnight ride through the woods, and I should certainly not have instructed him to manhandle me with such blatant lack of respect."

"Bevil, who is this woman?"

Ignoring his brother's question, the viscount continued, "If anything, sweetheart, I rather think it's for me to suspect you of a prior arrangement with our reverend vicar for some purposes of your own—"

"Ah, how you talk! Hear him, M'sieur Oakton, how he talks! It was you who said, let us stop here awhile, in this place, was it not, my good Lord Bevil?"

"Brother, *who is this woman and where is Miss Chevington?"*

"Miss Chevington?" cried the Frenchwoman. "Ah, Bevil, it is all clear, then—he thought to save the poor, pretty little Chevington from you with your wicked ways."

"No, it is not all clear. George, who the devil told you I had la Chevington with me?"

"But you are still engaged to the *petite,* no?" Marie went on. "Is it here the custom that brothers play the *chaperon* to each other until the marriage day?"

154

"My God!" said Oakton. "If it was not you . . . Bevil, do you mean to tell me you haven't seen her since leaving Rotherhithe tonight?"

"What? Worried, are you? Well, brother, I consider it damn well none of your business," said the viscount, still piqued at having been rudely interrupted and violently assaulted, with damage to his lace, at a most interesting juncture. "In future, perhaps you'll stay the evening out in your own family circle instead of leaving the party so deuced early."

"Be serious for one minute, Bevil. If you haven't seen Miss Chevington, she is in some unknown danger—"

"Whereas when you thought her with me, she was in known danger, eh? The possibility that my little fiancée might have been willing never occurred to your sanctimonious, busybody mind?"

"No more than the possibility that you really loved her," replied Oakton, keeping his temper with a violent effort. "By God, Bevil, I was to blame for letting this go on as long as I have!"

"So what do you intend now, brother? Since you cannot rescue Miss Chevington from my debauched clutches, are you going to rescue Mademoiselle Cluzot from me instead?"

"Ah!" cried Marie. "I was right, you see! It is a trick of yours—"

"Do be quiet, little cabbage. I want a woman, not a pennywhistle."

Lowering her voice an octave, to its usual pitch, she went on stiffly, "But you will learn, my Bevil, what it is to play tricks on the Comtesse d'Azalaine."

"Madam," said the vicar, "am I to understand that you came with my brother of your own free will?"

"I did, M'sieur le Vicar. As I will leave him of my own free will if he continues so wicked with me."

"Dash it, Marie—"

"And you know nothing of the outrage offered Miss Chevington this evening?"

"Nothing whatever," said the viscount promptly. Ignoring his sweetheart's gasp, his lordship went on,

"Now if you will kindly betake your prying nose elsewhere—"

He ended in a short cry of pain and anger as his brother reached out and seized his lace, pulling it tight.

"I tell you, Bevil, Miss Chevington has been taken from her friends by some person or persons unknown in the neighborhood of the hill. If you are half a man, you will come help us find her. Afterwards, you may go to—to Gretna Green and beyond with Madame d'Azalaine, and I will be the first to assist you in your elopement."

"Deuced sporting of you. The elopement was swimming along very nicely without you, many thanks, and the best assistance you can give us is to take your interfering beak elsewhere."

"No, no, Bevil, why do you tease him so? He is a very fine and good-speaking gentleman, your brother the vicar. M'sieur Oakton, he lies to tease you. He has saved the dear, pretty Miss Chevington from the wicked robber, and you will find her at the Grain and Grape, in my own little room."

"Is this true?" said Oakton.

"Yes, it's true, and if you're insinuating my future wife is a liar, George, I'll—"

"No, Bevil, you shall not use your seniority to bully me any longer." Slowly the vicar released his elder brother's lace. "If it were to come to fisticuffs, I believe I should have a decided advantage—I have no lace to worry about."

"Ain't you even going to thank me for saving her from that ruffian highwayman for you?"

As far as Bevil knew, Lady Cassandra's friend had been an actual menace; and in the dark his lordship could not see the vicar's smile. "For that, yes, I thank you."

"You'd dashed well better. Had her dress torn half off, he did."

"Your gallantry is touching."

"You're taking it damned coolly."

"Having caught you in a lie as to knowing her

whereabouts, am I now to trust your word in this matter of the highwayman's violence?"

"Begad, George, if you hadn't been so bloody officious about manhandling me, I might've told you where she was myself."

"I waste time here." Oakton turned from his brother to the Frenchwoman, groped for her hand, and stooped to kiss it. "Madam, I would wish you a happier fate than union with my brother."

"M'sieur the Vicar, I think together we will someday make him a very good husband, you and I, yes?"

"In such a task, madam, I can promise you no help."

"*Eh bien!* Then I will do it myself. But you have given me much help tonight already, m'sieur."

"And you me, madam. If I cannot persuade you to return to Tiptree—"

"Ah, *non, non, non!*"

"Then I can only wish you good success in your hazardous undertaking. Farewell, madam."

"Farewell, m'sieur. But I will bring him to your church to hear your sermons, you see, and so you will help me with him, after all."

"Confound it, Marie," muttered the viscount, after Oakton had departed. "What the deuce made you go and tell him where she is?"

"Because he is the *gentilhomme*, your good brother."

"He's a damned meddling puppy and he deserves to have knocked about in the woods all night looking for the chit."

"Ah, but no, my Bevil. You must not say every man is the *goddam* who annoys you a little."

"If you're so deuced taken with him, why didn't you just ride away with him, then?"

Marie giggled and put her plump hands up on the viscount's shoulders. "But he loves the little Chevington, *ma mie,* and *moi,* I love you. You are the one who wears the title, *n'est-ce pas?*"

"Bloody hell!" said his lordship, making a pettish movement as if to extricate himself from her hands—instead of which, he ended by embracing her.

"Besides, my Bevil, when we send him back to his pretty lady, we do not need to worry that he will be finding us again and again all night."

"Um—yes, there is that. Why didn't you say so in the first place, little cabbage?" He kissed her neck a few times and tried for her lips, but she turned her head at the last moment.

"No, no, no! We have lost too much time already, Bevil." Having been rescued by the arrival of the vicar just as she was on the point of succumbing, Marie did not intend to put her will to another such test. At least, not so soon. Besides, Gretta—no, Gretna Green was not walking down to meet them.

George Oakton, riding back towards Tiptree, felt no scruples of intrigue. Let his brother elope with the Frenchwoman—let him extricate himself from the parental wrath—having left the pair, Oakton allowed all concern with them to dribble out of his head. Although the possibility did not occur to his honest mind that the Frenchwoman might have been lying, he still felt the overwhelming need to find Deirdre, to see for himself, at first hand, that she was indeed safe and uninjured.

It was as well, then, that the information had come from the Frenchwoman instead of from Bevil. George would not have trusted his brother; he would have required the viscount to accompany him back to the inn. Yet, proven liar that Bevil was, he had succeeded in planting one doubt in the vicar's head, a doubt that grew as Oakton increased the distance between them. "Had her dress torn half off." What did Oakton really know of this Marblehead? Only that he had a compelling presence and that he was trusted by Deirdre's aunt. Might not Lady Cassandra have misplaced her trust?

This train of thought reminded him of his pledge to reunite aunt and niece with all speed possible. Therefore, instead of cutting cross-country to the north of the hill, he turned resolutely towards Ploverchase. Leaving his horse tethered at the post, he strode into the vicarage.

Parker met him in the hall.

158

"Is her ladyship awake?" said the vicar. "Miss Chevington may be found."

"Found!" The old servant made a gesture of exasperation. "Now her ladyship's lost!"

22

Rarely had any interruption been so welcome as the sound of a carriage; and yet, perversely, even as she rejoiced in Thomas's arrival, Cassandra regretted a little, also, the end of her conversation. When would she again have the opportunity to sit and talk philosophy or foolishness alone with her captain? Perhaps never in their lives. But for the constant underlying anxiety about a young girl in half-guessed danger, how delicious this platonic tête-à-tête by moonlight would have been—how impossible ever to re-create!

Nevertheless, nostalgia must wait. Sir Roderic had already hailed the coach—it was unlikely to be anyone except Thomas, but one must be sure—and when Thomas shouted in reply, both riders started forward to meet him. Unfortunately, both mounts did not respond equally well to their riders' signals. Sir Roderic's Gunpowder moved off in a trot at some cue invisible to Lady Cassandra; but Tully, having stood indolent for some time, had quite lost the slight momentum which had helped bring him here from Ploverchase, and now seemed more bent upon growing roots and becoming a tree than when he stood in the vicar's stable. A sharp application of the pointed spurs made him jump, but instantly he subsided again, with a sigh of determination, into lassitude.

Sir Roderic checked his horse, rode back, and

caught the bridle in an attempt to lead Tully, but even this expedient failed at first. Whether eventually his tugging combined with her application of spurs and toasting fork would have coaxed the nag into an amble remained uncertain, for the honest coachman did not wait to be met, but quickly drove forward to join them.

"What's to do, your worships?" he exclaimed, stopping the carriage a few yards distant. "Is the chase at your heels?"

"Worse, Thomas," said Cassandra. "The wrong man has taken Miss Chevington."

"Your ladyship? Lud, ma'am, I thought . . . do you know who 'twas?" asked the coachman, abruptly discarding his surprise. Lady Cassandra wondered if he had thought she was Oakton.

"We believe it to be Lord Fencourt," she replied, and she outlined to him what they knew and what they conjectured to have happened since the time he left the vicarage to collect her jewels for the supposed ransom.

Thomas listened gravely and competently, asking, when she had finished, "Shall I take the jewels on to the vicarage, your ladyship? If so be it was some real robber, and not his lordship, they might be needed yet."

Of all possibilities, that of a real ruffian was the only one which made Bevil seem preferable. Suppressing a shudder, Lady Cassandra replied, "Yes, I think that would be best. How did you fare, getting them?"

"Clara got 'em for me. Lady Harkendell was abed, and most of the hunt not yet back. All was still quiet when I left. Am I to wait at the vicarage, your ladyship, or help search?"

"Search, Thomas. You had best comb the neighborhood south of the road."

"Would it not be better," said Sir Roderic, "that he should raise the cry in the two villages?"

Cassandra turned in the saddle—to turn the horse himself would not have been worth the effort. True, Sir Roderic had established his character of an honest man of affairs on a belated journey, so far as Mr. Bellew and Mrs. Epworthy were concerned; but Cassandra's faith in the incompetence of the villagers to lay hands upon a criminal was not so strong as it once had been. "If it is indeed Lord Fencourt," she said, "how are we to ask the honest folk to interfere between him and his own betrothed?"

"By telling no one that we suspect the abductor to be their own local lordling."

Cassandra hesitated. To find Deirdre was her paramount concern. Yet to loose a general hue and cry over the countryside . . . "If he means dishonor, it will be done by this time. Can we let the child's shame be found first by strangers?"

"If we could be certain it is your precious viscount who has her, I would say no. But we cannot know absolutely it is not some rogue who means her worse."

"All the more reason not to throw him into panic."

"If you have any fears for me, Cass, remember it will look considerably stranger not to raise the cry than to raise it at once."

"Not at all, when we have explained it as an effort to keep the scandal contained as much as possible in our own circles. In the meantime, sir, I cannot see you detained half the night by the countryfolk, even with all assurances of your liberation before morning. You are of more use to us than any score of the local populace."

"As you will," he said, "since you know so much better than I how to keep me safe from the toils of the law."

She ignored the sarcasm; she thought he was speaking not from concern at how best to avoid danger himself, but from unselfishness in his efforts to help find Deirdre. "Tell Mr. Oakton's man," she instructed Thomas, "that if he has no word from any of us within . . . two hours, then he is to raise the villages."

"M'lady."

"Within one hour and a half from the moment you arrive at the vicarage, Thomas," said Sir Roderic. "And after that, you had best drive back at once and alert the abbey."

Cassandra was annoyed by his high-handed selflessness in thus whittling down the period she had named. With some effort, however, she refrained from protesting, which would only eat up more moments, and dismounted instead.

Teazle was no longer a young horse, having attained and slightly passed middle age for his species. She had had him trained to the saddle when he was still a colt and she a young maid, but in the past few years she had ridden him seldom. While at home in the country, she generally chose Creamline, the white mare who was Darnham's gift to her, for her morning rides. Creamline remained permanently at the country house and Cassandra brought, of her own three horses, only the versatile Teazle when they came up to London; but, during their last few sojourns in town, she had settled down into the habit of driving her light chaise about in the park to the exclusion of riding. How much the staid matron she had become! It seemed to her that Teazle quivered with anticipation when she transferred Tully's saddle to his back while Thomas and Sir Roderic harnessed the vicar's beast beside Beauty in the carriage traces. She felt a small twinge of guilt, and resolved no longer to banish Teazle to the carriage. Surely her relationship with Darnham was solid enough that she need not be forever riding his gift to the exclusion of her own faithful old mount! Yes; and she would take an occasional morning ride about the park even when in town—she was still too young always to be substituting a sedentary drive for true exercise.

These reflections passed spottily and all but unverbalized through her head between matters of more pressing debate. Thomas should not neglect to investigate the woods and fields to the south of the road, where possible, on his way back to Derwent Abbey. Sir Roderic and Lady Cassandra would attempt to find the *soi-disant* hunting lodge in Ploverchase Wood, in the hope of rejoining Oakton, and from thence circle east and south between the hill and Rotherhithe. If either party encountered any of the fox-hunters . . . well, their story was plausible enough in its outlines, and the manufacture of such details as were found absolutely necessary must depend, to some extent, upon circumstances.

"I would scarcely have called the vicar's beast a carriage horse," remarked Sir Roderic as the carriage drove off, "save in comparison with his performance as a mount. Some sort of mechanical contrivance, like a copying pen, attached to the first would do better—a metal horse with joints and cogwheels, its limbs to be governed, through a special system of harness and rods, by the movements of the real horse beside it."

"I doubt you will not become an inventor, Captain. Who would wish a mechanical horse when with less expense he could find a real one suitable to the work?"

"A man who, like our vicar, obviously keeps his horses for charity rather than utility." Sir Roderic turned his own horse's head and moved northward off the road at a slow trot. Cassandra followed.

"How well do you know this area, Cass?"

"Very imperfectly, I fear. I have been over it only as a matron confined to the roads and footpaths, and then only a few times in the daylight."

"And I have been derelict in my duty; I studied the land only once, and then only in the immediate circle between the road, villages, and hill." He laughed briefly. "A pretty figure we will cut, losing ourselves here!"

"Perhaps we should go back to the hill and try to find their trail from there?"

"We should only lose our time. He would hardly return with her to the scene of the abduction. No, we are as like to find them by chance as by art."

Cassandra sighed. "A very thin reed on which to base a young woman's welfare."

Having said this, she half expected him to make some response contrasting their present dependence on chance and luck with her own previous carefully plotted scenario. But, instead, all he said was, "I have some skill, at least, in finding my way by the stars."

After that, they rode in silence, as if they had each arrived independently at the same mental conclusion—that for them to call out into the night would alert the abductor; that if Deirdre were free to scream for help, she would do so at the mere sound of horses—or, if she were too far away to hear their horses, by the time their shouts could reach hers, be answered, and they could reach her, her captor would have time for violence; and that by riding without speaking, they themselves could listen more closely.

23

Deirdre woke and sat up in darkness. When she remembered where she was and what had happened to bring her here, it was hard to believe that she had not slept longer in her exhaustion. She should have slept at least until late in the morning and awakened to sunlight streaming through the windows. Instead, it was still night. She had not even slept until gray dawn!

Or, perhaps, she had slept the whole day through and it was the middle of the following night . . . but no, that could not be—surely someone would have come up during the day to see why the chambermaid was slugging abed, and, finding Deirdre in Mlle. Cluzot's place, have made a great to-do about her. They must surely know how she had been abducted; they would surely have exclaimed and rejoiced over her on finding her safe? Unless, perhaps, they had found her and let her sleep on, whilst they went to celebrate elsewhere. She thought she heard, very faint and far below her room, sounds of mirthmaking. She must have been sleeping very soundly; they must have seen she would be almost impossible to awaken easily. But would they still be reveling, all day and into the night, without trying again to wake her and learn how she came to be here, safe? Did they even know she *was* unharmed? Perhaps they assumed . . . or perhaps it was all a trick played up n her, and this was not the respectable inn of Little Tiptree at all, but the forest house of some Robber Bridegroom, and they were roistering below in vile anticipation of the moment when she would stagger down to them, innocent and helpless in a loose, borrowed nightgown . . . or when the Robber Bridegroom himself would mount the stairs drunkenly, to burst in upon her with his breath reeking of wine, and a great, sharp dagger at his waist . . .

She knew these were foolish, ridiculous notions; but the candle was out, the fire was all but out, the bedroom was unfamiliar, and she was alone in the middle of the night, a time and situation when nightmarish fancies came more naturally than wholesome common sense. It seemed as if, had they found her during the day and meant well, they would have left someone here, watching beside her bed until she awoke . . . or at least lit the candle and left a tray of food and something to drink. Or had Mlle. Cluzot left the door bolted from the inside, and did they assume the chambermaid was merely feeling indisposed? No, for in that case they should have pounded and hammered on the door, or put up a ladder and climbed in through the window, anxious about the chambermaid's health if she were truly sick, or demanding her to be about her duties if she were merely indolent. Besides, although it was true that the fire was almost out, a few gleeds were still faintly red in the fireplace, and, since they could not have glowed all day and half the next night, that showed that either it was still the same night as when Deirdre had come here, or someone had replenished the fire during the day.

The most probable explanation was that she had slept only a few hours, only long enough to take the edge from her exhaustion so that her nervousness and tension could push to the surface again and waken her —that she was really much more tired still than her excitement now permitted her to feel—and that no one yet suspected how she had changed places with the chambermaid. She was only able to arrive at this comforting theory, however, by dint of determined logic and slow breathing.

Having reasoned herself back into a state of mental calm, she got out of bed. Even that much took a certain amount of courage, and she might not have accomplished it, had she not needed to use the chamber pot.

In order to find that object safely, she needed light. In the darkness she could not even find a pair of slippers, and the floor was chill beneath her feet. Stepping gingerly, to avoid catching a splinter from some rough place in the floorboards, she made her way to the fireplace. There, blowing, poking, and adding bits of kindling, she coaxed the embers back up into a little fire. Then back to the bed, locate the chamber pot beneath it . . . she still could find no slippers, and finally guessed that Mlle. Cluzot had taken them. But where were her own evening pumps?

She took the candle and made another pilgrimage across the room in order to light it at the fire. Armed with portable illumination, she explored the chamber more thoroughly, finding her own garments and collecting them on the bed. She examined the rent in the bodice of her gown—it seemed larger than she had remembered, and she decided, with a blush, that she could not wear the garment without mending it first. Mlle. Cluzot's pincushion and cottons were near the window, so Deirdre retrieved them and sat for a few moments trying to mend the tear; but by candlelight it was difficult to chuse the right color cotton and thread the needle, the Frenchwoman's thimble did not fit her finger, and her hands trembled provokingly, either with nervousness or suppressed weariness. She gave it up, dressed in her underclothing and stockings, found her pumps and put them gratefully on her feet, and then, rather timidly at first, searched through the chambermaid's things for a suitable frock.

Deirdre had never considered her own circumstances particularly affluent or her own choice of wearing apparel particulary extensive; but she was shocked at the limitations of the chambermaid's wardrobe. She could hardly believe but that, in the poor light, she was missing some large clothespress. Good heavens, was it really possible that the working folk did indeed live in such austerity? If Deirdre had been puzzled before, and somewhat inclined to scorn Marie (even while feeling grateful to her) for eloping with Lord Bevil, the puzzle was now solved. Realizing that she herself had always been in a position to consider marriage only in its social and affectionate aspects (and remembering her own long and nearly fatal inertia even so), Deirdre could no longer look down upon another woman for considering it in a financial and material light. And Mlle. Cluzot must have been fairly well off for a member of the working classes, too! Her chamber was almost spotlessly clean, her few garments clean and well mended, her woodbox well supplied, and, of course, her food must have come as part of her position here. But for the thousands worse off than Mlle. Cluzot . . . in Deirdre's imagination, the interiors of all those dingy huts and town dwellings she had only glimpsed in passing, the tales of those grim factory towns—which before she had always accepted without really thinking of them—took on a new meaning . . . and the forest lair of the Robber Baron in her earlier foolish fancy seemed mild indeed, even benign, beside these new images.

She dressed, rather guiltily, in what, so far as she could tell in the candlelight, appeared to be the chambermaid's best frock. At least it would be her best remaining frock—she seemed to have possessed but three or four, and the best of all would have been the ones she wore eloping or carried away in her bundle. Even so, it seemed high-handed to take the better of another woman's dresses without the owner's permission; but, as Lord Fencourt's bride, had not Marie abandoned her things here?

Feeling not unlike something abandoned with the rest of the things, and chiding herself for such a thought after such luck and kindness as she had met this evening, Deirdre pinched up the excess cloth about her waist. Whatever her other privations, Mlle. Cluzot had surely eaten well! Deirdre found a long, slightly frayed riband and tied it about her waist for

167

a sash; but, not liking the bunchy, tucked-up effect, she untied it again and let the frock hang as it would. The neckline, being uncomfortably low, gave her more concern than the waist and hips. A riband was run through the top of the bodice, in the old-fashioned peasant way to be gathered round the shoulders and tied in front but when Deirdre pulled the riband tightly enough to bring the top high upon her shoulders, somehow the cloth would not gather as closely as she wished, and the result was a bulge almost as disastrous as the rent in her own gown. Alas, she had no brooch of her own with her. The only jewels she possessed worthy of being seen in Rotherhithe Castle were those which Bevil himself had given her, in that casually ostentatious way of his, as if to intimate that he might as well squander his money on ornaments for his future wife as at the gaming tables. She had forced herself to wear his latest gift, a pearl brooch, this evening; but the clasp must not have been equal to the night's adventure, nor had she so much as thought of it from the moment of her abduction until now. Most likely it had fallen to the ground when the highwayman tore her dress. It had been a valuable piece, too; at least, so she believed. She ought to make an effort to have it found, for she would have to return all Bevil's gifts. (Ought she return them at once, to his mother the countess, or wait until he returned with his new viscountess?)

Or perhaps the chambermaid had already taken the brooch, when helping her guest into a nightgown. This suspicion made Deirdre's indignation flare for a moment, but she chided herself quickly. How very dog-in-the-mangerish! Why should not Bevil's new bride have taken Bevil's loathsome trinket? Perhaps I even gave it her myself, thought Deirdre; I was very sleepy, and there seems a good deal I do not remember quite clearly.

Meanwhile, she must do something about the neckline of Mlle. Cluzot's frock. Using pins from the pincushion, she secured it as best she could. She was unable to find a shawl. The chambermaid must have had one, but had doubtless taken it with her. But she did find a large white kerchief and carefully pinned it round her shoulders to conceal the deficiencies of the frock's bodice.

When at last she was attired, she was far from content with the result, and realized she would have been still less satisfied had she been able to look at herself in a glass. In fact, she was much tempted to undress again, slip back into bed, and await the morning.

Throughout all her labors of dressing, those faint sounds of revelry had continued like a far background. Sometimes they seemed almost as distant and natural as the murmuring surge of water on beach and rocks at the small seashore town where she had spent two or three summers with her mother; but sometimes they swelled up loud enough that she could almost catch the words of some song or a line from what must be some anecdote. She no longer fancied they were celebrating her safety; but, if not, they must not have learned of her abduction, either. She could scarcely credit that Aunt Cassandra had failed to put out the hue and cry for her . . . unless—horror of horrors!— Aunt Cassandra were hurt, the coachman lying wounded or dead near her, and neither of them yet found.

No, it must be that Deirdre had slept an even shorter time than she thought. No doubt the news was still spreading of her abduction; no doubt someone would bring it here to the inn at any moment. Therefore, she must let folk know at once that she was safe, spare them a night of worry and fruitless labor. Moreover, she vaguely suspected that, if her appearance in a torn gown would have caused scandal and made it difficult to persuade folk she was entirely unharmed, then she would also do best to let them see at once how little time she had been in the brigand's power. Wait until morning and people might suppose she had been his prisoner most of the night.

The honest country folk below would not hurt her. They might laugh at the ridiculous figure she must cut in a frock far too large for her and clumsily pinned, but when she had explained the situation . . . She was

169

also very thirsty and not a little hungry. She would just go down long enough to tell them her story and show them she was safe, so that they would know and be able to get the news to Aunt Cassie. Then she would request tea, toast, and a few soft-boiled eggs to be brought up to her here . . . no, she would bespeak a better room . . . and go back to sleep until Aunt Cassie came.

Combing her hair with her fingers—Mlle. Cluzot had apparently taken the only comb and brush—Deirdre steeled herself to go down. Her hand on the latch, she hesitated again. They would not stop combing the neighborhood simply because she was safe—they would continue the search for her abductor.

Had he actually hurt her, she might have been hot for his blood, eager to see him dance in air. But he had not hurt her, after all. There were moments when he had seemed . . . fatherly somehow, like a great, strong taskmaster of a father, strict but solicitous for her learning. Even in those last few moments, she thought now in confusion, when he had ripped her gown, he had seemed less intent on hurting her than on making her scream and bring the approaching horseman to her rescue. Surely this could not be the usual behavior of highwaymen to their captive ladies? Perhaps he was no highwayman . . . but if not, who—and what—was he? A mysterious guardian who had come almost on the very eve of what would have been a tragic marriage . . . no, she had already decided, of herself, in the carriage, to talk with Aunt Cassie and find a way to break her engagement. But would she have followed her resolution? She had felt inclined to break the engagement very often during the miserable months of its duration, but had always shied away at last from actually broaching the subject. Her fatal indecision might have gone on until the very foot of the altar. Suppose the highwayman had been some ghost or guardian spirit, come in answer to a summons sent out from her own mind—the spirit of her own long-dead father, perhaps, taking on this guise and coming to strengthen her resolve and help her break with Bevil? Her mother's miniature of Papa showed a man of long,
170

dark face and stern mouth, but gentle and half-humourous eyes . . .

No, she must not yield to gothick fancies and country superstitions. If her adventure had never been, Bevil would still have run off with his Frenchwoman and freed Deirdre of him. A ghostly guardian spirit should have known that. Her abductor had been human—mortal—a being of mystery and unfathomable purposes, but flesh and blood for all that. He was probably still out there, somewhere . . . and did she really wish to see him taken and hanged, after the service he had rendered her, even though—probably—without knowing or meaning it?

Was that a lull in the merriment below? Was that a fresh burst slightly different, as if the party were about to break up and take its leave? If she did not decide quickly, they might all be gone before she could get down. Embarrassing as it might be to show herself in this makeshift attire before a crowd, if she were to go down and find the whole house dark and deserted, she was quite sure she would not be able to summon up nerve to call any of the inn people; she would go unfed and unattended until morning. No, she must go down at once, if ever. The highwayman would have had time to get some distance from here—he had seemed very confident in his power to look out for himself, and if he had not by now got a very good start, that was not Deirdre's fault. And Aunt Cassandra might need help. Yes, that must be Deirdre's first concern now.

Taking a firmer grip on the candle, she lifted the latch, opened the door, and ventured out into the hallway.

24

The hallways were drafty, dark, and labyrinthine; but Deirdre kept on, often pausing to listen for the sounds of mirth which were her only guide to ... to the common room, she supposed. Sometimes she had to go for a while in the direction opposite her goal, in order to find stairs. For the most part, however, she was reasonably well satisfied with her progress—but by the time she had reached perhaps the middle floor, she knew that she must now find the revelry, or at least the landlord, if she did not wish to huddle for the rest of the night in a drafty corner of the corridor. It was not likely she would be able to retrace her steps, unguided, to the chambermaid's room.

She might, of course, have been driven to the extreme of knocking on another door. That would be an audacious, forward act; but, if there were a guest inside, she could ask directions and assistance. Or if, as was more likely, she found the room empty, she could finish the night in another bed. Possibly one of the mirthmakers would come up later and find her in the bed he himself had hired; but, if that happened, she would at least be found. The doors around her grew more and more tempting as the noises she was following died out. They did not grow fainter as if from distance—she seemed still to be nearing their source; but they grew thinner, as if one reveler after another was leaving the group.

Fortunately, she was not reduced to knocking on a door, for some of the noises continued—now a straggling chorus of three or four voices, now a ragged burst of laughter—until she reached the first floor and found the common room.

At the entrance she stopped and gazed in with dismay. She had heard of the revels of gentlemen, but had never seen them, let alone their aftermath. What she saw now was actually the remains of a rather respectable party, but to her it seemed the ruins of a rakish orgy.

The atmosphere was heavy with tobacco smoke, the fumes of strong liquor, the odors of bodily effluences, the lingering smells of a greasy, meaty supper, and a suggestion of horsiness. Chairs were cast about helterskelter, spurs and articles of outer clothing lying limp and forgotten like old papers committed to a wind, wine bottles on their sides and glasses wallowing in rings of liquid on the tables, one candlestick overturned (the candle, fortunately, extinguished but cemented to the table top by a dribbled mound of wax), two other candles looking strangely decapitated, as if their tops had been snapped off or—perhaps— shot off in some contest or wager. Shooting off pistols within-doors! She had heard of such things, but that it might have happened in the very house where she had been asleep . . .

Much worse than the litter of inanimate objects were the human relicts of the riot. One was lying on a table, the other on the bench before the fireplace. Both were snoring wetly. For a few seconds Deirdre thought another was actually lying beneath the table, but then she saw it was merely a pair of empty boots, knocked on their sides, with the shadows behind them supplying the suggestion of a body. Indeed, both the snoring gentlemen were in their stocking feet.

At a smaller table in the far corner, three more gentlemen were sitting, still awake and apparently in a comparatively sober condition. It must have been they who had sent up the last few bursts of jocularity, though now they seemed to have grown subdued. They had dropped their voices and were talking quietly. One held a bottle tilted, as if pouring yet another round of drinks. One, even as Deirdre watched, slumped forward and put his head down on the table, as if to sleep or to cry. The third sat with his back to the doorway.

It was an expansive back, blocking her view of the glasses into which the first man was pouring wine and of the other man's head, once it was down on the table. There was something vaguely comforting in that gentleman's back, as if she should have known it at once in more familiar surroundings. Perhaps, if she looked closely, she might recognize those gentlemen whose faces she could see.

They must, of course, be some of the fox-hunters from Derwent Abbey. They had stopped here to do whatever gentlemen did to celebrate after a day's hunting—there had probably been many more of them here at first, but several would have already started for home, leaving two of their number in a state of drunken stupor, and three more to watch the two sleepers and either rouse them or see them put to bed. Or, perhaps, the remaining three were in process of joining their fellows—what was the phrase again?— "beneath the table."

These, then, were the men she had hoped to find, the men she had hoped, much earlier in the evening, might cross the highwayman's path and rescue her. She ought to have felt relief and rushed to them, or, at least, alerted them to her presence. Instead, she felt shy, confused, abashed.

As she hesitated between screwing up her courage and stepping forward into the room or retreating back into the safety of the shadows, the gentleman who was holding the bottle looked up, saw her, and gave a loud, incoherent exclamation. Deirdre's hand flew to the kerchief pinned round her bodice, and she would have retreated. But, while she stood momentarily paralyzed, the large gentleman took his hand from the shoulder of the comrade who had slumped to the table, pivoted in his chair, then leapt up with surprising speed for his bulk.

"Deirdre! 'Pon my soul, my niece!"

"Uncle Darnham! Oh, Uncle Darnham!" All at once forgetful of the surroundings, she rushed to him, meeting him part way, almost colliding with his portly,

174

comforting figure as she tumbled into his arms.

"Here, here, here, child, where did you come from? Chadwick! Go fetch Perry—better, Mrs. Perry, if you can."

At Lord Darnham's injunction, the gentleman who had left off his pouring in order to ogle Deirdre set down the bottle and, greatly to the young woman's relief, left the room on his errand. The snores of the third gentleman, he who had put his head down on the table, were already mingling with those of the gentlemen on table and bench, so she was, in effect, almost as good as alone with her dear, safe old uncle.

"Oh, Uncle Darnham, I've been so—and you really never heard anything of it at all?"

"An accident, was it? Here, didn't they have anything warmer to put over you?"

Deirdre realized she was trembling and her arms covered with gooseflesh. Seating her in the chair he had vacated, Uncle Crump disengaged a cloak that had been lying blanketlike over the gentleman on the bench and draped it around his niece instead. She accepted it gratefully; its warmth was welcome, even if her trembling was caused as much by agitation and relief as by any chill in the air.

She had suddenly understood the problem that now faced her—how to explain her presence alone at the inn without betraying the secret of Lord Fencourt's elopement.

"What were you doing wandering abroad so late without a good, warm wrap? Here, take a little of this." Uncle Darnham put his own glass of brandy into her hand. "And where's your aunt?"

Dear Aunt Cassandra! Of course, Uncle Darnham would be as concerned for her as Deirdre herself—more so, for he would not have anything else to distract him. Her perplexity about Bevil and the chambermaid falling to one side, she told him as coherently as she could and with numerous sips of brandy between phrases, of the attack by a highwayman upon their carriage, and her own abduction.

"Highwayman? Here? By gad, it was some young scoundrel's idea of a . . . Child, he didn't hurt you?"

"No . . . no, he . . . he frightened me very much, but he did not hurt me."

"And he did not hurt your aunt? He left her safe, eh?"

"Yes—yes, I . . . I think so, but . . . Yes, he threatened, but I do not remember that he hurt her," said Deirdre in confusion. Surely her last recollections of the scene on the road before that terrible horseback ride were of Aunt Cassandra standing unharmed and telling her to be brave, that help would follow . . . but help had not followed—Bevil's intervention had been quite fortuitous—and now it seemed that Aunt Cassandra had utterly vanished.

"He wouldn't have been Fencourt got up in disguise, would he? That young cockerel, we'll have his marriage settlement for this!"

"No, Uncle, the highwayman was not Lord Bevil. It was his lordship who rescued me." The moment she had said this, Deirdre regretted it. She might have told her uncle that it was the highwayman who had brought her here and arranged for her lodging, or that she had walked down to the inn herself after being abandoned for some reason unknown. Either story would have given her difficulty explaining her present attire—and also the fact that her presence would take all the inn people completely by surprise—but at least she could more easily have kept Bevil's secret.

Fortunately, Uncle Darnham did not ask what Lord Fencourt had been doing abroad in the vicinity. Instead, his brow instantly cleared of confusion, though not of anger, as if he now understood the situation in its entirety.

"Ha! Then it was some friend of Fencourt's. Damned young bullies with their notions of amusement. We'll see the earl hears of this—"

"He was too old to be one of Lord Fencourt's companions." Again Deirdre wished she had not spoken. There was no need to have contradicted Uncle Darnham's theory; indeed, if Uncle Darnham had continued to believe the highwayman a bosom confederate of Bevil's, then both highwayman and elopers would have had the rest of the night to get clear away.

176

Once more, to her relief, it seemed to come out well despite her own overready tongue. "Too old? Not necessarily. They ain't all youngsters, these rakes. Some of the worst would make your old uncle look like a puppy, m'dear. And if it wasn't Fencourt's chum, it must have been his servant. Infernal young prankster! You won't want to marry him now?"

"Oh, no, Uncle Darnham!" Her eyes filling with tears, she jumped up and flung both arms round his neck. By good luck, the brandy glass, which she had forgot to put down, was now empty. "Oh, no, I will never marry him!" How wonderful of Uncle Crump to side with her!—For it had seemed to her in her narrow experience and her reading that men were more likely to put loyalty to those of their own sex above loyalty to those of their own kindred.

"Well, then! Well! We'll see to it first thing in the morning. Devil of a mess it'll make 'em, breaking off the frills and hubbub." He chuckled briefly. "Your mama won't like it, m'dear. Now,"—he grew serious again—"what was he like when he saved you? Fencourt? How did he . . . um, behave, eh?"

"Oh, respectfully enough." Sitting again, she poured a little more brandy into her own glass. Relief was beginning to make her feel not quite herself.

"Respectfully? Hardly sounds like the young villain."

"I told him at once that I no longer intended to marry him." Deirdre was not going to make the mistake of talking too openly a third time. "He brought me to the inn and left me here. I think he was rather piqued."

"Piqued, eh? Gad, so I'd think! But he left you alone, did he?"

"He was the soul of respect. I—I think he did not much want to marry me, either." Deirdre tried to swallow too large a sip of the strong liquid, and choked. "But what of Aunt Cassandra?"

"Um. Let's think this through." He seated himself across from the sleeping gentleman and drank meditatively from another brandy glass. "Friend or servant of Lord Bevil's dresses up like a robber and kidnaps you.

177

Obviously a prank—no danger to her ladyship there. We'd expect her to set the villages ringing. She doesn't. Remarkable woman, your aunt. Brain deep as Darkmere. Fencourt comes and 'rescues' you—clearly what he's set up the demned prank for. Treats you with respect, agrees to break off the marriage—couldn't be what he'd had in mind to do, that. Brings you here . . . Where did you get those clothes, child?"

"My—my own gown was . . . dirtied, rather badly. I . . . fell, you see."

"Um." Thank goodness, he accepted it without further question. Perhaps she should have invented a tree branch to give her gown the tear it actually had, instead of mentioning dirt which would not appear on the garment when it was examined, but this was not the time to change her story.

"Well. He agrees to cry off, brings you here safe, and leaves," Uncle Darnham repeated. "Not what he'd originally had in mind, we can take it. Now, why does he change his plans, eh? And why does your keep quiet? Answer: She got wind of it somehow . . . maybe sensed it herself, maybe bumped into Fencourt on his way to you . . . and put him straight."

"Yes. Oh, yes, yes, that must be it!" Would there have been enough time for all that to have happened whilst Deirdre had been with the highwayman? And why had not Aunt Cassandra come along with Bevil, or been waiting here at the inn? And why would Bevil have set up such a comedy on the same night he planned to elope with the chambermaid? Perhaps to . . . what was the word that military men used? . . . set up a diversion? Well, no matter. It was a very good explanation; it promised to stop Uncle Darnham's questions, and it put Deirdre's mind at rest. Indeed, the brandy, in her empty stomach and in her state of weariness and dissolving tension, was already putting her mind to rest, subtly but forcibly. She wanted to be safe and to know that everyone else was safe, not to think.

She picked up her glass again, and it swayed, almost turning in her hand. She put it down without taking another sip. "Uncle Darnham . . . I should like above all things a few boiled eggs and toast and to go back to my room and sleep."

25

Lord Crump Darnham sat in silence, drinking coffee and staring into the fire.

Demned odd business. Neither Perry nor Mrs. Perry had known anything about Deirdre's presence in their honest establishment. The girl said one of the maids had seen to putting her up the first time—wouldn't say which one. Said the maid was surely asleep and shouldn't be waked. Carrying good-heartedness a bit too far there, but it wasn't her old uncle's place to throw stones. All the same, maybe he had made a mistake, telling Mrs. Perry to stop trying to coax it out of the girl, let it wait until morning. Then back down comes the landlady after seeing Deirdre up, and tells him the child won't say which room she was in before, but insists on a different one now. (Second floor, fourth on the left—best to know these things.) Something wrong in it all.

Harkendell, Thompson, and young Bassworth all snored on around him in the otherwise empty room. Well, let 'em sleep. They would none of 'em be of much use in their condition. Maybe not even awake and sober. Chadwick was out seeing what he could find. Not that Chadwick would likely be much use, either; but he was better out somewhere on his feet than here getting in the way of Darnham's own thinking.

Best to keep the child calm and quiet; but Darnham had not laid his own misgivings to rest, not by a quarter. His niece was safe and unharmed, he'd take her own word for it; besides, she would have been hysterical if the bastards had done it—but where was his wife? Probably safe, but . . . the situation called for action, but better try to think it through first, before rushing out like a cockamamie to blunder around and make a bad business worse.

Maybe he had hit it right at first; maybe young Fencourt had run up against Cassandra and got a fine dressing down, to make him fetch Deirdre on his good behavior. But it was not likely. Fencourt would still have come stumping into the Grain and Grape like Caesar coming home to Rome in triumph, get a hero's glory out of the affair, at least—not slipped in and stowed the girl away without even shaking up old Perry. And why would Fencourt have set up the thing in the first place? Poor girl was to have been all his in a fortnight or so. Why not set up the prank somewhere else and with some other young woman? Unless . . . by gad, if he had planned to get her dishonored as an excuse to throw her off . . .

But he would not have told Cassandra about it first, even if he did meet her on his way. She might have guessed, got it out of him—gad, the woman should have been a queen—but she would not have trusted him to ride on alone to the so-called rescue. She'd have gone with him, been on hand to gather Deirdre in. She'd have got her back snug to the abbey in short order, or at least seen to the inn lodgings herself. Not disappeared. Not unless she were party to the whole scheme, knew right along that Deirdre would be safe. But Cassandra hand in glove with Fencourt? As likely look for Whigs and Tories to praise each others' politicks.

Darnham had reached this stage in his examination of the evening's events, when the sound of hammering at the front door penetrated to the common room. Loud, even knocking, forceful but controlled.

Mrs. Perry had said she would wait up in case she was needed again. "Lord bless us, what a night! I'd sooner watch than be pulled out of my warm bed every ten minutes," was how the good woman had put it through her yawns. But she seemed to have fallen asleep in the kitchen. More important to see who it was at the door than to stand on ceremony. Darnham heaved himself out of his chair and took on the role of doorman.

For an instant after the door was opened, the older gentleman on the threshold and the younger one on the step stared at each other in temporary loss of memory. Darnham knew Fencourt's junior brother, the young cleric; and Oakton knew Deirdre's uncle, Lord Darnham—but their previous meetings had been of a formal and infrequent nature. Certainly neither had been looking to find the other here at the Grain and Grape on this particular eventful evening, and it took each of them a moment to clear away his confused preoccupation so that the other's identity could stand out clearly from the general crowd of acquaintances. It was an instant of hesitation in which the feeling of "I know this man, but in what context?" coupled with the overriding concerns of each about a much dearer face, took momentary precedence even over good breeding.

The younger man spoke first. "Lord Darnham? Thank God! Then she *is* here!" This was Deirdre's uncle; therefore, Mistress Cluzot had spoken the truth and Deirdre herself must be here also, safe. It did not at once occur to Oakton to ask how his lordship had been apprised of the matter.

"Mr. Oakton, is it?" At first, his lordship had applied the boy's use of the feminine pronoun to the woman whose unknown whereabouts were giving himself the most concern. What the deuce did it mean to have the young vicar scuttling about in the night looking for Lady Cassandra? Then came recollections of his niece and Oakton, the glances that passed between 'em, the self-conscious efforts not to look interested in one another. Thought they had kept their faces well masked, belike. Lord Darnham chuckled inwardly. "Who's here?"

"Who?—God, sir, your niece! Miss Chevington—you don't mean you haven't—"

"Yes, yes, she's here, snug as eggs." Taking pity on the young man, Darnham pulled him inside just as

181

Mrs. Perry, awakened at last, came bustling down the hall toward them.

The landlady was soon dispatched again to fetch a light supper for Oakton, and the two men settled in a private parlor, where they could talk without the accompaniment of snores. Much needed explaining on either side. Each man realized that he knew only a part of the story and guessed the other held the key to fuller understanding; but in the vicar this realization was a minor matter. Deirdre was safe—reassured twice of this fact, Oakton's only question was how Lord Darnham had come to be here with her. The question was speedily answered: fortuitous circumstance. The fox-hunting party had got separated into several groups, and Darnham's group stopped here at the Grain and Grape to indulge in a bout of good fellowship before returning home.

Darnham's questions were most pressing and less simply answered. His lady was still unaccounted for; and how the devil had Oakton come asking for Deirdre as if already aware she would be at the inn? "Well now, Oakton, what do you know of all this business, eh?"

"I know that it was . . . that it appears to have been someone's twisted idea of a prank."

"Your brother Fencourt's, from what Deirdre told me."

"My brother's?" Oakton felt in his pocket for his pipe, and discovered, as was hardly surprising, that he had either set off without it or else lost it during the course of the evening. He felt the need of something to do to cover his confusion while he thought how to answer Darnham. That Lady Darnham had taken Oakton into her confidence was one thing; but had she authorized him to repeat the tale to her husband? True, in the eyes of God and society husband and wife were one, and should keep no secrets from one another; but was it not for the partners themselves to make all such revelations? Especially one like this . . . no, the vicar decided he could not betray her ladyship's confidence. It seemed comparable to intruding unasked into a boudoir.

But perhaps Darnham was already in his wife's confidence? Perhaps he had knowingly steered his companions to the Grain and Grape in order to be on hand in case of need? Still, if this were so, would not her ladyship have informed the vicar? "What did Deir—Miss Chevington say of the matter?"

"Seems a gallow's-bait, or some rascal got up as one, kidnapped her out of the carriage, from under her aunt's nose. Fencourt came by in time to rescue her on the hill and settle her here for the night. The devil of it is, what's happened to Lady Cassandra?"

"Ah!" Oakton sat back and crossed his legs. "Lady Darnham appealed to me. She's at the vicarage now."

The older man brought out his snuffbox, offered it to his companion, and, on the latter's politely declining it, indulged in a pinch himself. "Explains it all, then. The one thing I couldn't account for—why they were both keeping so mum."

"Sir?" The vicar realized that Lord Darnham had been cogitating his own theory to explain the night's events. It would hardly have been natural to refrain from asking what his theory was—though this point did not occur to Oakton until he had already asked.

"Thought Fencourt might've set up the charade; but why the deuce not go through with it? Answer: Her ladyship met him and dressed him down before he reached Deirdre. Told Deirdre so. But then, why didn't Lady Cassandra come along with Fencourt, make sure he behaved? Answer: She was on her way to you." His lordship grinned. "Deuce take me if I don't think they were in it together, after all. Oakton, I may have been doing that brother of yours a wrong."

"I doubt that very much, sir." Any good turn Bevil might do another would come only incidentally, when the chance fell his way during the pursuit of his own ends. It was well, Oakton reflected, that tonight's opportunity to rescue Deirdre from Lady Cassandra's masquerade highwayman had come to Bevil when he was deep in another concern of his own and pressed for time. "Nor do I think her ladyship acted in concert with my brother. Her concern was genuine."

Darnham chuckled. "If Lady Darnham had chosen to go into intrigue, lad, you wouldn't find a cooler hand at the game in Europe. I don't say they planned the thing together from the beginning, but depend on't, if she met your brother and changed his plans for him to her own satisfaction, convincing you would be a piece of cake."

The thought crossed the young vicar's mind that he was, perhaps, acting dishonestly in allowing Lord Darnham to continue thus building his own fancies. Still, caught between the demands of honor and of discretion, Oakton decided to continue the middle course of pretending to less knowledge than he actually possessed, and saying no more than necessary to maintain appearances. "What purpose would they have had?"

"If you can't think that one out yourself, lad, she may have lost her effort," replied Lord Darnham in almost the same words his wife had used earlier.

Oakton wished his supper would be brought. He began to feel more than a little confused himself. He had thought he was on top of the situation; but Darnham's placid assurance was causing him doubts. Lady Cassandra had not sent him directly to the Grain and Grape—had not even hinted he should come here. Did his lordship realize the lapse of time? But Bevil —or, more accurately, Bevil's mistress (at Bevil's coaching?) had sent him here. Who had first proposed that the vicar ride to the old so-called hunting lodge in Ploverchase Wood? But that was my own idea, thought Oakton, or . . . no, Parker suggested it. But her ladyship could not have conferred with my man . . . aye, but Bevil might have, whilst I was with Lady Cassandra and her friend. And why should Bevil and his Frenchwoman have lingered in the ruined cottage, instead of sensibly pursuing their way northward, if not to wait for the vicar . . . Good God, it began to seem a vast conspiracy indeed, all aimed at bringing Oakton and Deirdre into close proximity under unusual circumstances . . .

"Believe I'm a bit of grit in the wheel," said Darnham unapologetically.

"How so?"

"You should've been the one she found here, Oakton. Doubt they didn't plan on the child's having only her old uncle to come down to."

"You surprise me, sir." The vicar spoke rather drily. "I had begun to assume that you, also, were party to this great web of intrigue."

Again Darnham chuckled. "Be sure I would have been. Only too happy to help 'em out, instead of getting in the way. Well, well, as I say, it was probably the inspiration of the moment, and no way for Lady Cassandra to get me word if she wanted to. Problem before us now is, how to make up for lost opportunity."

"I disagree with your lordship. I see no problem. All that remains is for us to return home."

"You don't seem to catch the drift of things, m'boy." Darnham shook his head. "You got here too late. She should have come down and fallen into your arms, not mine. How do we rectify that slip, eh?"

Oakton rose and began to pace before the fire while the older man calmly took another pinch of snuff.

"Am I to understand by all this, sir, that under the proper circumstances, my application for the hand of your niece would meet with a favorable reception?"

"It'll have to be improper circumstances."

"Sir!"

Darnham sneezed, nodded, and put away his snuffbox. "Can't very well apply for her yourself while she's already spoken for. Have to be bolder than that, lad."

Lord Darnham could not be aware that at this moment Bevil was journeying to Gretna Green with Mlle. Cluzot. "It happens I have certain knowledge that my brother is merely searching a reasonable pretext for breaking the engagement."

"Well, then give him one."

"Lord Darnham," said the vicar in a low voice, "are you suggesting that I should—"

"No, no, not if you're so set against it. Does you

185

credit, in its way. I'm only suggesting, my boy, that you make it look as if you have."

Oakton noticed that his own fists were clenched. Deliberately he unclenched them. "Five years ago I would have called you out for that suggestion, my lord."

"Sit down and stop thinking with your feet, Oakton. I'd have declined your invitation with a polite apology. Fought one duel, thirty years back. Pistols. Demned uncomfortable, having a ball dug out of your arm. Not worth the 'honor,' or whatever y'call it. Now sit down."

Oakton's attempt to express righteous indignation foundered in face of Darnham's cheerful, imperturbable, heathen pragmatism. Somewhat against his own will, the younger man sat. "Surely another excuse would serve as well, and once the match is stopped, an honorable application on my part—"

"You don't know her mother. I do. My sister. Mrs. Chevington would go into a flutter and call it almost as much as to marry dead husband's brother. Real reason, of course, is that she wants a title for her daughter."

"Then my application would be refused," Oakton said bitterly. "If Mrs. Chevington would not accept my honorable offering for her daughter, it seems highly unlikely she would—"

"Give her no choice, lad."

Oakton rose again. "I think you forget, Lord Darnham, that I have a certain reputation of my own to maintain."

Darnham shrugged. "Your own choice. Reputation or wife."

"What an example to my flock," said Oakton. "Their vicar engaged in scandal!"

Lord Darnham nodded gravely. "Might want to find another living. Likely to have one at my disposal in a year or two—pretty little place. But choice is all your own. Scandals die down, though. Ten or twenty years, and you may wish you'd chosen Deirdre."

"I think it best, sir, if I leave you now. In the morning, when I hope to find you more sober, we can, perhaps, talk like Christian men."

"If I were one of your hot-blooded fellows, now," observed Darnham genially, "and you were anyone else but a man of the cloth, that'd be a dueling insult."

"Since I am a man of the cloth, consider it a merited admonition." Taking his cloak, the vicar quitted the parlor.

In the hallway, he stood still for a few moments. His soul was in serious turmoil, yet he was not sure whether he must pause to allow his anger to cool or to try to find his anger. Was he the more enraged by Darnham's pagan suggestion . . . or by the fact that if he were any other but a man of the cloth, he could have considered himself free (but for the harm it would have done Deirdre's reputation—and that he would speedily have repaired at the altar) to act upon her uncle's advice. He glanced at the stairway to the upper rooms.

"Second floor, fourth door on the left," came Lord Darnham's voice behind. Glancing round, Oakton saw the old reprobate standing in the doorway watching him. "And if you're still thinking of her reputation, m'boy, remember she'd be better off compromised by a local vicar than by a highwayman who's vanished into air."

"Good night, my lord."

"Good night, Mr. Oakton." With a last chuckle, Darnham retreated into the parlor, shutting the door.

Oakton took a few deliberate paces towards the front door. Then he hesitated, turned, and looked at the stairs.

Beyond the stairs, he heard Mrs. Perry's brisk steps returning down the hall from the kitchen. He remembered that Darnham had bespoken supper for him, and he was seriously tempted to stop and take advantage of it.

He started back towards the hallway, intending to ask Mrs. Perry to bring the tray to another room than the parlor occupied by Lord Darnham. But the stairs abutted into the hallway. Whether by absence of mind or for another reason, the vicar found himself on the stairs instead of in the hallway. And, having reached the third or fourth tread before realizing his mental lapse, he continued on up.

The landlady arrived even with the foot of the stairs in time to glimpse the reverend vicar disappearing in the shadows at the top. "Lord love us!" she ejaculated softly.

"In here, Mrs. Perry." Lord Darnham had opened the parlor door a few inches.

"But he'll want a light, sir."

"Not on your life, ma'am." Opening the door wider, his lordship urged her inside. "Break the spell now, and we can't answer for the consequences. He'll find his way without a light, never fear."

"And his supper, too!" Mrs. Perry set down the tray with a hint of having had her good nature imposed upon. "Such a nice cold tongue as I sliced for him, too—"

"Well, well, we won't let it go to waste, will we?" Darnham settled down in front of the tray and began to lift the covers appreciatively.

"But what's to do, sir. I can't have folk wandering about like that upstairs."

"I will answer for his conduct myself." His lordship began by investigating a pigeon pie. "Ah, excellent! Excellent! Now if you'd be so good as to fetch me up some burgundy, Mrs. Perry, I think we can all rest in the knowledge of a day's work very well done.

26

Lady Cassandra and Sir Roderic had found the "hunting lodge," the half-ruined cot in Ploverchase Wood where Bevil and George Oakton had played as boys . . . and it was empty.

"Perhaps it is not the same one," said Cassandra.

"Perhaps. Or it may be they were never here."

"No—wait." In the moonlight, Cassandra noticed a small scrap of ragged white on a mound of dark earth or detritus. Dismounting from Teazle, she approached the white thing and picked it up. "Lace. A bit of torn lace."

"Clean?"

"Very clean, I think." It felt fresh and pliable in her fingers, not stiff, as it would have had it been lying here in the dirt and rain for any length of time.

He dismounted and came up beside her. She spread out the fragment, first on her hand, then on the dark material of the cuff of her borrowed coat.

"From you niece's gown?"

"I . . . can't tell." She could not even tell how wide the lace had been originally. "It is very badly torn." A spasm of horror went through her, almost as if it were a bit of flesh and not of tatted thread they had found. Still holding her left arm, with the lace fragment on the sleeve, out before her, she groped with her right arm for her friend's hand, found it, and gripped it fast. "There has been a struggle here," she said.

"Not necessarily. It may have been loosened when I tore her gown, and only come off here."

"*You* tore her gown?"

"Confound it, I thought it was her vicar coming, and she would not scream and alert him."

"Forgive me." Cassandra retrieved the lace from her sleeve and rubbed it between her fingers. "We do not even know it is hers. The viscount, too, was wearing lace this evening."

"As did I, in my salad days." He took the lace from her and felt it himself. "This at least constitutes additional evidence that it was our young nobleman who took her from me."

"Yes. It is also evidence that they struggled here." Moving away from him, Lady Cassandra leaned against the broken wall and buried her face in her hands, her will and energies paralyzed for a moment by the horror of what appeared to have happened here to her niece, and the knowledge that she was responsible for it.

Sir Roderic came up behind her and put his hands on her shoulders. "And if there was a struggle, can you be sure which of them had the better? Your niece has spirit, Cass. I experienced that much for myself, and I had time to give her a few brief lessons in how to use it."

"And do you think she could have . . . held him off?"

"I doubt she could not have held me off indefinitely, not without further instruction and a deal of practice. But such a green fop as I conceive Fencourt to be—"

"He has shot men in duels."

"Which is nothing to the present case. It is one thing to stand at twenty paces and discharge a couple of pistol balls at one another, or even to slash out at the distance of a sword. But if she were able to attack him strongly enough in a vulnerable member—a little finger, or a favorite bit of lace—"

"You do not seriously believe they could have struggled here and she come to no harm?"

"Do you insist on believing the worst? From one scrap of torn lace, are we to hypothesize an entire battle? Or spend the rest of the night searching for other signs of struggle?"

Cassandra looked around the ruined cottage. There might be other signs of fresh disturbance here, but the darkness kept them well hidden. It had been little more than chance which showed her the lace. "God knows what we might see with a lantern," she said, "but at least it is better to think that she is with him than with some murderous ruffian." They might have found Deirdre's bleeding corpse—the image made a single bit of clean lace seem innocuous enough. I must control my fancies, thought Cassandra.

Sir Roderic drew closer. "Would he have taken her from here back to Rotherhithe or one of the villages?"

Cassandra leaned against him. For a moment a classical image appeared in her mind of herself as a dryad and him as her solid tree. She fought it down. This was a time to submerge her romantic side and bring the faculties of her practical side into play. "Yes, he might have done that—to Rotherhithe most likely. Or perhaps to his brother's house." (Had I waited at the vicarage, I might have been there to receive her!) "But if he has done that, she is safe. If he has not, then she may be still in danger, and we shall not help her by looking for her at Rotherhithe or Ploverchase."

"If we were to separate, you could ride to the castle and thereabouts while I continue on through the woods."

"You think that Teazle and I cannot keep pace with you and Gunpowder, eh?" Putting her hand on one of his, she pulled away from his chest and turned to face him. "Captain, Captain, suppose you were to find them. What sign could you give her to win her trust?"

"I rather think that would not be so difficult as you suppose, Cass. You did not see us together. I became quite fatherly for a time. But come along," he added, "and I may leave it to you to handle Fencourt."

"With a will, Captain."

A slight pressure passed between their hands before they turned to remount their waiting horses. "North, Cass?" said Sir Roderic.

To the south lay the villages, to the east

Rotherhithe Castle, to the west, although at some little distance, Derwent Abbey. Had Lord Bevil taken Deirdre in any of those directions, belike it was with a view to her safety. North would be the direction he would probably take if he meant further mischief. "North, Captain."

They found what might possibly have been a bridle path leading northward from the cottage. It was neither wide nor particularly straight—nowhere on it did they venture to ride, in the darkness, at more than a medium-slow trot—but it seemed their best way north.

How long should they ride? wondered Lady Cassandra. Until they found Deirdre? And if they did not— if she were indeed safe at one of the havens behind them? Should they turn back before morning, or continue their search on into the day? And if I am not back again at the vicarage before anyone knows of my expedition tonight, she thought . . .

Well, she would weather that storm when it broke. Meanwhile, having engaged herself in the task, she had no time now for second thoughts.

Marie sat drumming her fingertips impatiently on a mossy boulder. "Yes, yes, it is charming, this little *étang* of yours. We will come back some day and see it in the light, *n'est-ce pas?*"

"The word is tarn, sweetheart. And it's much more fascinating by moonlight." Bevil tossed a pebble or twig into the water. The blurred reflection of the moon broke up in ripples and then slowly formed again.

Marie yawned. That Bevil must stop here for a moment, *oui*, that had been for him *necessaire*. But that he should then insist that she, too, must climb off the horse and sit with him to rest for a moment beside this *étang*, this tarn he called it, which was nothing more in the dark than a black smoothness with a spot of moonlight like a dead white fish floating, and a faint sound of water flowing as if someone were still making the *pipi* somewhere—that was what was *ennuyeux*. "Yes, yes, yes, it is *très intéressante, mon ami*, but now we ride on, eh?"

"Have you no romance in your soul, little cabbage?

Have you been deceiving me all these months with false pretenses, mistress mine?" He put one arm round her waist and drew her close.

She sighed. It had been very well, this sport, earlier in the evening; but it became fatiguing. "*Mon gallant escargot*, is it that your Gretta Green comes down to meet us while we wait here?"

"Gretna, sweetheart, Gretna."

"Ah, yes, yes, yes. Will she not miss us in the dark?"

Pushing aside her hair, he kissed the back of her neck. Despite her resolution, she giggled. He said, "Gretna Green will still be there this night week, darling."

"And your tarn here, it will not?"

"Rest easy, chuck. There's no way we can reach the Scottish border under two days."

"Two years it will be if we stop twice in every hour."

He lifted her hair again, tickling her neck with it. "We must stop somewhere for the night. Why not here?"

"You have not enough money for an inn?"

"Dangerous. Much too dangerous. Might be known."

"*Ouf!* And if they know you? They will set the dogs at you? They will come at you with their guns and cannons and demand you do this and do that and be the good little bridegroom of honor?"

He blew in her ear.

She tossed her head angrily, hoping to shake some of her curls into his nose and make him sneeze. "No, no, *mon* Bevil, I wish to sleep on the lovely featherbed between the nice, clean sheets, and to drink the hot chocolate and eat the fresh, warm rolls in the morning."

"I thought as much." He moved his arm up from around her waist to around her shoulders. "You've betrayed yourself now, sweetheart. Beneath that façade of noble romance dwells a soul of pure *bourgeoisie.*"

"Ah, you have slept in your featherbeds until the

193

middle of the day today, and they brought you chocolate on a silver tray, *n'est-ce pas?* Me, I have been at work today before the light, and now I wish to sleep in a warm featherbed and have another maid to bring me chocolate on a tray, myself."

"If you're tired as all that, m'dear, you should be glad of a lovely moss-covered rock beside a still woodland tarn whereon to rest your beautiful, soft body."

"No. I will have the warm featherbed, *mon* Bevil."

"Then I'll be your featherbed, eh, sweetheart?" Blowing into her ear again, he began to feel her as if he had offered that *she* be *his* featherbed, and not the other way.

"*Ciel!*" Out of patience, she jabbed her elbow into his ribs. "I will push you off into this still woodland tarn of yours!"

"You will, eh?" He threw both arms around her. "Why then, love, we'll go together!"

"Bevil! *Mon Dieu,* Bevil, you are mad!"

"Come on then, dear heart—a nice, chilly dip in the cold waters of the tarn, and then we shall both have to strip out of our wet clothes."

They were on their feet now, somehow—she did not know whether she had arisen and he with her, or whether he had dragged her up—but they were closer to the edge than they had been, and she did not like it. "Bevil-devil, you are the madman, you will make us both to take the *rhume de cerveau—*"

"We'll have to strip and then snuggle very close together to stay warm whilst our clothes are drying, *n'est-ce pas,* sweeting?"

She tried vainly to get one arm loose of his encircling grip. "I have the change of clothing, myself!"

"But I have not, only one clean shirt and a cravat. You wouldn't let your *chou* die of the cold, would you now?"

"I will let you die of what you choose, and go back and marry a *gentilhomme—*" She ended with a scream, as he began to sway back and forth with her. *Mon Dieu,* did he really mean it, then? "You will spoil your pretty laces and brocades "

"Good as spoiled already."

He swayed further. She thought he was making the sport with her—she thought he did not really wish to fall into the dark water—but it went too far.

They would be safer not to stand. Breathlessly choosing her moment, she caught her leg behind his knees, gave a violent wiggle, and carried them over backwards, back down onto the rocks.

"You witch!" he cried as he struck. "You've near cracked my shoulder!"

"I too, I am bruised. It is better than to be wet."

"Ah? We shall see about that!" Hugging her fiercely, he began a tussle of rolling and pulling.

"Bevil! Ah, *monstre!*" Momentarily on top, she half succeeded in heaving herself up off his chest, with designs of getting her hands on his ears, but he rolled and changed their relative situations. And then, *mon Dieu!* He began tickling her ribs!

"*Monstre!* Stop! Ah, stop it, you wicked Bevil!" Laughing and shrieking, she freed one arm and began to pummel upwards at his chest and face . . . and all the while they swayed, he was trying to roll towards the water, and she trying to roll back away from the edge . . .

27

Deirdre, now dressed in a nightgown lent her by Mrs. Perry, had finished the eggs and two slices of toast, but, to her great embarrassment, dozed off sitting in her chair, with the teacup still in her hand. She awakened with a little scream as a dollop of tea—fortunately, no longer scalding hot—sluiced down into her lap. Blushing, and extremely grateful that no one else was there to see, she mopped it up as best she could with her napkin.

But she could not go to bed in a wet gown. And she was sure it must be one of Mrs. Perry's best, too! She went and stood at the fireplace, holding the drenched part of the voluminous nightdress and fluttering it carefully in the dry heat.

"Oh, Lord!" she thought once, "If I should doze off again and fall into the fire . . ."

Just then there was a knock at her door.

Uncle Crump? Mrs. Perry? She dreaded to let the landlady see what she had done to her nightgown. "Who's there?"

"Mistress Chevington?"

Oh, God! George! It was George!

It was the one person in the world above all others —except, perhaps, Aunt Cassie—yes, even above Aunt Cassie, since Uncle Crump said she must be safe—whom Deirdre longed to see—and she was in no fit condition to see anyone! "Mr. . . . Mr. Oakton, I am quite all right, thank you, good—good night."

"Miss Chevington, may I come in?"

She glanced around the room, vainly hoping to see a peignoir miraculously appeared somewhere since Mrs. Perry had left her here. "No—no, I'm very sorry, but you must not. I'm quite alone and ... and hardly ... prepared for callers."

"I've something very important to tell you."

She felt something cutting against the backs of her legs, and found she had been twisting and bunching up her nightgown until the hem was pulled tightly across her calves. "In the ... Can it not wait for the morning? We can call at the vicarage ..."

"Alone. I must speak with you alone."

Ah, she would prefer that too, but not here, not now, not when she must look such a fright. "I'm ... very sorry, but you cannot come in."

He rattled the latch. It was not secured. Ought she to—With another desperate glance round, she decided to run for the bed.

"I trust you are decent, mistress." The latch lifted. She ran. She was on the edge of the bed, about to dive beneath the covers, when she looked up and saw him standing full in the open doorway.

With a small scream, she ducked beneath the coverlet. When next she looked, he had come all the way in and shut the door behind him.

Then for several moments they simply looked at each other in awkward silence, he standing just inside the room and turning his hat in his hands; she sitting in bed and holding the covers hunched about her.

"What ... what did you have to say to me?" she ventured at last.

Throwing his hat onto a chair, he strode across the room to the bed and—knelt beside it.

Realizing that, though the covers shielded the front of her body, there was nothing between her back and his eyes except the thick muslin nightdress, she lay down and drew the covers up to her chin. Then, realizing that this might seem almost an invitation, she sat again, nervously pushing herself back against the pillows, bolster, and headboard, and still clutching the coverlet protectively. And all this while, she thought, he was trying to speak.

"For some time now," he began at last, after several false starts, "I have suspected that you may, perhaps, feel . . . not entirely happy in your commitment to my brother?"

"Not happy a bit!"

"I hoped that perhaps I had not . . . imagined it."

"But it's all over now, thank goodness!"

He tried to say something else, did not quite succeed, and reached out instead to try to take her hand. She snatched it away, a little frightened at what she had said. Her engagement to Bevil would have been a better protection than the blankets, if she had not admitted frankly that it no longer existed. (Or did it? *She* knew, to her great relief, that the viscount had no intention of marrying her, but for all the rest of the world, they were still officially betrothed, and would remain so until his elopement with Mlle. Cluzot was revealed.) But did she really want protection from George Oakton?

"But . . . I may have imagined something . . . more than I should have?"

Deirdre decided she did *not* want protection. "No, no, you didn't imagine it. Not if . . . not if you mean what I think you must mean." Then she remembered she was a respectable young woman and he a vicar. "But I think . . . I think you had better go now."

He reached for her hand again. This time she did not pull it away.

"Does anyone know you are here?" she said.

"At least two persons, I should think."

"You mean ourselves?"

He shook his head.

"Then hadn't you best leave at once? Your . . . your reputation, you know."

He pressed his lips to her fingers. "Deirdre, will you . . . be my wife?"

"Yes! Oh, yes!"

"Then I cannot leave you yet."

She thought this over. "Have you been talking with my Uncle Darnham, downstairs?"

"Yes."

"But he couldn't have told you why, because I

didn't tell him. Oh, Mr. Oakton—George—your brother's eloped with—" Ought she to say with whom? "—with someone else!"

"I know. I met them, looking for you. With the French chambermaid from this very inn." He began to laugh. Deirdre had hardly ever heard him laugh before. It was so beautiful that she began to laugh with him. "The earl will be furious!" he went on. "I could make my fortune out of this—if I wanted any more fortune than you." Then he suddenly grew serious again. "But he may not intend to take her all the way to Scotland."

"George?"

He frowned, got up, and began pacing the room. "It might have been another of his tricks all along . . . God! That poor woman, alone in a foreign land, and I left them . . ."

"George, you don't think . . ." Deirdre half jumped from beneath the covers, crawling along the mattress. "Oh, George, you're not going to go back and try to *stop* them?"

"Stop them? I may have been derelict in my duty not to have tried, but . . ." He paused, turned, and looked back at Deirdre. "No! He may be serious, and if he's not, I'll see he makes her a handsome allowance. In any case, may Heaven forgive me, tonight my place is here."

He sat beside her on the bed, putting one arm around her.

"But you need not stay now," she began halfheartedly. "If only nothing stops them . . ."

"But if anything should stop them, he may claim you again. No, darling, this is the surest way."

"But your reputation . . ."

"It will weather the storm."

"How very noble of you!" She sighed.

"But yours . . .? Dearest, if you would rather I left on that account—"

"Oh, no! I shall be as noble as you."

"More noble." Holding her face between his hands, he kissed her forehead. "More noble, because more dependent on trust."

For answer she clasped her hands around his waist. He embraced her in return, and they swayed gently back and forth on the bed for a few moments.

"Is there not something more ... to being compromised," she inquired at last, dreamily, "than this?"

"Not for us." He kissed her again on the forehead. "I will compromise you only in the sight of the world. In the sight of Heaven, we will come to our marriage bed with honor."

She leaned her head on his shoulder and relaxed utterly. They rocked for a few moments longer, Then he realized she had fallen asleep. Feeling a swelling in his throat, he gently disengaged her, slipped her between the sheets, and tucked her in.

Then he drew up a chair on the other side of the fireplace, arranging it so as to afford himself a view of her slumbering face. Within a few minutes, he was fast asleep himself.

28

No questions, no comments passed between Sir Roderic and Lady Cassandra when they heard the screams. There was no need. They did not even pause to exchange a glance with one another, because the woods shut out most of what moonlight there was in the sky. They simply turned and rode at a trot, making no effort to approach unheard. Minutes counted, and the sound of their coming should be enough in itself to check his immediate assault.

But when they reached the pond in its clearing, it appeared deserted, except for one horse standing patiently, tethered to a small tree.

Sir Roderic stopped, dismounted, and tied his horse to another tree, some yards away. Cassandra did likewise, securing Teazle near Gunpowder. "They could not have gone into the water," she whispered. "There was no splash."

"I heard none. And it is hardly likely they would have slipped in softly," he agreed. "He's hiding with her here somewhere."

"He would not . . . harm her now."

"Probably not, if he is indeed Fencourt."

"They may take us for robbers and assassins. Shall I call out?"

Sir Roderic shrugged. "They know we are here. To let them know who you are should do no harm."

She nodded and stepped forward until she stood about midway between horses and pond. "Deirdre!

201

Lord Bevil! Deirdre, answer me—it's your aunt! Fencourt, blast you, let her answer me!"

Silence.

Sir Roderic advanced to her side. "Whether you are Lord Fencourt or another rogue," he said in a voice all the more menacing for its calm, "it will be better for you to come forward at once than to wait for me to find you."

Silence.

He turned to Cassandra and put a pistol into her hand. "Unloaded," he whispered in her ear. "Powder only." He lifted a small pouch of ammunition inquiringly.

She shook her head. She was a good amateur marksman, but even a good marksman could miss too easily in the dark; and the abductor was probably holding her niece very tightly.

"You to the right, I to the left." He groped for her other hand and pressed it for a second before turning away and moving towards the horses.

After a moment's hesitation, Cassandra likewise turned and began tracing a semicircle on a line with his, but in the other direction. She was ashamed she had taken even an instant to gather her wits and realize the plan, which was, of course, to cover the ground between here and the water's edge, methodically searching all possible hiding places, inevitably closing in.

If the kidnapper broke cover, he would almost certainly make for the horses; therefore, Sir Roderic chose to work on that side, better positioned as well as better equipped by strength, profession, and practice to foil any such attempt at escape.

The search was not without possible danger. That someone was here was evidenced by the horse—she thought she had recognized Bevil's newest mare, but quick identification by moonlight was far from sure. Fencourt was hardly well advised to remain in hiding after Sir Roderic's threat; she could not credit that the young man meant bloodshed—but what freak, then, *did* he have in mind? Nor was it sure that Fencourt was, indeed, the man they sought. Even if that were

202

his new roan, she might have been newly stolen from him. For an instant, the hideous vision flashed through Cassandra's mind of both Deirdre and Bevil lying somewhere unconscious or dead, having been attacked by some desperado in need of the horse. Resolutely, she dismissed the image.

Yet one fact remained clear. Whoever had ridden this horse to this pond—whether Deirdre's abductor or some countryman uninvolved in the affair until this moment—and for whatever reason—he now meant mischief. Why else continue hiding from them? An uninvolved, innocent person should have come forward at once and explained the mistake.

She soon realized the most probable explanation of a silent third party: a poacher. The thought made her tread all the more warily. The poacher—still hypothetical but growing more plausible in her mind at every step—could be a poor, harmless countryman wishing only to supplement his family's diet, but he could also be a ruffian able and more than willing to crack a few skulls in order to escape capture. She half wished the pistol she held were loaded.

If it were Deirdre and her abductor they would find here, then they would find them together. Clearly, he must be holding the girl tightly, to prevent her calling out or making a dash. Any man not holding a girl could not be the viscount or some other kidnapper, but a poacher or perhaps a chance thief. There could not be more than one kidnapper, because there was only one horse. So firmly persuaded was Lady Cassandra by this logic that when, as she began to push aside some branches, a pair of hands caught her arm and wrenched fiercely, she knew at once they belonged to the poacher. The kidnapper would have needed at least one arm to constrain Deirde.

With a cry to alert Sir Roderic, she braced herself and pulled back. Instead of standing fast in a contest of strength, her attacker came forward with her, breaking out of the bushes and bearing her to the ground. He aimed a fist at her head. It missed—due to darkness and her struggles—but smashed into her shoulder instead.

She, in turn, struck upwards with the pistol. Its barrel smacked hard against some part of his body, and—whether jarred by the force or by an inadvertent tightening of her finger, the weapon discharged.

Her attacker screamed with the pain of gunpowder going off so close. In the instant that his guard was down, Cassandra managed to roll over and on top.

Only to be grappled at once from behind by a second pair of arms.

She struck backward with her elbow, heard the gasp and felt the new stranglehold loosen, but it had given the man under her space to surge up again and knock her flat.

"So I'd regret it if you'd had to come find me, eh?" He drove his fist into her stomach and was hauling back for another blow when his arm was arrested.

A woman screamed, and Lady Cassandra knew, albeit a little confusedly, that it was not herself.

"Yes, you will regret it," said Sir Roderic jerking her assailant away from her.

"Wait—not yet!" she said, aware that in an instant her captain would begin pummeling the other unmercifully.

"What in God's name—" cried the younger man. But it was a few moments before Cassandra could get her breath back and continue. Meanwhile, the scene seemed frozen around her, like a charade tableau in almost total darkness. She herself was not only shaken but nauseated from the blow to her stomach and aware of the great bruise that was forming on her shoulder. Near her was another woman, panting in fright—it must be Deirdre, yet it was not Deirdre, she knew it was not Deirdre, and why would Deirdre have aided her abductor?—yet who else could it be but Deirdre? And Sir Roderic was only awaiting her good pleasure before visiting she did not like to think what chastisement upon her erstwhile attacker . . .

"Be careful with him, Captain," she said. "For now at least. It is Lord Fencourt, I think, by the voice."

"Lady Darnham? By God, is *that* you? Good Lord, madam, I took you for—"

"You took her for me, hey?" said Sir Roderic, and

the scene became suddenly very noisy, with Fencourt shouting and protesting, and the other woman speaking rapidly in the strident tones of a low-pitched voice gone tense and high, both at once, causing such a spate of confusion that it took Cassandra a moment to realize that the woman was speaking mostly French. Deirdre would not speak French like that—it was all Deirdre could do to remember the conjugation of *être*.

"Please—stop it!" said Lady Cassandra. The force with which she tried to speak hurt her own head, but if they heard it through their stream of protests, they paid no attention.

"Be still!" cried Sir Roderic; and, at his voice, they were. "Now," he went on, "we will sort this out like creatures of reason before I take the skin off your back."

"Who are you?" said Cassandra. "*Qui êtes-vous?*"

"I believe I have already tendered her ladyship my apologies," said Lord Fencourt, rather stiffly.

"*Qui êtes-vous?*" repeated Cassandra. "What have you done with Deirdre? *Mademoiselle Chevington, où est-elle? My God, answer me! Répondez!*"

"And who are you, yourself?" The Frenchwoman's voice rose as if in the last stages of exasperation. "*Mon Dieu, mon Dieu!* Bevil, you have put them everywhere!"

"*I* put 'em! You think *I*—"

"So this is the way you will treat me, *hein?* So this—"

"Silence!" commanded Sir Roderic. "I am very angry," he said when they quieted again. "I am trying to remain the master rather than the slave of my rage, but if there is another such outburst, I will not answer for my actions. Now, madam, who are you? Answer in French if you will, but answer directly."

In face of his intimidating voice, the Frenchwoman hesitated only a few seconds. "I am Marie Cluzot . . . d'Azalaine," she added, not quite defiantly. "I have done nothing—your pretty Mademoiselle Chevington is safe, very safe. Quite safe."

"Thank God!" Lady Cassandra released a long, shaken sigh. "Where?"

The Frenchwoman hesitated a little longer. "I do not think I will tell you. We do not know what it is that you wish with her."

"Lord, Marie, tell 'em and be done with it before this brute breaks my arm!"

"It is because he is a big man and can break your arm that I do not wish to tell them where they can find the poor little Chevington," said the Frenchwoman with a considerable degree of *sang-froid*.

"Mademoiselle d'Azalaine," pleaded Cassandra, "I am her aunt. We mean her no harm."

"Ah, no! You must prove it is true what you say by letting milord go free, so *poliment, hein?*"

"This is ridiculous!" said Fencourt. "You'll find her safe and snug in Marie's room at the Grain and Grape."

"Bevil! You are the fool—the silly goose! You spoil all—"

"No, madam, you are the goose," said Sir Roderic. "Lord Fencourt has at last, and for once in his life, shown a grain of sense, assuming it is not a lie. How came she there?"

"I rescued her from some brute of a highwayman who was about to do her, to put it politely, bodily harm," said the viscount surlily. "Go chase down that rogue if you wish to take the skin off someone's back."

"And you left her alone at a public inn rather than restore her to her family and friends?"

"Stop," said Cassandra. "I think I see. He was on his way to a tryst with Mademoiselle d'Azalaine, and he did not wish to set aside his own plans."

"You find it plausible, Cass?"

"I find it entirely of a piece with Lord Fencourt's character. Yes, Captain, I believe them."

"I'm grateful that one of you, at least, is a person of sense," said the viscount. "Now, sir, if you will be so good as to release me—"

"You claimed a few moments ago that you had apologized to her ladyship," said Sir Roderic. "I heard no such words."

"Nor have I heard any apologies tendered to myself

and Mademoiselle Cluzot for this—" Bevil began, but ended with a sort of grunting sound and after a moment went on in a humbler tone, "Lady Darnham, I beg you to accept my most profound apologies."

"Better," said Sir Roderic. "But words alone will not mend the damage."

"Perhaps not, but a little time will." Lady Cassandra got to her feet. "Let be, Captain. I'm not badly hurt. Having chosen to wear male attire, I should not complain of the consequences."

Sir Roderic must have released him at her request, for in his next words Fencourt resumed his indignant tone. "By Heaven, my lady, if you were truly a man, I think I should have grounds to call you out for your remark concerning my character."

"If *you* were a man, Fencourt," said Sir Roderic, "I would have called you out long before now."

"Since you are both men," said Lady Cassandra, feeling more nearly herself, "pray stop talking nonsense." Then, turning to the Frenchwoman, she said privately, "Forgive me if I seem impertinent, Mademoiselle, but does he mean marriage, or . . ."

"We are going to Gretta—Gretna Green," said Mademoiselle d'Azalaine. "If people will not stop us to fight and quarrel at every two steps."

Cassandra groped for the other woman's hand and pressed it tightly. "Then be sure you get him there safely, madam, and do not show him too many favors on the way."

Mademoiselle d'Azalaine returned Cassandra's grip. "It is not always so easy to keep back the favors, dear lady, and they say that the way is not short. But I am Marie d'Azalaine, and I will bring him there at last."

Impulsively, Lady Cassandra leaned forward and touched her lips to the other's cheek. Then, aware that the two men were hardly likely to come to a similarly amicable understanding, she released the Frenchwoman's hand and turned back to Sir Roderic. "I think, Captain, the place for us now is the Grain and Grape."

"My opinion coincides. Shall we take along our glib coxcomb until we know he's told us the truth?"

Reflexively, Cassandra shook her head. "No. I think we may safely—"

"Afraid we'd intrude on your nice, cozy late supper, eh, Lady Darnham?" said the viscount.

"By thunder, whelp!" said the older man. "You make me forget myself."

"Overlook it." Cassandra hurried to Sir Roderic and murmured in his ear, "They are eloping. Don't stop them."

She was close enough to feel the shrug of his shoulders. "Be off with you, then. But if we should meet again, someday when you have grown up, by God, sir, be careful how you cross me!"

Fencourt began a retort, but the Frenchwoman came forward to cut him off. "Come, my Bevil-who-rhymes-with-devil, you will bring me to a safe and comfortable place *aussitôt possible, hein?*"

Still half fearing a further violent clash between the two men, Cassandra did not breathe easily until Fencourt and Mlle. d'Azalaine were mounted and their horse moving away. From the saddle, he called back, "Don't worry, dear lady! I'll be discreet." The taunt annoyed her no more than the momentary buzzing of a midge, but she felt Sir Roderic's muscles twitch.

"You believe him, Cass?"

"I see no reason not to." She leaned wearily against him. "For all his undesirable qualities, he is not a complete monster."

Her highwayman put an arm about her shoulders. "The point is debatable. But I, too, think that for once in his misbegotten existence he was probably telling the truth."

"Umm?" For the moment, Lady Cassandra was feeling languid with relief.

"I've just remembered that, as Oakton and I passed the inn a few hours ago, I glimpsed the tail of a knotted sheet disappearing into an upper window."

"Why did you not speak of it before?" she asked lazily.

"I dismissed it as a probable illusion of moonlight and shadows." He pressed her a little more closely, not quite hard enough to hurt the bruise in the hollow of her shoulder. "Forgive me, Cass. Had I stopped then to investigate, we might have been spared much."

"I should have missed a great adventure." She rested her head on his shoulder, dreamily noticing how it heightened her sensations of her own voice. "Forgive me, Captain. No doubt you have little taste for additional adventure in your life."

"I chiefly regret that we have given that young whelp the wherewithal to spread gossip about you. I would have preferred to give him a sound chastisement at once."

"Don't you see, Captain? No, I suppose not—you did not talk with her. They are on their way to Gretna Green."

"Hmf!"

"*She* means marriage, at least; and I think she may well succeed. At any rate, I wish to put nothing in their way."

"Thus freeing your niece, eh? Well, I will not argue. One woman of resources should know another." He rubbed his hand up and down her arm. "Meanwhile, we had best get back to the Grain and Grape."

"Yes," she murmured, "we had best."

29

Harkendell had been moved from the common-room
table to the best bed in the house. Young Bassworth,
like Lord Roger, had had to be carried up. Thompson
awoke long enough to make it upstairs to a room under
his own power, and Chadwick, something to Darnham's surprise, stayed in condition to ride back to
Derwent that night.

All in all, Chadwick had been the most troublesome
of the lot. Only a nodding acquaintance, did not know
any of the principals more than passing, not even
Fencourt; but now wanted to hear the whole story
from the start, including everybody's life histories. Not
content with a simple message like, "Everyone safe;
stopping at the Tiptree Inn for what's left of the
night." Kept insisting on what would he do if Lady
Harkendell asked (as if he was her closest gossip; in
fact, Darnham had watched the pup bore Lady
Harkendell more times than once). Still, not a bad
thing to have someone to ride on back to the abbey
and tell folk what had become of Lord Roger and three
others of his party, not to mention Lady Darnham and
Miss Chevington, Fencourt's betrothed. (Darnham had
not trusted Chadwick with the developments of Deirdre's romance; there was a limit to what a man could
blab of family matters.)

Well, Chadwick should be well on the way by now,
and not likely, with a ten-minute start, to turn around
and come back for something he might have forgot
210

here. Oakton had been up there long enough with Deirdre to serve the purpose. Darnham thought of going up and rousting him out; but, remembering his own first courtship, he was not eager to cut in on the young folk. Oakton was trustworthy. Yes—Darnham nodded to himself—Henrietta would come round in time and see her daughter had got a better man than if she were married to a title, after all.

Meanwhile, a man could do worse than go collect his own wife. Cassandra was pretty well the exact opposite of the first Lady Darnham—one of the reasons he had offered for her, knowing his first marriage had been so good that attempting to recreate it would likely be disaster for the family and the new Lady Darnham as well. Best take a second wife who could shine in her own light, or else stay a widower. Indeed, if he had not met Cassandra, Darnham would probably have followed the latter course.

He was surprised she had stayed at the vicarage all this time. Cassandra could be patient, but Darnham would still have expected her at the inn long before now to see how matters had fallen out.

Well, she might have dozed off in an armchair. Or, being Cassandra, got engrossed in some book of philosophy and lost track of the time. Maybe, confident that things were going well here, she considered that she would only seem a duenna. Or maybe the vicarage clock had stopped. In any event, there was no reason a man should not take a stroll over the hill to the neighboring village and bring back his wife.

He bespoke a room for himself, looked it over to be sure it was satisfactory and the bed was double, and then remarked that he was going out for a moonlight walk, and if Mrs. Perry would be so good as to leave the door on the latch, she need not wait up for him. He had more of an argument than he expected from the good woman; Mrs. Perry, it seemed, had had almost her fill of strange comings and goings in her establishment during the small hours of the night, especially when no one saw fit to explain things fully to her, and she would have a pretty mess of it in the morning, what with at least one servant, as she suspected, up to some mischief, not alerting her at once when Miss Chevington came. No, she did not intend to leave her door on the latch, not with strange folk roaming the neighborhood all night, and—though she was not one to meddle in the business of her betters, it was her opinion that his lordship should stay close and not go outside at all. But if he must, he must; and if she was too drowsy to wait, his lordship would find Perry waiting up to let him back in and get him anything else he might want. "But it's my belief," she added, "you'll do best to get up to bed at once, if you want to get full value for money, now while there's still night left to sleep in."

"Plenty of night left." Still, no point in wasting any more of it. Wagering with himself that the landlady's curiosity would outweigh her drowsiness and he would find her, not her husband, waiting up when he came back with Cassandra's arm in his, Darnham began to put on his cloak.

He had his hand on the latch, Mrs. Perry hovering behind him with an air of guarded disapproval and a lantern for him to carry to light his way, when, on the other side of the door, the knocker sounded yet again that evening—a few short but authoritative raps.

"Lord bless us!" muttered Mrs. Perry. "Will they be at us the whole night long?"

Darnham guessed it was his wife, finally come to the Grain and Grape just in time to save him the walk. When he opened the door, however, and beheld a pair of soberly dressed but rather bedraggled gentlemen, he was taken somewhat by surprise. When, in the next moment, he recognized the younger of the two gentlemen as his wife's brother Cassius in unwontedly dark attire, he was still more surprised. And when, the instant after that, he realized it was not his wife's brother, but Cassandra herself, he was not unpleasantly intrigued.

"Well," said the landlady, her placidity increasingly ruffled, "let them as want to go out go out, and them as want to come in come in, so as to close the door and stop the drafts."

"Quite right, Mrs. Perry." Darnham stepped back, opening the passageway. "I believe no one will be going out for a while. Supper, I think, for three."

Mrs. Perry shrugged and disappeared towards the kitchen, taking the no-longer-needed lantern with her.

The moment in the open doorway, Cassandra realized, had been much briefer than it seemed. How far Lord Darnham's hitherto ironclad complaisance would withstand the shock of seeing his wife in the condition of adventurer and the company of a not unhandsome stranger, she was not sure; their marriage had until now been two years of almost stodgy comfort, each partner acting more as anodyne than stimulant on the other. Her adventures had been confined, during that period, to explorations of the mind into the realms of philosophy and quasi-scholarly romance, his—as far as she could tell —to the hunting field and to quiet gleams of surface mischief. How deep her hunsband's sense of humor went, or how great a shock it might withstand, she had never until now had occasion to test.

Nevertheless, she recovered only an instant after he did. Stepping into the passage, she said with as much calm as if they had met at a soirée, "My lord, allow me to present a distant cousin on my mother's side, Mr.—"(What was the pseudonym he had given himself?) "—Roger Marblehead, formerly a captain in His Majesty's service. Captain Roger, my husband, Lord Darnham."

"Lord Darnham." Sir Roderic gave a short nod. From the preoccupied manner he adopted, Lady Cassandra guessed she might actually have shown too much *sang-froid* for the situation. "We have been searching for your niece, and have evidence she may be here," he went on.

"Safe and comfortable," said Darnham.

"Thank God!" said Lady Cassandra, as if she had not already known the fact, and thinking even while she spoke, Now I've gone too far in the opposite direction.

"Asleep by now, I shouldn't be surprised," Darnham continued equably, and then went on to exchange more conventional compliments with the highwayman. "You'll sup with us, of course, Captain Roger?"

"Aye, and break my journey here for the night. But first, if you'll excuse me, we have horses to stable, and at this hour I prefer to see for myself that the boy does not fall asleep while unsaddling them."

It occurred to Cassandra that if he so chose, he would thus have the opportunity to slip away. It also occurred to her that if he did so, his part in the evening's events would be still harder to explain away. "Captain," she said, turning to him, "you *will* sup with us?"

"In all probability I shall join you again before the table is laid."

She knew there was a message concealed in the look he gave her with these words, but she was no more confident of its exact meaning than she was that her own words and look had conveyed the meaning she intended. She *thought*, as she watched him go out again and close the door behind him, that he read the situation as she did and would be back. Meanwhile, she discovered in herself another reason for her reluctance to see him go. For the first time in her married life, she felt uncomfortable to be alone with her husband.

"Where is Deirdre?" she said.

"Probably asleep, m'dear. I think we'd better let the child rest till morning." He tried to lead her into a small parlor, but she held back.

"No, I think I would prefer to look in on her, nevertheless." She smiled. "Woman to woman, you know, Darnham. Besides, I feel the need to refresh myself a bit."

"Charming as you are now, m'dear. A bit unexpected, but charming. Come and tell me a little more about this new cousin of yours."

"There will be time enough. I think you must have many relatives of whom I have never heard either, do you not?" She smiled again, more serenely than she felt. It was not that she wished to be away from him, but that she dreaded the need for less than candor
214

with him. "At any rate, I really would like a few minutes to refresh and tidy myself."

"As you wish." He told her the location of Deirdre's room, then that of the room he had taken for himself. "You may not find it quite convenient to tidy up in Deirdre's room, y'see," he remarked, and she was not quite sure, but she thought he winked.

She mounted the stairs with a sense of mixed escape and regret, found Deirdre's room, and leaned against the door. She heard nothing within except a gentle snoring. She tapped softly, and got no reply. Judging herself justified by circumstances, she tried the door and, finding it unlatched, opened it softly a few inches.

Deirdre lay asleep in the bed. Across the room, his feet on the settle, the vicar of Ploverchase slept in an armchair.

Lady Cassandra considered them, thinking over her husband's gentle efforts to prevent her from looking in on the young woman, his parting remark that she might not find it convenient to spend any length of time in Deirdre's room. Then she nodded, closed the door as softly as she had opened it, and found the room Darnham had taken for himself—and, she guessed when she looked it over, for her as well. No doubt George Oakton, believing her to have remained quietly at the vicarage, had told her husband he would find her there. Darnham must have been just setting out for Ploverchase when she arrived to spare him the trip.

After lighting several candles at the small fire in the fireplace, she made what toilette she could. To change her clothing was, of course, impossible; but she could straighten it, dust or rub out some of the worst of the stains, wash her face and hands, take down her long hair and replait it, gathering it in an almost satisfactory (at least by candlelight) knot at the back of her neck. And all the while, she thought ... of her husband, of her highwayman. And of a young man who would have meant so much more to her than either of them, but who had been long dead and towards whom, she found with mild surprise, she felt no sense of

215

betrayal, so different was her emotion for him from her affection for the other two.

Sir Roderic was already sitting in the private parlor, drinking and conversing with Lord Darnham, when she came down to them. "I fear I've kept you waiting," she said as they rose at her entrance.

"Since the supper has not yet arrived, it hardly signifies." Sir Roderic settled again in his armchair.

Darnham poured and handed his wife a glass of sherry. "Did you find her comfortable?"

"Completely so." Accepting the glass, she pressed his hand and returned his wink of ten minutes ago. "You were quite right, Darnham."

"Was I? Glad to hear you say it, m'dear. Appearances deceive, y'know."

"They do." She settled herself on the small sofa beside him. "For instance, anyone not aware of the situation, seeing me riding about the country by night with my cousin, might have found appearances deceptive indeed."

Sir Roderic raised his glass to her, at the same time cocking one eyebrow, as if he were the interested spectator of a whimsical play. She raised her glass in reply.

"Bad business, this, of highwaymen," said Sir Roderic. "I only regret failing to catch the rogue."

"Fancy you'd have been his equal in every way, Captain." Darnham chuckled and glanced at his wife. "Better equipped to teach him a lesson than an old dog like myself. Captain Marblehead's been telling me how he happened to come into this affair. Was on his way to Endercombe on business, did you know?"

"How should I not have known, Darnham? Do you think Coz Roger would have kept it secret from me?" Lady Cassandra found her husband's hand and pressed it, meanwhile smiling across at Sir Roderic. Smiling, also, at the distaste she had felt a little earlier at the apparent need to deceive her husband. Darnham, she now realized, had read the situation as clearly as she had read George Oakton's presence in Deirdre's bedroom, and, having recognized the general relationships, if not the details, had chosen to enter

216

the game as a genial co-conspirator rather than as a hoodwinked husband.

Yes; it was there all the more surely for being unspoken. Understanding this, Lady Cassandra knew that she, as well as her niece, had won a better marriage that night than either had expected before.

About the author:

Phyllis Ann Karr was born in Oakland, California, and grew up in Indiana. She wrote her first book when she was in the second grade. After taking a degree in languages at Colorado State University, she worked for several years in the Indiana library system and later earned a Master of Library Science degree at Indiana University.

Ms. Karr lives in Rice Lake, Wisconsin, where she enjoys playing the flute and the recorder.

Isaac Bashevis Singer

Winner of the 1978 Nobel Prize for Literature

A CROWN OF FEATHERS short stories	CB 23465	$2.50
ENEMIES: A LOVE STORY a novel	CB 24065	$2.50
THE FAMILY MOSKAT a novel	CB 24066	$2.95
IN MY FATHER'S COURT non-fiction	CB 24074	$2.50
PASSIONS short stories	CB 24067	$2.50
SHORT FRIDAY short stories	CB 24068	$2.50
SHOSHA a novel	CB 23997	$2.50

8003

Buy them at your local bookstore or use this handy coupon for ordering

This offer expires 12 31 80